Roll The I

Corbin Cases – B

Ken Hughes

Windward Road Press
LOS ANGELES, CA

Windward Road Press

11923 NE Sumner St Ste 879426

Portland, OR 97250-9601

Book Layout © 2017 BookDesignTemplates.com[1]

Cover © 2022 by Sleepy Fox Studio

Roll The Bones/ Ken Hughes—1st ed.

---

1.   http://www.bookdesigntemplates.com/

To Elizabeth
— who herds judges and transplants mice

CHAPTER ONE: THE MAGICIAN

I had the door locked, I know that. But she swung it right open.

"I need your help."

The woman's hushed voice was a poor match for how she walked boldly into the little library room, as if she were the one who'd put her name on its time slot.

A dull green coat hung over her, and a shapeless old hat hid most of her dark hair. Her face was pale—too pale, like makeup trying to soften the contours of her beauty and make her look barely eighteen. Nobody that young walked like that.

The song line came to me again, *A face that takes all in...* This time I heard it as *A face that glides away from all*, but that would only make the song harder to finish. And I was writing it about Helena, not this stranger.

I nudged my tablet on the table as she closed in, nudging it next to my bike jacket and blanking the screen from her. Two new reports of strange phenomena had been peeking out there, along with my database of possible allies for the Plan. Officially I was just here for some privacy to help the library with their website.

"It *is* Adrian Corbin, right?"

Her eyes flicked over the jacket and the tablet, the room I'd gotten at the library. I waited for her to ask if I'd been out of college long enough for detective work, but then she took a closer look at my face.

"I said I need your help. Two men have been harassing me—as in, threatening to set things on fire."

Two men... It couldn't be the Duvals, not yet...

I rose to my feet before she could settle herself in one of the wooden chairs. My height gave me an edge there.

"Sounds like you need the police." I could hand her the card for one cop I knew, simple. Except, if this *was* magic, it was exactly what the Plan was for.

"Sure I need the police." She flashed a sharp, rueful smile. "And sure, Jericho's Finest need a solid crime before they can step in. I don't have time for that, so I had to track down someone who could help me."

"Flattery?" She looked too thin, too hunched under that coat, to have any guess what kind of danger she could be under.

I wished my magic could read her. But of course the Bones were sealed away in their thick box in my pocket, and I could barely feel their cold. Instead I watched her sink into a chair, soft as the library's murmurs outside the door.

She watched me as I sat back down. "You made Jan Reynolds's boyfriend back off. You tracked down a witness about the library water's contamination last year... or that's what I think Ms. Travers was hinting at."

She talked to Helena? I kept my eyes on hers. None of that proved she actually was dealing with the Duvals, not while the Plan was still coming together. This could be a simpler threat.

And Helena sent her here because she expected I could handle it. The thought brought a curl of warmth inside me... and then a more cramped side of me added, *Or Helena's noticed my interest in her, and she thinks helping this woman will distract me.*

I frowned. "Just what are you asking me to do? I'm not a PI, or a bodyguard—"

"I want you to *fix* it," she said. "The way it's getting, it's not safe for a girl to do magic anymore."

A card skittered over the table toward me, but her hands never lifted from the wood—

I jerked back, the sudden word *magic* ringing in my ears—

That card. Beside the bright red name *Maya Grant,* it featured a shower of multicolored ribbons erupting from a classic top hat.

She added "Sorry to startle you. I've worked hard on that one."

And she, "Maya," brushed both her thumbs against her middle fingers, and the card twitched on the table again before I saw hair-thin strings sliding free of her hands. I'd never seen a trick so flawless.

"I may be a victim of my own success," she went on. "I've built up a whole set of techniques, sleight of hand and escapes—"

"Like opening locks." I waved at the door behind her.

Maya tilted her head to the side, studying me. "Mr. Corbin... tell me, if you ask someone for help and they say they can't do it, what do you do then?"

"Then? I try to ask them something they can't turn down. But after that..."

"You find another way," she nodded. "From what I hear, you've been finding ways for a while now. Helena Travers doesn't seem like a woman who'd hire just anyone. But those two men are stalking me, and they seem to be stuck on the 'asking louder' approach. Twice now they've come to one of my gigs and said they need me for something. And they keep saying it with fire."

Her voice caught, just for an instant before she pushed the word out of her throat. I could *feel* that fear, even with the Bones boxed up in my pocket.

Of course it was the Duvals.

But I had to ask, "What fire?"

"It's their signature. They'll push in close, like—"

Maya leaned in. The pale-washed lines of her face sharpened into a scowl of warning at barely a foot away, as she brought up her hand between us.

"Then there'd be a tight burst of flame, right there," and she gave her fingers a sharp snap, and finally leaned back. "In fact I still have a professional interest in how they do that. But they said they 'have a job for me'—I could almost hear the *offer you can't refuse* part."

"And I'm the one to fix that?"

I wasn't ready, not for them... but I felt the eagerness starting to build in me. This was still the Duvals, not the Eye.

The door rattled open.

Maya pulled back, hunched down a fraction, stealing a glance from under her hat back at the figure in the doorway.

Barry Alonzo had a tall stack of books in his hands, pinned expertly under his chin. "Adrian? You almost done here?"

I took the chance to stand up and cross past Maya. Better to get some distance from her before I tried this. "Something up?" I asked Barry.

The young librarian grinned, and his words started gathering speed. "Oh, just an idea that would reshelve everything faster. I thought I'd run it by you before I wrote it up for Gina."

"To make the books more available... just in time for my new webpage on what's getting read?"

"It wouldn't hurt, would it?" He rushed on, oblivious to Maya watching us now. "See, we tweak the algorithm that tracks the shelf locations of what books are returned. Then when we've got a few ready we bundle them together and run them right back out, no waiting to fill up a cart. Easy, if we just get the numbers that pace it right—can't be running up and down all day either—"

"It could work, sure."

I glanced over his shoulder at the familiar floor of the library. Two boys were strutting between the stacks, the wild waving of their hands a contrast to their hushed whispers about the band displayed on their shirts. Beyond them, some kind of nervous rumble came from the stairs toward the first floor.

Turning my side away from where Maya sat, I slid my hand into my pocket. Just long enough to slide the thick wooden box open.

The four dice slid free of that insulation. The Bones felt cold as blocks of ice, as the magic of the Pulse stirred against me.

That *was* a trace of fear downstairs—that certainty sprang into shape along my nerves. That was the one emotion the Pulse wouldn't miss, even with Barry's eagerness whirring away right beside me.

"—get the size right and we get the books back out there even faster."

"If," I made myself add, "you get someone taller for the high shelves."

"That too." He laughed.

"Sorry to break in," Maya said. "But I do need him first—understand?" She smiled, looked at him.

"Sure, sure…" Barry stepped back, and I saw his feet catch and almost stumble as he pulled away. The stack of books never slipped.

Steadying my senses, I shut the door and moved back to my chair. "So, you're certain I'm the best one to help you?"

And I stretched my will into the Bones' coldness, to the Pulse running through their ivory that carried and pushed at the emotions all around me.

Maya's were fluid—cinnamon amusement rippling to metal-bright irritation, shifting so smoothly it felt unnatural for anyone's to be more simple. But I needed to know what I was dealing with.

That drifting restlessness contrasted with the focused look she fixed on me. "I heard you've taken on problems like this before. Unless you lost your nerve."

I clicked my teeth to drag myself back from the flow of emotion. "Cheap shot. I'm trying to see all the angles you could take here. I do know a bodyguard or two, and a cop that might listen to you. We want the best answer for this, right?"

"Right." She leaned closer, just an inch now. "But, I think now you're curious."

I felt the frown bend on my face—she was right. But with the Pulse ready, I'd pick up more if I kept her arguing. I centered it on her—

A force dragged my focus away, a roiling anger outside this room, this floor, fierce and demanding—

She was searching my face as if she'd already seen my attention wander. I locked my eyes on hers. "Curious? Are you so sure?"

"Sure enough. People say it's the weirder stories that you listen to. And the people in the most need."

That presence below us, someone paced back and forth, not just angry but frustrated, or searching.

It could be anything. Stranger, wilder people had pushed into the library before... but my feet shifted under the chair. I should be out there now.

"Right," I said to Maya.

"I've had to stay away from my home," she went on. "Yesterday these two came right up to my show, and they could have gone after the audience. Just seeing those bruisers sent a scare through them, believe me..."

The pressure I tracked drew away a fraction—how far, how near the stairs up was it? My fingers twitched, a bit of motion to push back the Pulse's numbness.

"I bet it did," I said.

"They *should* be scared. These two are enormous—are you listening?" and her voice went sharper.

"One big man, with a scarred face, right?" A smile was tugging at my lips. "And the other's even bigger?"

Her eyes narrowed. "You know them. You know who they are... alright, what does that mean? How do we get them off me?"

"Willard and Dom Duval. Cousins. From what I've heard," and my fingers tapped against the tablet, and the Plan's files in there, "they've been seen near several crimes, but I think not connected to anything solid. And a couple of those do involve fire."

The threat below came nearer, nearer through the building...

"We should get out of here," I said.

"What?" She searched my face. "Are you helping me or not? If it's about your fee, I hear you can cut that way back. You know this isn't some petty problem anyone could chase off—these 'Duvals' are real trouble."

"Not that. Can we just..." How could I explain it?

I pushed to my feet. The pressure was closer still.

"Are you alright?" Maya's voice softened. "If you're not up to it now I can look after myself, until—"

"No—"

My phone buzzed.

The sound at my belt shocked us into stillness, like all the colliding problems of the world would always stop for someone's message. I grabbed the cell out.

A text from Barry said simply *trouble.*

And with the sharp flare of anger I could feel outside, that could be all he had time to send.

"Something's wrong out there." My voice came out low and certain. "What are the odds that—"

"They followed me here? Didn't think so, but..." She shook her head, not a denial but a brisk motion like throwing off what she'd assumed.

"We need to get you out of here. If you're fast enough, they could think you just ducked through here to shake them off, and move on."

The Duvals could *not* be coming back here looking for more traces of her. For one moment I had an image of them turning their fire magic loose in the stacks...

One motion scooped up my riding jacket, another slid the tablet into its inside pocket. I shrugged the heavy leather on for protection as I made for the door. At least the Duvals hadn't met me, wouldn't see me coming.

I cracked the door open and looked out, toward the rage.

The floor looked almost clear—but I spotted the two boys crouching behind a corner, staring helplessly at the broad reference desk. Where a huge figure of a man leaned right over it, right into Gina's graying face, while Barry stood frozen at his elbow.

"So I duck out back?" came Maya's voice behind me. "I'll find my way."

I nodded. As I pushed outside, I heard her slip away in the other direction.

The Duval—my guess was Willard, reports had him as the leader—was just a scrape of black hair above a massive jacketed back, bending over the desk and ignoring Barry beside him. Whatever threats he was saying to poor Gina were too low to carry, even with the floor frozen so still. My footsteps were clear, and so was every rustle and murmur of the people scattered around the stacks and tables.

There should be two Duvals. I kept my eyes on the first Duval I closed in, but I took a moment's tug at the Pulse.

A second, even steadier spark of violence moved among the shelves off to my side, working in the other direction. Toward Maya, if nothing drew him away from there.

"Hey!"

I shouted it, and the volume pushed my feet faster, and roused hushed sounds of reaction from the people watching.

Willard ignored it.

Closer now, I could catch a glimpse around him, around where Barry stared at the intruder.

Staring at the open bottle Willard had set on the desk, full of sinister gleaming liquid. At the rag in his gloved hand, as the scarred face growled "Where'd she go? Before I—"

Flames burst from the rag.

Gina shrank back. One wild breath later Willard crushed the fire out within his glove—playing that all these were simply tools that could have turned that bottle into a flaming Molotov, as if he needed them.

Barry lunged past him to grab at the bottle. Willard swung an arm and sent him stumbling away.

The Duvals could crush them in moments, or one stray spark from their magic could wipe the whole floor out. If I let them strike that spark.

I seized Willard's wrist, with my other arm straining for a grip around his huge midsection. I had a moment to wrench him backward before I felt his startled grunt, and him catching his balance.

Barry was gasping *"Sir, we've got this—"* as if acting like he knew me and Willard connecting me with the library was the greatest danger here. No need.

I let the Pulse loose.

The Bones were only in my pocket, but with my hands full of my target their magic only needed me to release it, to flood the Duval with the emotion at the root of their power: fear.

Cold, shattering fear, the Scarecrow's lesson to me, like pouring freezing water on my enemy's rage. Willard Duval shook, crumbled, and I twisted him around to his knees.

"Too late for your tricks now." My voice came out cold too, but Willard had to believe what I said. "One move and I'll break you."

Willard's free arm flailed, scrabbled in a pocket. The stubborn bastard was going for his own weapon, to get the magic right into his hand.

I yanked him around. My strength wrenched his flopping bulk over and slammed him into the base of the desk, then shoved him to the carpet.

A flash of yellow-brown metal skittered from his hand, bouncing away across the floor.

I stared after it. If I'd just disarmed Willard's magic... his cousin was still out there. I pressed Willard down harder and forced more terror into him—too much of the Bones' energy used up, already. Then I leaped clear and ran after the fallen magic.

Dodging around one table brought me almost colliding with an old man, all wild white hair and flailing cane as I veered past him. Where, where was—

Something moved from the shelves off to the side. Dom Duval stepped out, looming like an unscarred copy of his mountainous cousin.

Metal glinted under a table ahead, still my best chance to shut their power down. I scrambled toward it.

Orange flame flared on the ground in front of me, what someone might have taken for a small splash of burning liquid on the lime carpet. It leaped up right beside a rickety easel crowded with papers.

I wrenched my jacket off and slammed the leather down over the flames. A scream rang out behind me, that an instant later was choked off by a fire alarm's shrill howl.

He could have torched the papers, or the whole wall. The thought crashed into me as I whirled around: Dom Duval had used just a fraction of his power, to get my attention.

He stomped toward me, a full head taller than me and even wider than his cousin. My fists came up—Willard had been on the slow side, like any avalanche that hadn't gathered speed yet. At least facing him hand to hand might limit the flames.

Over past Dom, I saw Willard struggling to his knees already. I braced as Dom closed in, tried to picture the block and the grab that would let me unleash the Pulse again.

Something arced through the air. I caught one glimpse, of Maya ducking back between the stacks, as something hurtled across the room. It struck the corner where the corridor branched away, ricocheted back...

And thumped into the side of Dom Duval's face. Just a wad of tight-crumpled paper, it must have been wrapped around some kind of weight to fly that far.

Dom froze, looked around.

Then he spun, and stomped over to scoop up the bit of fallen metal, and he lumbered toward the corner where the missile had bounced off. Away from her.

I caught at my coat, crushed a shoe over the last embers in the carpet. The alarm was still stabbing at our ears.

Willard Duval staggered after his cousin, keeping a warning eye on me.

I reined in the urge to rush him again, and stepped backward in among the bookshelves. A pull at the Pulse let me track the growing haze of fear and confusion, louder than what voices I heard under the alarm. But the two Duvals' rage was drawing away into the next wing, still chasing the false trail she'd "thrown" at them. So, the cleanest answer was to get her out safe and see if they stayed to make more trouble here.

High, familiar shelves of metal flew by me as I raced for the wall at their back. No time to pick out emotions from the haze—instead I glanced through the gaps in the books, and the breaks in the rows of shelves, for a glimpse of where Maya might be among them.

I, we, had taken on the Duvals and gotten away, so far. But they'd come *here*—after years of my slow searching and building the Plan. All that slower-paced searching for traces of other magic, looking for who might have met the Scarecrow, or traces of whether the Eye was real, but now...

I reached the back wall. Three rows away, Maya stood pressed against a shelf row's end, sheltered from the sight of everywhere except this edge.

Her smile flashed out at me, gleaming under her shapeless hat and through the pale makeup—all crafted to blend in. I grinned back, and motioned her forward along the wall. The emergency stair back there would be perfect; even the alarm it would trigger might tell the Duvals we were done with the library. If they could hear that sound over the shrilling their fire had already set off.

She scrambled for the door, quick and quiet. I started after her, and the alarm went silent.

I slowed, tried to search the suddenly-clear murmurings around the floor for any screams or fighting, anyone else the Duvals might be going after.

If we made it out without more fires... then I'd have every chance to pick my moment with those two, and dig up what they were after. Maybe bring the cops down on them after all, if I got enough leverage and someone who'd listen.

A footstep sounded, behind the shelf I'd just *passed*—an aisle that had been clear an instant ago. I twisted back, reached for any emotions.

"You could lose this place."

A dry whisper behind me, close as the prickle on the back of my neck.

I spun around, but the figure was already sidestepping away behind a shelf. Simple dark clothes, face out of sight. Leaving Maya to pull away ahead, I lunged in after him.

The aisle was empty. A few steps brought me to the narrow gap within the shelves, and the next aisle stretched out twenty uninterrupted feet with nobody within it. No footsteps, now that my own had stilled. Even the gaps between the books showed nothing moving in the row beyond it.

But, the Pulse. I let the magic flow through me again, straining to separate out the scattered, dazed sensations around the floor, Maya retreating somewhere at their edge. Nothing like the Duvals' sharp violence was lurking nearby.

Only one quickly-deepening fear—my own. *It can't be* him!

And a presence close behind me: deadly calm, barely a ripple within the magic.

I should look back, but... was it the Eye? Did anyone ever see the Eye, when even the Scarecrow hid from him?

Here?

"You could lose it all."

Now I did turn. But there was nothing, not even a retreating shape. Not a sound—the first time, had there been footsteps at all?

The same cold, certain voice whispered behind me:

"If you want to save it... then bring me the key to Maya Grant's magic."

Maya's—

Another alarm blared. That would be the door I'd sent her to, telling me and the Duvals that she'd made a way out of the building.

I looked around one more time. The Eye was gone.

CHAPTER TWO: NEVER

The door's alarm screamed behind me as I clanged down the fire escape. The afternoon April sun showed no sign of Maya among the people scattered around. I dashed past a chattering couple, along the broad orange side of the Jericho Central Library.

My motorcycle was waiting. I pulled off the chain that locked the helmet beside the wheel, and shoved the helmet into place as I climbed on.

One more pull against the Pulse—but emotions only swirled around me, too many dotting the streets, each presence different and nothing that stood out as Maya.

A press of the starter and a twist of the throttle sent the compact little Ninja surging forward. I swung wide around a repair scaffold along the back wall, staring around, riding in spurts with my feet tapping the sidewalk every time a passer-by forced me to slow. The helmet and the engine roar swallowed my hearing, but I couldn't see her nearby, and no glimpse of her up the side-road that branched off at the far side of the street. Where'd she get to?

The Duvals could charge into view any second.

Or they could stay inside and bully more of the people I knew. My stomach twisted—I was gambling everything on them knowing from the alarm that their target was gone.

And how are those tricks going to work against a whisper I can't even get a look at? That voice had to be the Eye. Even the Scarecrow, the madman that killed—killed *Ray*—with a thought, had lived in fear of the Eye. Said he was everywhere.

And he wanted Maya's "magic," that had to mean more than her card illusions. Or else "you could lose it all."

A shiver swept through me. I should be furious, but instead I fought to keep the bike steady at this halting sidewalk speed. I wobbled past a family clustered around a parked car, spurted clear to slice by and pass too near the building. There were too many people dotting the sidewalk to let me move, and a solid fence of cars along the curb keeping me away from the street.

The next street opposite came in view, still no sign of her dashing away among those houses.

The woman came to me for *help*. No matter what threats the Eye made, helping people was why I had the Bones, it had to be.

The bike jolted, rolling over a lump in the sidewalk I'd never have felt at a real speed. I stole a glance back, all around, for any trace of the two Duvals—nothing.

I wasn't ready to take them on. No way in hell I was ready for the Eye himself.

If Maya Grant just slipped away from all of us, it would make so many things easier. I could go back inside and try drawing the Duvals out... My hand twitched around the handlebar's throttle; I could just let that go and pull over...

Instead I weaved on. The block's corner and the front of the library were up ahead.

A shout broke out behind me, loud enough to reach through my helmet. I twisted around—but, just a man sprawling over the sidewalk, just picking himself up from tripping.

Slowing down made my bike teeter, and I slammed a foot down before it tipped. The solid pavement gave me a moment to breathe deeper. I reached for the Pulse again... still too many currents, waves of feeling from everyone around. Maya's shifting emotions would have been swallowed in this; even the Duvals' aggression was still hidden. I roared on.

Turning the corner ahead brought me along the library's front, to the pale steps and the long ramp beside them. I headed on past them, keeping my eyes on the sidewalk and the people there, trying not to think how I was turning my back on the door where the Duvals could come charging out.

The building's next corner was up ahead; I was halfway to making a full circle around it, with nothing to show for it. I nursed the bike along, faster when the path was open and easing back when more people broke up the sidewalk ahead. A frustrated pain was digging in behind my eyes.

Motion broke out ahead—out of that cluster of people and stepping toward me. A slight figure, peeling back the green coat she'd huddled in and sliding through the crowd to walk toward me. Maya.

I pulled the bike up and let my hands go to take a full glance around. No Duvals in sight.

My helmet slid off, and I realized Maya had never seen it or known I could be on a bike. But she could see a rider searching the sidewalk for something, and she did know my jacket—she was nobody's fool. And here I'd been thinking of leaving her.

As she came closer, I held out the helmet.

Her eyes twitched wider, but then she shoved it over her head and climbed on behind me.

She said "So where do we go?" Like escaping was just another question, like she'd take any answer I had.

"Away. And then..." Then I had to hide her somewhere safe, while I took on the Duvals. But how could anyone deal with the Eye?

One last glance around, and we roared forward. For another moment the clogged sidewalk held us back, and then we swung out the parking lot entrance and onto the street at last.

The fresh speed steadied the bike—I slid it between two slow-moving cars, felt the wind on my unshielded face to warn me I had no head protection if I slipped. But Maya was pressed in close behind me, matching her balance to mine, her arms warm around my jacket.

Warm, safe. And we *did* beat the Duvals, between her trick and my guidance.

For now.

I zipped us past a yellow light—another amateur risk for a helmetless rider, but every second's distance might be the one that got us out of sight before they stepped outside. And speed was all we had right now, with Maya's problem triggering while the Plan was still trying to take form. I just didn't have the contacts or practice or preparation I'd need to stop and face a menace like the Duvals. And *no* chance against what I'd just seen of the Eye.

So, I'd have to adapt.

The traffic in my mirror showed the library was long out of sight down the street. First, I'd get Maya more distance and some shelter. Then I'd track the Duvals and pick out a way to shut them down—find what they wanted with her, how to bring the police down on them or scare them off or whatever worked. With the Bones' cold burning in my pocket, there had to be some way.

So, hide Maya, and do it fast enough to let me go on the attack. I only had one option.

Another twist slid us between two cars ahead, these moving slow enough that a family of joggers could have streamed by in safety. Maya's grip on me didn't even twitch.

She did squeeze tighter when I swung us around the next turn, into thicker traffic and then out again to edge through an alley, a space tight enough to throw the engine's roar back at us doubled. After that it was simply block after block of clear sailing.

And then we scooted into the vast Travers Bros building, into the cool dimness of the garage, and settled to a stop in an empty corner.

The end of that momentum, trading the engine's throbbing for sudden stillness and pavement under our feet again, let the moment freeze.

And she... *is she holding onto me longer than she needs to—* The thought stirred, just at the instant she drew back and climbed off.

I watched her, studied her face as she slid the helmet away. Before we went inside, I could sound her out about the Eye, about if all her "magic" really was stage tricks. Except she was only looking at the helmet in her hands, with no sign she felt a need to break the silence at all.

A car rumbled by us, turning in from the street. Another pulled into view on its way out—had I thought we were alone here?

I motioned for the door inside. We'd get a better chance to talk soon, once she was settled in.

The Travers Insurance corridors were as busy as ever. People scurried down the carpeted halls or crouched at their desks as if some invisible tethers pulled them along and kept their voices chattering. A few of them glanced at me as I strode in with Maya behind me, but none of them got in our way.

The assistant outside Helena's office was new, nervous-eyed. I told him "We'll be taking one of the conference rooms for a while—or we may be here late. You can check with her if you want," I added.

Then I led Maya off a side corridor, past a pair of small trees in huge pots. Two of the handful of people we passed gave me an uneasy look, no doubt remembering some of the things I'd poked into before. Simpler problems, about frauds or grudges.

I swung a glass door open. We stepped into a small conference room, one mostly filled with the table and too many chairs.

Maya leaned against one of the chairs, staying on her feet as she looked at me. "They did make you sound important this morning. I asked about their 'troubleshooter,' and the boss herself made some time for me."

I looked away, forced my feet not to start pacing. "It's not like that. But right now..."

The Duvals. Dealing with them started with knowing what they wanted with her, and what the *Eye* was up to. He said she had real magic too—was she still hiding that from me?

Well, why wouldn't she? The last thing anyone would do was open up with a secret like this, to a stranger. And now our lives might depend on it.

The door opened behind me.

"Maya? I didn't think we'd see you here again, after you found our Mr. Corbin."

Helena Travers swept into the room—all flawless blonde poise in her trim suit, and the *confidence* to talk about my work as if the whole floor was her trusted friend. The familiar tingle edged through me, for the fascinating woman who'd taken over a corporation and was still barely a decade older than me...

I glanced back from her to Maya again. Convincing Helena we needed her help could be the first step toward making Maya see how deep this had become.

"I had to bring her back here," I said. "She's in real trouble, worse than you were when we met." That clash hadn't even been against any secret powers—I'd still never told Helena about magic, not yet. "I need to hide her here for a few hours, maybe more."

"I see." Helena took a step closer to me, and dropped her voice to whisper "Still, do you think bringing her here is appropriate?"

"She *needs help*." I kept my voice up; Maya had to hear this too. "When have I been wrong here? That man you fired looked like just another employee caught in a lie, until he pulled his gun—and believe me, he would have used it."

Would she listen? Being around Helena was a constant temptation to use the Pulse and know what she really felt. One that I'd always resisted.

She said "I do believe you—but now you're calling that in as a marker? I thought we trusted each other more than that."

I was working on that. But I said only "Then listen to me. I've been catching your frauds and your embezzlers, and I've been right before. Today you gave Maya my name because you saw she needed help. Now I'm saying she does need that, more than anyone I've met in, well, years."

Right then I *did* draw on the Bones in my pocket, only to brush at Maya. But all I touched was the same shifting worry and resolve and quick-reacting awareness she showed before, with no spike of recognition as I hinted at the Duvals' danger, their magic.

"Nobody's turning you away." Helena smiled. "I'm simply saying, we need to talk about what being on retainer here means, if you think you can bring your off-hours cases in here. After this one, that is." Then she turned to Maya. "Sorry if we worried you. Adrian surprised me, but he says you need this. If there's anything we can do, let us know."

"I'm sorry, but no."

Maya rose to her feet, eyes on Helena.

"Thank you, both of you. But the more I think about it, the more I know it's not safe for any of you if I stay here. I need to go."

And her hand moved at her side, hiding one glint of something between her fingers. Like she'd been checking her phone.

"After we talk," I added, and I moved in front of her. Maya sighed, nodded, and I looked back to Helena. "Sorry. I guess we won't be long."

Helena looked at her a moment, some expression I could never read without the Pulse. "Alright. If that's how you want to handle it." And she stepped out and walked away.

When the door whispered shut over the carpet, the last fragments of corporate talk outside fell away. Maya drew back along the table, still not sitting down.

"Helena has seen a bit of this, you know," I said.

"I noticed. But, I didn't think those two would follow me. Or think about what that fire could do to anyone."

Their magic. Like she had no idea what that was, or about the Eye and his interest in her... Or she was keeping that secret and its burden, knowing how much it demanded from anyone to believe it.

I knew that feeling, better than anyone.

She reached over the conference table and lifted up a glass pitcher, half-full of water and melting ice. Judging by the water's surface, her hand didn't shake at all.

Still looking away, she said "I... was wrong, coming to you. I can't ask someone to get involved in this kind of craziness."

"I already am. And I've seen crazier." The Bones felt colder than ever in my pocket. "You think I'd run away? Especially when that message on your phone has to be trouble—"

"*No.*" She set the pitcher down with a low thump on the table, and glared up at me. "I'm saying I don't *want* help, from someone who doesn't have to be. I can barely pay you a thing for this. And I've tried the cops, they gave me the whole explanation about how they can't step in until those thugs have already done their worst. I need to get out of this my own way."

"And *I* said I *am* involved. I promised Helena, and myself and a few people more, I don't turn someone away when they need me." I took a slow step closer, a soft scraping footstep in the stillness between my words. "Hey, I should have gone after the Duvals weeks ago..."

But this was more than a pair of firebugs, if the Eye was involved. There was no way around it, I had to tell her about him, about all the magic, when she still might not have one reason to listen.

The old pain spread its tendrils through my chest. My throat was suddenly tight, and I took one glance at that pitcher of cool water.

I added "That's because I do know about their fire."

"That's more than I do." A smile twitched on her lips. "As a pro, all I can say is it's a hell of a magic trick."

"That's half true."

I grabbed onto her word and latched my answer onto it before it could fade, before I could hesitate. Maya's face flickered, with what could be surprise or a greater secret underneath, I couldn't tell.

Because I wasn't *using* the Bones, even with them unboxed and ready in my pocket. I was still letting myself guess whether she was one of the few people who might have come across actual magic, or they'd dragged her into these schemes by mistake. And I could just picture how her pale, haunted face could sharpen into a knife of doubt once I said it.

I don't have to read her, I insisted to myself. Maya was a client, a victim, not an enemy.

"I'm waiting," she said. "Are you going to explain that or not?"

I took a long breath. "I mean it's magic, and not a trick. The Duvals have weapons that conjure up fire. And, someone thinks you have something like that yourself."

There it was. Her eyes jolted wide, then narrowed—just the picture of shock and suspicion, the *I'm staring at a madman* look.

The shame flared through me. I could still grab at her emotions for a hope that she was faking that, if I could risk *feeling* that kind of doubt if it was genuine... I left the Pulse still.

"Real. Magic," she said. "I do one illusion of sliding a card toward you and you think... you think *they...*"

She edged back a step. Like anyone would, even in this cramped little room and its table that gave no room to slip past the crazy-talking stranger.

And if she did run, if she ran into the Duvals and whatever had been on her phone?

I could only push on. "It's more than the Duvals. You know about the Eye?"

"What?" The shaken, unnerved look on her face didn't change at all now.

"I don't know much. I was lucky I even heard the name and survived—"

She drew back another step, when I mentioned surviving. But this time I let the Pulse work, and I felt something else. Her fear stretched and throbbed through her, but she *gripped* it tight, same as she'd held that pitcher steady. Not as shaken as she looked.

I went on "The Eye is supposed to have a presence everywhere. That was all I heard, until today, just when you were slipping out the library door."

That fear in her tightened, but she glared right back at me.

"The Eye spoke to me. Or he appeared around me, I still can't say what he did or what force he was using. And he made a threat against everything in my life, if I didn't get him the secret of your magic."

She shut her eyes. "My magic. A voice in your head said—"

"Not in my head!"

The words burst out of me, rang off the walls.

Maya froze, but I shoved the thought down. Forced down the image of—

My mother, "hearing ghosts," but this time it was all too real—

"Sorry," I whispered.

At least Maya was still facing me, standing her ground.

I tried again: "You've seen the Duvals work. You've seen it yourself, they've got something you can't explain away..."

No, I had to give her the whole truth. I reached inside my jacket to draw out my tablet.

"They've got the secret of magical fire, and they've been using it. I was already sure of that, just from this, and this."

I pulled up one news report, a picture of a local hardware store in smoking ruin. Then another burn site, with the word *unsolved* leading the headline.

Maya's face didn't stir at all.

"As for the Eye... the first question there is *how*, but he's supposed to be the most elusive person in the whole city, and that's all I know about his magic. And I need to know it.

"Because I've got my own."

I forced the last words out and braced for the derision that could twist her away. And her fear... it tightened again, and her control tightened along with it.

"You have... no, it's too much," she said. "You want to talk real magic, you're going to have to show me."

My eyes clenched shut. She had to go right to that, to actually meeting me halfway—except that the Pulse wasn't something like the Duvals' fire that you could *see*.

Or I could tell her I was tracking her emotions, or how I could try bending how much someone felt a thing. Just the way to put her at ease.

I let my sense of her fade away, and said "There's not much you can see of it, not right now. It's most obvious around enemies, like when I dropped Willard Duval. Or..." The thought burst through me. "Or, when we were first talking, before I got that call about them in the building. I sensed them coming—I was already trying to get us out, remember?"

Her head *dipped,* in the faintest nod. She was listening.

Then she said "So... I should just trust you about this?"

"You should," and I managed a smile. "You told me the Duvals had some use for you. Now the Eye wants your magic—that makes two sides that think you're hiding something."

And I drew on the Pulse one more time. The guarded tension behind Maya's eyes drew back, tighter still, maybe too much for just the fear of an awkward question.

"Well, I'm a *performer,*" she said. "I'm paid to fool people for ten minutes at a time, with the best deceptions I can find."

Not for the first time, I wished the Pulse could catch some clear spike in emotion when people lied. Still, she read like someone with a secret to hide, and of course she'd turn cautious when I'd just admitted the Eye was after her.

She shook her head. "These Duvals just have their tricks, and I guess they figure they can add mine for some new racket of theirs. All of that adds up to... I can't stay hidden here. What I need is to get out of their reach, my way."

"Escape?" I moved back a step, as I added "And how does that go with that phone message you saw before you told Helena you were going?"

Her eyes flickered, and I nodded. Yes, I'd been waiting to play that card, even if she thought I'd forgotten.

She sighed "You don't want to know."

I smiled again, kept it a small, gentle thing. "I think I've just been showing you that I do."

And with any luck, her staying to argue meant she was willing to tell me, and let me help.

I fought down one treacherous urge to try the Pulse at muffling her fears, at *making* her more willing to open up. You don't force things like that—least of all to get real trust.

Then, she seemed to shrink, to settle as traces of tension eased out of her face.

"The text was from my landlord. He says the Duvals are lurking around my apartment, and I bet they'll be making threats to him soon."

"Good bet."

A flush of heat swept through me, a chance and a need to do something, that shook through the coldness of these confessions.

"I'll see about that. Maya, this is still about them wanting you for some job, they called it?" And suspecting the magic she denied having.

"Yes. And that's all they said, no idea what I was so damn important for."

"I'll try to find out, when I get them away from your friend." I felt the smile stretching all over my face. "Now that we know where they are. And our firestarters don't have us caught between walls of paper."

"I told you I'd handle it—"

Maya broke off, looked away. Then she looked back to meet my eyes.

"Or, we can. If you're so determined to show me this magic of yours."

That's not what I said... but I *did* have to show her the danger from the Eye and all the rest. And I'd missed my chance to make her stay back, unless I could make her listen.

"Let's go."

* * *

"No, we're as quiet as, well, a library again. No sign of those two bruisers." Barry's voice on the phone slowed, impressed. "You really just tackled that bruiser."

"Guess I'm that crazy—but I'm glad it worked. Thanks."

I glanced around the sidewalk, at the late afternoon foot traffic cramped in between the high apartment buildings' walls. How did I get so caught up in this that it took me this long to check back on Barry and Gina and the rest? But then, I knew the Duvals had moved on.

The street Maya and I walked along had its own kind of tight echo, as kids scurried around and cars rolled along the narrow space. I looked past the scraggly trees along the walk ahead, to where one style of brick and masonry made a subtle shift to another design for a different set of apartments. Just how close together the windows were told me each living space here was smaller than how I lived. Not many places to hide out here, either.

Maya halted, sidestepping closer to the wall.

"That's Sheffield Apartments up ahead, so if we come any closer the Duvals could see us through the windows. Unless they're somewhere out on the street, or they're long gone." She spoke softly and clearly, tucking the private words in below the raised voices of an older couple arguing up ahead.

"And you still don't know why they're so interested in you." *Like the magic the Eye thinks you have, that it feels like you're lying about?*

She only shook her head again. "Interested, that's all. They kept saying to stay in town, and be ready for some 'job.' So I'm hoping you've got a way I *won't* have to find out what that means."

I looked back up at the buildings' faces ahead. I'd never said what I had in mind here, because there was no way to choose until I knew the situation.

Squaring my feet, I gave one leg a faint stomp; my thigh felt close to numb from keeping the Bones outside their box for so long. Then I drew on their power.

Currents of emotion stirred around me, one stream along the street and others scattered behind the walls, like water bubbling behind glass. The pressure should have been a flood, but I'd used so much of the Bones' stored power in shocking Willard Duval and then searching for Maya...

Shards of tight anger floated within the lake of emotion ahead, the same deep-rooted rage I'd felt before. Even clearer was the single spike of fear they clustered around.

"The Duvals are up there. In the next building, alright, yours." I held my breath and tried to distill the sense down to one spot, dozens of feet ahead. "I can sense them... up at the building's front."

"You sense them? This is your 'real magic' again?" She smiled—and somehow the small grin was straight enough, clean enough, that it might not be mocking me. "At the front, at Gordon's office?"

I'd treat that as taking me at my word, better than dwelling on how much doubt she could still be holding onto. "Gordon must be the one in there with them, and he's scared. But I'll see."

I closed my eyes to focus on the three presences, then drew my eyes slowly open again to hold that clarity, to match it against the lines of brick beside me. The Duvals were standing back from the windows.

Slowly I walked forward, edging nearer the side, passing a step's railing covered with flaking brown paint. Maya moved a few steps behind me, as people flowed on past us.

The building's face shifted to paler, cleaner bricks, her own apartment group, and I pressed in closer to the shelter of the wall.

The word *magic* jumped out at me—written on a sign hung beside a door, with the same hat-and-ribbon logo I'd seen on Maya's card. Some kind of apartment promotion she was in next week.

I could just make out the windows ahead, and the blinds hanging over them. I moved close along the wall, out of view in case the Duvals stepped over to peep out between those slats. A boy glanced over at me, then a pair of women, but they kept walking.

A camera dangled above the building, at some limp angle as if it had been broken long ago... The Duvals still hung back inside the room, away from the window just ahead...

One moved. One knot of hostility moved, toward the window—

I flattened back against the wall. People around me stared, but that couldn't matter now.

Maya pulled backward a few steps, out of the window's view as well. No doubting, no arguments from her this time.

Then the wandering Duval moved back deeper into the room. I waited, tracked them all, smiled at the passing people until I'd taken four slow breaths.

I crouched down and crept over to the edge of the window, and the crack of the blinds. The Pulse put him right about...

The sliver of the room showed me a graying man with a bushy beard, sitting in a chair with his gaze locked on something further in. I felt him soaked with the kind of constant dread that never quite numbed the nerves. His face was screwed up tight trying to hold that fear in.

Back behind me, Maya kept her distance—she might look like any one of these passers-by, who had no idea what happened behind that window and only wondered what I was up to. Still, the people around her were the ones she had to live among.

I drew out my phone, and angled it to snap a picture through the crack. More heads turned to watch now, but I'd have to deal with that later.

When I pulled back from the window, Maya walked right up to join me. I held up the phone.

She said "That's Gordon Weber alright. But maybe the Duvals don't have him at gunpoint. Yet."

I nodded. I could sense the same thing—if *terror mostly under control* counted as a stable situation. "Well, I'm not waiting to see what they're up to. And you're sure as hell not giving them what they want."

"So you've got a plan?"

I winced at the word. For years now, the Plan had always been to collect information, options, allies, try to find any other dangerous magic out there and come after it on my own terms. No surprise it couldn't be ready enough: no Plan survives contact with the enemy.

"We've got time to pick our choices," I said. "So, the safest way to stop the Duvals from torching everything in sight is to use something they won't want to burn."

"And there *is* something they won't?" An eyebrow rose.

"Some one. *Now* we call a cop."

I had to flip my phone past a screen to find Detective Jenson Poe. I'd met him helping Helena and a friend of hers with a stalker, and Poe had seemed honestly concerned—enough to take information from me, at least the kind I could let him know. I kept meaning to sound him out more, to see if he was the ally I needed against what else I'd seen. One more part of the Plan I put off.

The phone rang. It just rang, with Maya watching me and at least one man on the street still eyeing us after my skulking around the window. It would be just my luck if my best answer to all this didn't answer the phone...

"Mister Corbin, is it?" Poe's voice was hushed.

"Glad you remember me, Detective. Here, I'll get right to the point: we have a man being held hostage." And I sent him the picture.

For a long moment, the line was silent.

Then:

"Hostage? He's just sitting there. And how'd you get this—peeking through windows?"

What? I clicked the picture open, looked at it again. There was the fear in Gordon Weber's face, not as clear as when I'd first seen him or anything like the dread the Pulse showed me. But Poe must be missing all that...

I shifted my grip on the phone. On the phone I couldn't read Poe to sense how deep that skepticism went—but I didn't need the Bones every time. *"He* needs help. His name's Gordon Weber, and he was texting for help. See?"

I looked up at Maya. Her phone was already in her hands.

Gordon's text to her pinged onto my phone: *two thugs watching me* and an ominous lack of anything since. I sent it along to the detective.

A sound came through the phone, some kind of crowd's roar, loud enough to reach me. Wherever Poe was when I called, he could barely hear himself think.

"That went to Maya Grant?" he said. "I don't see much court time on her, but from her juvenile hints... well, you'd do best to stay out of her business."

What did he... did Poe just search *Maya's records, and write her off at one glance...*

Slowly, carefully, I tried to push the thickening anger out of my voice. "I said, this is about a *hostage*. And it's Willard and Dom Duval—the ones at the Central Library an hour ago, that almost *burned* it all down."

"Library?" The line went still, for barely a second, and then he added "First I've heard of it. No reports from there at all."

So they hadn't filed it yet... or Gina panicked or something... I might as well be feeling Poe's mind closing off now, it sounded. "I'm telling you, just call them! They'll tell you what happened."

"You call them. Or call 911—but remember there's a law against fake reports there. And Peeping Tom photos too. Stop wasting my time."

He hung up.

I stared at the screen.

Of course it couldn't be that easy. I'd only called Poe because I had his number, and what had sounded like a hint of cooperation from him once. I hadn't even tested him with the Pulse back when I had the chance.

I looked up at Maya. "So it's up to me. Us."

CHAPTER THREE: REVEALS

Maya led me around the side of the building. We slid past an ice-cream cart that had just begun to gather kids around it, and into a narrow alley that the high walls cast into twilight. Then she pulled open a quiet little door in the wall.

The sounds of the streets vanished behind us, replaced by the scattered noises from the rooms. The corridor pressed around us with its doors and smudged tan carpet.

She said "Were you thinking of sneaking up and, say, getting Gordon away from them?" Her voice changed as she spoke, from a hesitant start to a firmness as it came together.

"I could. Or I get more evidence for a 911 call, or jump them—if I get a chance..."

I paused as a door opened, and a little girl with a dog as big as she was walked by us to the exit.

The trouble was, the Bones had only so much magic left for now, after my full-on assault on Willard Duval. And even without trying to sense the Duvals now, I could still remember how volatile they were.

Maya said "I thought you'd want to let them get a glimpse of me again. It got them away before."

Did she sound reluctant or not? I was trying to keep her with me, where the Pulse and the crowds could help screen her from them—but *you don't get to be bait, ever* wasn't an answer she'd listen to. Instead I said "They chased you last time. But then they came here, to your home, so if we shake them again they might simply come back here. And they're *angry.*"

Except... how did the Duvals' rage fit with them saying they had "a job" for her? And, Poe had said Maya had something shady in her record...

But then, she hadn't been afraid to ask the cops for help once, and now she was asking me. And the Duvals' threat was bigger than that.

She led me around a quick turn and onward. Our footsteps padded over the carpet, echoes in the narrow corridor fading in and out against the one or two people we passed at their doors and the sounds of more behind them.

This had to be too many emotions between us and the Duvals to spot them now. I wished I could slip away to recharge the Bones, even a little.

A kid leaning against the wall looked over at Maya, and pulled out his earphones to wave at her. "Hey. Old man Gordon was looking for you." He straightened his ratty shirt.

"Hey—" She stopped, like she'd forgotten his name. "Looking for me?"

"Could have been ten minutes back. He had a couple big guys with him, looked like bad news. That or they want you for that sales thing someone's doing now. Pull some bucks out of a hat?" He waved a hand.

"If I could pull dollars out of hats, I wouldn't be doing favors for Gordon, would I?" Her laugh sparkled, then died away. "Guess I have to remind him I only signed on for the community thing next week."

"Unless the boss says different, right? Nice gig, though—"

Ten minutes ago, just before we got here, or were they still out in the halls? I reached out with the Pulse for a moment. Instead of the Duvals' anger, I felt the constellation of feelings around the corridors, and one churning knot of them ahead that drowned out so much of my senses. Still, a hard edge beyond them made me think of the rage I'd felt in the Duvals before.

Maya was walking away, just in the moment I'd lost searching. I moved after her, and she kept her gaze straight ahead, almost embarrassed.

"I think they're still at the front office," I said. "But, how many people is this 'sales thing'?"

"How many can they get? If they're in the rec room it could be a dozen or more."

Maybe it was our talking about it, but the murmurings around us seemed to gather, into a thickening sound of voices up ahead.

"Maya... can you get them out of here? Get them to the other side of the building, or make them call it off?" Her eyes widened, and I added "You can't sense how mad the Duvals are now. But you know what they could set off here."

"Get those people away, because of your invisible warnings? You think that's easy?"

She just couldn't feel how short those two fuses were... but I had no words to make her see. And no good way to help her—even if I were someone who went around using the Pulse on people's fears or trust, the Bones didn't have power to spare.

Just the fact that the Duvals' hostility could stand out made me wonder. Could using enough fire magic *make* them "hotheads"? I'd spent so long after the Scarecrow trying to ease into magic safely.

People milled around where a glass door stood open ahead, the source of those voices. The room was dotted with chairs between a pool table and a ping-pong table, and there were people for half of them—mostly our age and up for a challenge, some older, singles and couples, curious or impatient or laughing.

Stepping up beyond that doorway let me probe the corridor in front for one instant. With the tangle of emotions behind me, I could make out the sizzle of the two Duvals somewhere ahead.

I glanced back into the room. One balding man in a suit was in the center, whirling back and forth between checking the snacks on a table and nodding to different people.

I waved Maya toward him.

She gave me a long, slow sigh, and headed in. I moved behind her, threading past the chairs and the people shifting around.

She looked at the busy leader and called to him over a woman's shoulder: "Hey, um—"

"Ah, it's Maya?" He turned right to her; he was younger than I thought. "Let me guess: you're looking for the funds to upgrade that old coat. And some new venues to perform too, am I right?"

Was that supposed to be some hard-sell sales pitch, for his... the signs and pictures only showed generic happy families that could be selling anything from medicine to mortgages. More likely medicine, since they let him sell it here.

I saw Maya wince, before she said "I'm doing alright. But—"

The woman beside him said "We almost ready?" and he turned away.

The voices closed in around us, drawing him another step away.

Then Maya seemed to *swell,* to straighten, and her voice settled in a low, resonant tone that pushed those sounds back.

"I thought I'd give you some help here. If you put this on hold for half an hour so I can set something up, I'll give these people a demo they'll never forget."

The leader looked at her, slowly, appraising her.

Then: "Can't, I'm afraid, it's already planned down to the minute. You see why you need to get in to these opportunities early? Now next week we're—"

"Not then." Her voice rose, just enough to cut him off. "This is a once in a lifetime chance. And believe me, I'll make it worth your time."

She held up one of her cards, and with a flick she sent it high into the air. It sailed upward, spun down, and landed right in a bowl of nachos to stand on end with a corner wedged between the snacks.

For a moment the room seemed to hush, as if even the people across the room had felt some of our reaction around the stunt. My mind's eye replayed that card's flight... what kind of wires could do all that with no setup...

The sales leader eyed the card. His hand slowly stretched toward it.

He pulled back. "Now I know we have to talk, *after* this is done. There's just no time now, and this can't be one of Gordon's plans or he'd have come himself. But you just watch us here and—"

I felt myself stepping forward. "You should listen to her. Or aren't you the one that grabs at opportunities before they're gone?"

And I reached out with the Pulse.

Just a twitch, trying to draw out a bit of hesitation, then uncork a little of that cloying greed... *I hate this, trying to remake someone's emotions...*

Maybe that was why my touch slipped. I saw his gaze go dull for a moment, but then it gathered sharper than ever, focused on me. "You're a, a friend of Maya's? You sound like you know how the world works." That greed I'd tried to draw gave his voice a hungry edge. "As soon as we're done here—"

"Sorry," Maya cut in. "I said you had one chance, so there's nothing left to talk about."

And she swung away, pulling me back through the crowd. I saw her give one glare back at the snacks and the people around them, and then we stepped outside.

She muttered "Upgrade my coat... you think he'd listen if I'd worn my best one?" Then, more gently, she added "But I hope you're wrong about what the Duvals could do."

"So do I."

She led me up the corridor again. It was a dozen doors later that her first angry rush slowed and let us drop into a more cautious pace.

The range I'd felt the Duvals at, how did that match with the distance we'd covered? They had to be near that intersection ahead, one side or another of that T shape.

And the Bones weren't empty yet. I reached out for a quick scan.

Heat, that made me flinch back from those smoldering, growing, *approaching* wills—

I waved at the corner ahead. "They're coming!"

Too many long steps stretched between me and that turn for me to reach it and ambush them—and behind us it was another forty feet before another branch in the corridor, and they'd hear us running, they were so close to the T ahead.

A wash of confidence welled up from Maya beside me, and she grabbed at the nearest apartment door. It swung right open to let her dive inside, with me at her heels to shut it behind us.

An older couple stared up at us, from a tiny dinner table set for two. Their mouths opened in shock.

"Shhh!" Maya said. *"Please..."*

I didn't move, didn't speak. But I grabbed at the Pulse—made one tickle of trust at their emotions, no more. Inside I cringed at my having another moment of weakness.

The man's eyes swelled wide. "You can't just break in... do I know you..."

"Please!" Maya's voice was a raw whisper of fear. "That's my ex out there."

Simple as that, she slipped into the role of a woman in hiding. And she'd been dressed for it all afternoon, with the nondescript coat and shapeless hat all chosen to help her slip past a pursuer.

The couple broke off. An uneasy look flicked between the man in the thin glasses and the woman in her multicolored sweater.

I pressed back against the door. Just outside it, heavy feet tromped toward us—that steady pace was our best promise that the Duvals hadn't heard us, even as it brought them closer.

The couple watched us, still frightened, but less certain now what they'd been caught up in.

Behind me, the footsteps passed close. Marched by.

A harsh gasp broke from outside, a sound that must have been wrenched loose by pure terror. The Pulse confirmed it with a thought: sharp fear leaped up there, spilling past the simple rage of the two Duvals. Like a man just realizing he could die.

I cracked the door open—

To see the backs of the two massive Duvals walking away, one with an arm locked around Gordon Weber's shoulders. A smell floated behind them, just a whiff like burning hair.

Or beard. Like one instant of fire before it was snuffed out.

"She'll come, she'll come!" the prisoner was wheezing. "She's still an orphan fighting her way up, she knows I'm the only one who gave her a chance..."

The sound faded as they drew further away. One last hushed word broke through the distance,

"*tombs...*"

and their voices faded away.

I shut the door, the softest whisper of wood clicking against wood, as I used the Pulse to keep tracking how that *dread,* that violence, moved away.

I couldn't stop them. My hands shouldn't have shivered as I closed the door, I'd already beaten Willard Duval once. But that had been just one of them, and now the Bones were mostly drained, and I couldn't even stop myself from trickling out more power just to stay sure that those two were heading *away.*

Maya looked at me. Her mouth twitched, struggling to hold in some emotion of her own.

The woman in the sweater gasped "What is it? Who are you people?"

"Sorry," I said. "I think they're gone now." The words sounded like I'd had someone else say them, so calm. As if it didn't matter how much fear I'd brushed against, once there was someone else to keep from panicking.

Maya moved up to brush my side, a question in her eyes.

I whispered "They're still holding him, as bait for you." Guilt flashed over her face. I added "And I've got no way left to attack them." Not in this tile and concrete environment, with no way to recharge the Bones, even if Maya wasn't watching.

"If we can't stop them... the police? A distraction?"

"It has to be. Their frustration's been brewing so long, I know they could boil over any time." They were already singeing their prisoner—but Maya didn't need to know that. "They could burn—"

"A fire alarm," she hissed. "Get everyone out, and hope the confusion gives us a chance."

"That... could be it."

I met her gaze, her sharp eyes watching me, needing that confirmation. Were there any flaws in that plan, at least compared to leaving that prisoner with the Duvals?

"Okay," I nodded. "But one thing: they were heading near that rec room, so we need to get that crowd away from them. I'll do that—well, if I have a chance to duck in behind the Duvals, anyway."

"But—"

The man at the table broke in, hesitant but gathering force again. "Please! Just tell me what's going on. Do we need to call the police about you?"

"M-maybe you should." Maya's voice trembled as she looked back at them, even more than when she'd calmed them before. "Tell them, tell them we're running from Willard Duval and his cousin. We need help!"

"You *want* me to call—"

"Yes!"

Maya turned and edged the door open to sneak a look out.

One moment later she ducked back and thumped the door shut, and a flash of rage sparked on her face before she turned away from me.

"You alright?" I breathed.

"Sure."

She *sounded* okay. "Maya, we have to move. They said something about needing tombs."

And I reached for another scan. The Duvals were still up there, almost at the pool of emotions that would be the rec center, and Gordon Weber's fear was still beside them. But Maya's own fury burned like a blowtorch at my elbow.

In a tight voice she said "Around the corner, away from them and toward the office they came from. I think there's an alarm up there."

"Okay." My hands twitched, wanted to go to her shoulders as I said "One step at a time, you can do this. We can do this."

She still looked away from me, but she nodded.

This time I edged the door open.

The Duvals and Gordon were out of sight, far down the length of the corridor and screened by a family with a knot of kids moving toward us.

Maya headed toward them.

Not that way, not you—I caught at her, but she dodged clear and scrambled out of reach. I bit down a wave of worry and moved the other way, toward the corner the Duvals had come from before. This made twice the two of us had settled into a plan to split up, but this time she'd grabbed the dangerous role.

When I turned the corner, the fire-red alarm handle hung right there on the wall. So, pull it now or wait for Maya to get to the rec room...

Except, the Duvals really had felt near that spot. Was I expecting Maya to slip in there right behind them, that close? I turned toward the alarm.

Something moved on up the corridor—a flurry of motion as a figure in a doorway pulled back out of sight. One movement, one glance toward me, one impression of a beard nothing like Gordon Weber's, something huge and red. And the door closed.

For an instant it looked like he'd been avoiding me. I tried to place where I was—that could be the apartment office I'd seen from outside.

I shook my head, looked back up the corridor toward the rec room. The family, chattering kids' voices and all, was coming closer, giving me just a few more seconds to duck back and grab the alarm before they saw me with it. Another breath...

Then I got a glimpse of Maya beyond them, racing on up toward the rec room where the crowd would be.

My grin stretched over my face. *That girl's lucky, or just crazy.* So I'd let her get to the rec room before I moved—

She turned aside, toward the wrong side of the corridor, and ducked in through what had to be another apartment door.

What was she doing? I stared, up the tight, pale corridor and the approaching family, the handful of other people scattered around it. If she was running from the Duvals, I couldn't see them.

My hand was leaning on the corner, holding me up as I shook. I fumbled at the Pulse, but now the Duvals' anger felt lost in the distance and the tangle of different emotions between us, and the family's whirling, half-meshed patterns walking past me...

I wrenched myself back from staring. The little group turned off one way at the T, so I turned the other way and walked numbly past the alarm.

That alarm had to happen soon. Voices sprang up around me, not only the ones receding behind me but sounds in an apartment I passed, and up ahead. More and more people would be settling in for dinner—and any of them could roast if the Duvals started their fires.

I reached the office door, saw its blinds covering the windows.

But right now I didn't care if that Redbeard had been looking at me or what. Instead I noted the door out to the street just beyond it, one clear exit people could head for, and spun to stroll back toward the alarm.

This had to be now, Maya or no Maya. At least the corridors looked clear for the moment. I stole one glance back around the corner.

Up at the far end, Maya was striding straight toward the rec room door. Sweet relief rushed through me, and I grabbed the alarm switch.

One quick yank brought it down—so easily the sudden stop at the end jarred my fingers loose. And then the fire alarm came jarring at my ears.

I swung around the corner at a quick walk, craning my head different ways and hoping it fended off anyone's suspicion from settling on me. Far ahead, Maya reached the rec room as the voices around me roused.

"What the—"

"Dammit to hell—"

"Someone shut that thing off—"

The alarm wasn't even the loudest sound, against all the echoes crowded into the corridor. It was its demanding tone and mechanical relentlessness that forced doors open, forced people into the corridors.

"That way, right out there!" I shouted once, waving back toward the office and the door to the outside. Faces flicked toward me, some angry, some starting to turn for the exit, moving in a daze.

The Duvals... the thickening crowd in the corridor cut off any sight of them, and the turmoil of emotions would deafen any try to use the Pulse. I sidestepped and twisted my way onward, searching. The people around were young, old, angry, dazed, but slowly gathering momentum to flow past me. Filling more and more of the corridor.

Maya stepped into view up ahead. She was calling out something that the clamor swallowed up, standing boldly among the people she waved out from the rec room. Some trudged slowly, some quickly, some dispersed away into the corridor—probably checking on their families—but she had them moving.

Doors opened along the corridor, and more bodies filtered in to thicken the crowd. Sweat seemed to gather in the air, as figures pressed closer around. I slid along the wall, on the far side from Maya, peering through the shifting shapes ahead for a first glimpse of the Duvals.

That was our best hope, that I could spot them before they saw me. A large woman popped out of the doorway I passed, and I spun myself away and staggered against the wall.

Motion—another shape *ran* through the crowd, and that graying bearded face was Gordon Weber himself, dashing past me.

He'd broken free. We'd won.

Something in me relaxed as I turned and slipped back in among the current of bodies. A furious young voice shouted something by my elbow, and a shriller sound tried to hush him—and I waved them both on toward the exit. Up ahead, Maya was picking her way out too.

A bald man toppled to his knees, bumped by someone behind him, then a young woman helped him up. I looked around for anyone else at risk.

Dozens of feet back, the huge figures of the Duvals were muscling through the crowd, with what looked like suitcases in their hands. I turned away to hide my face from them, and ducked in around three men that were moving ahead. Now we just had to slip away.

"Maya!" someone bellowed.

The full-bodied shout cut through the tangled voices and the alarm—I turned, saw her sprawling on the floor, struggling to her feet against the press.

A flash of russet behind her. The red-bearded man kept his eyes on her as he backed away into the crowd. Now that his shout and push had given her position away.

The Duvals surged toward her, eyes locked on their target. One shouldered a tall man aside without a glance at him, closing in fast. I dodged toward Maya as she twisted away among the crowd ahead.

Then someone screamed.

A raw, far-too-real scream ripped loose from somewhere up beyond my sight. Somewhere beyond the crowd—then figures recoiled back to reveal one of the apartment doors covered in leaping flame. Another flash of orange light and the fire spilled out along the floor.

Shouts and frantic motions exploded in the corridor. One woman trying to cover her face and steel herself for a leap across the barrier of flame. Another dragging her back. So many instants, so many different people thrashing in the trap.

Oh God. Once I pulled the alarm, the Duvals had nothing to lose...

The press of bodies ahead hid how far the flames had stretched. Smoke bit in the air, a first whiff made all too real by the coughing sounds ahead. That *heat* on my jacket couldn't be real yet, it had to be from the people crammed together or pure desperation. Bodies struggled, tried to push back through each other.

Maya was swallowed in that frenzy. The shouting, the alarm, blasted all hearing away.

The two Duvals lumbered closer, and what people could get free fled around them like a stream around rocks. They looked right past me.

I eyed the distance to them, the cover and the obstacles that the fleeing people would give—and the *size* of the two cousins. With the Bones this drained, I might do better rushing the wall, but it could be that or burn.

Gordon Weber stepped from the edge of the crowd. He stumbled toward the Duvals, waving them toward somewhere back behind him—toward the wall where Maya crouched.

Traitor... survivor... The two thoughts flashed together, and the part of my head that should pick one lay still.

The Duvals pushed in. More shapes poured by them, closer now but never slowing them. I gathered myself, watched for the break in the stream that would let me charge them. The shouts hammered at my ears.

A tall man twisted into my side. I spilled to the floor, something slammed at me as it passed, then another body—I rolled away and got a foot under me, forced myself to my feet.

"This way! This way!"

That shout must have been going for some time—the sheer repetition of it worked through the clamor the way no volume could. Down behind the Duvals, Redbeard was waving people toward a small, open door, and people streamed toward it.

And that current pulled more bodies away from Maya up at the flames, left her hemmed in by a shrinking rush of people racing and fighting past her, with the fire beyond her and the Duvals closing in.

A stocky man rushing past Dom Duval swerved, staggered and fell right onto his side. The bigger man shoved him away with a grunt. I gritted my teeth—that could have been my shot at them if I'd been closer.

Willard Duval grabbed Gordon's arm. Why wasn't the landlord long gone by now, safe?

Another man stumbled and sprawled against Dom. And a woman toppled against his back, another man fell against those as Willard tried to pull his cousin out of the pile-up. Another body crashed against his back.

And Maya slipped right past them, a fierce grin on her face.

I charged after her.

Willard's hand never let go of Gordon. I heard Dom snarl "We've still got tombs—"

The flow of the crowd swept me through the door. I tried to catch Maya, but we were losing Gordon again—

I fought to look back up the corridor. And there, the Duvals were hauling their prisoner away past our door behind us... and then more firelight flared up from somewhere in their wake, after the door. People still poured in behind me, pushing me away.

This last fire didn't corner anyone, but it covered the Duvals' retreat. No way back.

And suddenly it was all speed—running *with* the crowd and not thinking about losing our balance, closing in on Maya and the door to the outside—

On the floor lay a small mound of russet red. From the man who'd led us here, that beard had been *fake*.

I burst out into the open air, and my ears filled with the wider echoes and the sheer space of seeing the people fall back and spread out. Had I ever called this huge urban canyon a *small* street?

Maya grabbed at my arm.

"Gordon! They caught him again!" I said. And the man who'd led us here had tried getting Maya caught once... I waved in the direction I'd seen the Duvals go, and we dashed along the building's side.

Weaving through this crowd was different, the way it freely thinned out into the street and left the sidewalk almost clear. The clatter of voices was a duller roar with so much space to soak it up. From out here the building still looked untouched.

Maya led me along the block, both of us watching doors and searching as the crowd pressed back a nervous distance from the building. As we ran, the first sirens howled out in the street—at least our early triggering the alarm might have given the firefighters a head start.

Then I realized we'd run all the way around the block, with no sign of the Duvals and their prisoner. I grabbed Maya and pulled her across the street, up into the next block. Whoever had been under that beard could still be watching... he might even be the Eye.

We stumbled off the street and up some small flight of steps toward a small apartment, out of the shifting crowds, and we sagged against the railing there. I gasped for breath, felt the chills and the wobbly, wrung-out exhaustion work their way through me. I managed to glance up and notice the place's door hung open; everyone must want a look at the fire now.

"I'm sorry," Maya whispered. Her voice was faint, ragged.

"So am I, about all of it. I'll find them, I'll find Gordon... but did you see, he tried to turn you over to—"

Her hand moved, waving that aside. "I'm sorry I lied to you."

Lied? I opened my mouth to answer, but she went on:

"When you said you had magic. Of course I believe you, and I do have my own. It's all the different ways I can just... *pull*."

She looked up, at the building's open door.

The door moved, in one swift motion it swung shut. I could hear it thump closed.

"I could have told you. And now, all of our homes..." Her head sank to look at the railing, keeping her gaze far away from her block. "We could have done so much more to stop those maniacs. Your senses, my tricks..."

"You pushed those people into the Duvals. Telekinesis." I studied the slumped figure beside me. "And... you opened those locks—that's how you grabbed the nearest door and knew we could hide behind it. Did you steal magic from the Scarecrow too?" I heard myself add.

"Who? No, this is about *me*."

Her head lifted now. She looked smaller, with something haunted in her face. Or like something had been scoured out of her, a woman all out of denials.

She said "These two, they must know something. I mean, I saw them go into my room, and they came out with bags of my stuff. I had to check."

The room she went to, before the rec room meeting. That had been her room?

She added "And, tombs."

Tombs, sure. I swallowed—how bad was this going to get? "What tombs?"

"Not what. Who."

A tiny smile flickered on her, and then it was washed away.

"If they're after me, I think they're after Floyd Toomes too. He was my foster father for a year... but that was before I found my magic, he's got nothing to do with this. Or I thought he couldn't—I don't *know* anymore..."

Her hands slammed onto the railing.

"But if he's next, we have to find him."

CHAPTER FOUR: SECRETS

The bike swept around the blocks, gliding and weaving for what speed we could make with the fire engines and the shifting crowd moving around us. Every shift drove the fear into me, of how the flames might have reached Maya's home by now—while the image of Gordon Weber being pulled away floated in my sight.

We never saw the Duvals.

Long blocks later, the traffic on the street thinned out to leave us with just the rising winds and the truth that we'd lost our enemy. I settled us to a stop, and Maya climbed down and started tapping a number on her phone.

She stopped midway and had to retry it. Her fingers were trembling.

"Calling Toomes?" I asked.

She nodded. I looked away—Maya wouldn't want me to notice how shaken she was.

Instead I tried to dredge through my own ideas. The Duvals took Gordon, and they said they'd *got* Toomes already... all I had was the small file I'd started on the cousins when I began to tie them to fires and intimidation... But what did that tell me about what they were after?

Go back to what I have. I'm on retainer for Helena's insurance company, and I have a contact I know works late.

Maya was still on her phone, drumming fingers in some limbo of waiting. I put my call through to Johnny Reece.

"Hey. You busy?"

"I am now, I bet."

I could hear his voice perking up in mid-word. Johnny's corner of Travers was a world of reports and statistics, and I'd first gotten his attention with a bet that I could dig up an answer that his charts had missed.

He asked "You on another arson case?"

"Yep. But, remember when I asked about all the fires that could be suspicious, or unexplained?"

"Oh, like those apartments that went up *half an hour ago?*"

Away through the street and the rumble of traffic, I could imagine I heard some siren blaring, some firefighter yelling to quiet a crowd... Calling Johnny was a mistake. "I guess."

"You guess? Listen, I've got a poker buddy who's a cop—and he was just asking about you, and you calling about the same place. And the sparks in the library too."

I tried a laugh. "Seriously? Since when do you play poker?"

"Since I'm trying to hear more of what's out there. But listen up, the cops want answers from you. And that loose cannon you called them about."

"Loose cannon?" Now I was just repeating him, like it could stall anything.

"I mean, he wasn't giving details, but he made her sound like she'd been dodging jail time for half her life. Foster kid, he said."

Maya was still on her own call, not looking over.

"He said that, but no details? Sounds like..." Like rumors, and a cop just trying to rattle Johnny to see what shook loose.

So how did I tell them Maya didn't torch anything? That they should be chasing two men who could burn a place down just by walking through it? Simple, I couldn't risk the time to try—when the Duvals still had Gordon.

"Johnny. I'll talk to the cops, soon as I handle one thing. Can you leave that to me? And, that wide search we did about fires... can you send me an updated version? Leave the Sheffield apartment out if you think that information's too, well, hot."

"Hold up, did you just ask me to keep my mouth shut? You *do* know something."

"Please. Just think what kind of answers I could dig up to pay you back."

Just his pause told me his curiosity was digging into him. Even without the Pulse, sometimes I guess right.

"Okay, okay. And you keep your head down."

I watched the phone, waiting for the files to slide in.

But instead of flicking through the first reports, my thoughts went back to all this police talk about Maya. I'd seen her risking her life for people, but the cops just wrote her off. I rubbed a hand at my face; something felt wrong over it, like a patch of soot lingering from the fire.

"Floyd Toomes isn't answering," Maya announced. "And he has a girlfriend now, and she says he's been missing all afternoon. You find something?"

"Something, that's all. Just incidents I'd been looking at for the last few weeks, fires that I thought might be the Duvals' magic..." I was trying to reassure her with part of the Plan, when I'd never properly talked about it, or magic, with anyone before. "Wish I'd pushed sooner—I might know more about what they want. Or how they found out about you."

"I've got no idea. Really," and she looked straight in my eyes, a more direct gaze than she'd taken with me before. "They saw my act and guessed there was real magic giving it a nudge? They wanted sleight of hand good enough to make a problem disappear? They did just grab a bagful of stuff out of my room—maybe they think there's something in there. Or they want something to track me down, or just sell it for quick cash."

"Wish I knew. I've been looking at burn sites..." One figure on Johnny's files stood out, a date. "This one was two nights ago. About when the Duvals were leaning on you too?"

"Right then. And..." She frowned. "It's two blocks from Floyd's home."

"Looks like just some fire at a house's door, but it could be someone tried to burn their way in. Only ten blocks from us." As a clue, it was more than we had. And the area itself might give me another edge.

* * *

Riding through the spring evening, the thought kept playing in my head: *could* we help Gordon, or Toomes, this time? I thought I'd been preparing for this, for facing a danger like the Duvals. The police weren't ready... but I was turning them against me just by staying around Maya...

Nothing was going like I thought. But it *was* what I trained for, it had to be.

And, the street brought us near the river. That could change everything.

"Pull over!"

Maya's shout was right at my shoulder, pushing against the engine's roar. I brought the bike to the side, and she wrenched my helmet off her and pulled up her phone.

"From Floyd."

The text said simply *hurry*. And a picture that had to be Floyd Toomes, an older face pale with fear. His wild stare looked stretched, as if the sagging folds at the edges of his face had begun shrinking, shriveling up.

And a map. A single dot by the Western Square... right where our guess had us heading.

"We're almost there." I tasted the words as I spoke them, savoring just how lucky we were. "And, the Duvals don't know we're this close."

I studied the shape of the Square, the small open space beside the river, the half-circle of shops around it. My finger tapped it as my thoughts came together:

"This time, we can look around first, find anyone out who'd get caught in the crossfire—and hope there's no *fire* in that," I added. "This is all near Toomes's house, right? So you know the area, you circle wide and check up *there*, I'll come around *this* way. Keep your distance from them until we meet up again, but you know that. Sound good?"

"If you want us to split up again, just say so." That was almost a twinge of hurt in her joke.

"We do want to be sure the street's clear, right? And, I need to recharge my magic, alone."

I simply *said* it, no evasions. And Maya only nodded, handed the helmet to me, and walked away up the dimming street.

I got the bike parked and started out on my own path through the blocks. The street was already quiet out here, with nothing but a few people on it and the growing winds to distract me from my thoughts.

Recharge my magic, from somewhere around here, I'd simply trusted her with that much of the truth. But then, I'd already had to tell her I had magic because there were two other forms of it taking aim at her... and the Eye called her magic a secret to learn, just like I'd learned the Pulse from my glimpse of the Scarecrow... and I'd seen Willard Duval kept his magic in a weapon like mine...

Maybe I had let too much slip. But I'd learned more about other magic in a few hours than I had in years of the Plan.

I crossed the last block, passing only scattered people on the street, as the broad length of the city riverbank came into view.

The Pulse was faint, the Bones barely even cool in my pocket anymore. I reached out with the last of it to feel for anyone behind some corner I couldn't see, for any trace that felt treacherous or secretive or hostile, I was gambling *everything* that I could spot the Duvals if they were near, or the Eye.

Because if either of them saw me now, if they learned the power to *see* the terror they spread...

I climbed down the embankment's steps, toward the soft, vast rippling of the river under the shifting winds. This had to be safe, it had to be.

The water felt almost clean, clean and spring-cold, when I knelt down and dipped a hand in. My fingers cupped it, then daubed it against the soot on my face—just like some trusting fan of our city's decades trying to get the river pure. Or that was what the few passers-by would see.

My other hand trailed in the water, hiding the Bones in my grasp.

"Shalassa lua."

The words I said were the softest whisper. A sound fit for curling around the brightest and darkest corners of a heart.

I had the words, and the bits of ivory I'd made like the Scarecrow's, and all that expanse of water for the words to draw on. Power began to gather, quiet and invisible, cold as if unseen ice were spreading across the river from the Bones.

When my hand felt too cold to feel at all, I drew it out and fumbled them to the other, more responsive hand to pocket them.

The buildings above the embankment looked silent, like this whole end of town was barely used anymore. Was that emptiness why the Duvals came to this neighborhood again, after trying some other scheme here just days ago?

But there they were. One pull on the Pulse could feel their coals of rage now, up and across the square. And shards of fear beside them that had to be their prisoners.

They waited behind the row of shops at the square's back. Only a handful of figures moved around the square now, willing to brave the cold evening wind. So few emotions out... but my sense of the Duvals and their prisoners felt off, not right for four people.

The wind muffled my footsteps as I crossed the square—at least this paved-over world wouldn't burn up like Maya's home had. The dry cleaning shop at the row's end looked already shut down. I peeked around its corner.

The back end of the shops had a wide space between it and the next row, big enough for delivery trucks but now empty. Except for the people I'd sensed: two frightened figures sitting against the wall, and three very different shapes crouching around a low pile of objects and open suitcases. All three of those fumed with different levels of anger, none looking across to spot me twenty feet away.

There *were* three of them. As the Pulse had told me.

A quieter knot of emotions crept up behind me. I glanced back, stepped away from the corner to let Maya have a look.

Then we edged back to a safe distance from them.

"How is there a third one?" I muttered. "Some hired thug, or—"

I shook that outrage off. Maya's face was right in front of me, waiting for a solution.

I said "There's Gordon and Toomes there. Our best chance is to move soon—while they think we can't have gotten here yet."

"That's the stuff they grabbed from my room. If they want it so much, let's see how far they'll chase it when it blows away." Resentment tightened her voice, and she rippled her fingers open, closed.

Simple as that, the two of us had a plan, better than most and far better than hesitating. "I'll charge whoever's left; this time I've got enough fear to take them all down if I can grab them. And we get those two out of the way. Can that 'pulling' of yours slide them back here? Or hit the Duvals?"

"Not like their fire can. *Please,* don't let them get you." She looked back toward where our enemies waited. Her hand was on my arm.

Then she pulled away and led the way back to the corner. The only sound was the wind.

I stretched up to peep around, and she leaned in under me.

The wind eased for a moment, as one of the Duvals glared over at where their prisoners sat. He waved at the pile of loot. "Look at it! Some of this stuff you've got to know!"

Floyd Toomes looked even more frightened than in the picture they'd sent. "I don't..." The wind swallowed the rest of his words.

The Duval—Willard—waved at it again. "You sold stuff like this, remember? Look!"

The wind swelled again. And an instant after it rose, the pile of things flew apart, tossed against the Duvals' bodies and tumbling away down the pavement, pushed away by magic under cover of the gust.

"Get it, *get it!*" screeched the third goon, and they spun after the objects. I charged.

Two hulking figures, one leaner one, all turning away. And the two prisoners against the wall.

A small object, maybe a bound pack of letters, settled on the ground. Right where it made Dom Duval stop with his back to me,

I made one motion to the slumped prisoners as I passed, waving them to run—

Gordon's head lay slumped against the wall, unconscious, and Toomes sat frozen—

My gaze swung back. Dom Duval's eyes were locked right on me.

Bright orange flared up between us, a geyser of flame out of the asphalt itself, making me twist and stagger and skid aside as I flung up my hands against the wave of heat.

A fist slammed in. Pain whirled, muscles went limp but tried to roll, roll and tumble over the pavement. My head wouldn't stop spinning... that *smell,* was that the asphalt smoking...

The three of them loomed over me. Blurred shapes in heavy coats, two huge and one lean, hanging back behind the others.

Wait for it, save my power. Maybe I can make another opening.

One Duval glowered at the dark behind me. "Come on out, Maya. I know you're here too."

How would he know, rattled a thought in my head.

Floyd Toomes gasped "Maya? You think she's—"

The leaner figure stepped toward where Gordon lay unconscious. A gloved hand flicked, a tongue of flame sprang up around it.

That firelight showed the face of a woman, a hard, scowling young face half-hidden under a wool hat. She reached the flame down toward Gordon.

I twisted to get my feet under me. "Don't hurt him!"

Maya stepped around the corner, without a word.

The two Duvals drew back a step to keep me at a safe distance.

But the woman pulled away from the prisoners and peered at Maya. "Never thought you'd stick your neck out." And that hard, knotted face twisted tighter with wrath.

Maya stared. She floundered *back* a step. "Sihh... sihh..."

"Damn—" The strange woman spun around and slammed a fierce kick into Floyd Toomes's head. He spilled sideways, and she reached down to him.

A hypodermic needle slid into his neck.

I was on my feet, just dodging clear of one Duval when she spun around and raised her other hand toward me. Flames surged, ready.

"One less witness, in case she starts screaming," she said. "Glad we got these. This'll be over when these two wake up, if we let them. But we only brought two needles." She frowned at me.

"Maybe we want him to feel what's coming," Willard Duval said. "You think she'll play nice with her boyfriend on the line?"

He leveled his own hand toward me. I halted, tried to steady my breathing and find the moment to move. From the corner of my eye I saw Dom step away, to Maya, and drag her back to us.

Maya's eyes never left the strange woman, and she gulped:

"Sihh... *Sibyl*... that's Floyd Toomes you just kicked! He raised us, for a whole year! He said we could be like sisters—"

"You'd like that, right? Anything to hide behind me." The big woman, Sibyl, took a step toward Maya, and the smaller girl flinched back against Dom Duval's grip. "Poor Maya... did you ever learn to drive?"

"*You* stole that car." The words came out fast as a reflex, but her voice was weak. "You would've wrecked it anyway, if I'd just sat there and let you."

"Always think you've got an answer, don't you?" Sibyl's teeth flashed in a cold grin.

Maya leaned toward her, like struggling to push against some current of fear. "Please. Sybil—whatever the Duvals offered, they're just using you."

"There it is again. Must be how you hooked your protector here."

Sibyl brought her hand back up toward me, but she never looked away from Maya.

"Now, 'sis,' we talk about your magic."

I shifted my weight, trying to test my balance. Willard was covering me too, but if I could dodge behind him away from Sibyl... if I had time, had a chance, to talk them down from just blasting us...

Maya gave a weak laugh. "Magic? I'm a *performer.* I do illusions, like those flame-throwers you're wearing... Oh."

Her voice softened.

"Is this about the stories my dad told? I told you, I was six."

"I remember."

Sibyl's voice was quieter. Was Maya really getting through to her, making Sibyl wonder if she'd wasted her time on someone with no actual power?

Maya went on "And we were thirteen when I told you—I don't know how I remember him anymore. You didn't even listen then. But now, all that kids' talk is why the fearless Sibyl Morgan has joined up with these thugs?"

"It's Sibyl *Duval!*"

The words cracked in the night.

"I told you," and she smiled as she motioned to the two men, "I told you I'd find my cousins someday. But you..."

Her face, the craggy features not so different from the two men's, tightened into a snarl.

"You sit here and lie that you've got nothing. You were hiding it all the time—all the time! *Laughing* at me. Or, you think I'm so stupid I'd think you never read that bracelet?"

Maya's head twisted up in surprise.

"Yeah, the bracelet—no more lies! About that, and the other stuff your dad left you. Don't you tell me the bits I swiped had the only thing with a real spell clue on it."

Sibyl swung her hand around from me and toward Maya. The flame on it narrowed now, tight as a cutting torch.

"Your turn! You show me your fire!"

Maya flinched back.

Sibyl brought that hand toward her, slowly. "Use your fire! Because either you snuff this out, or I swear I'll..."

No, no—I glanced at Willard, saw his face was all too alert on me, and I clawed for other ideas.

"Magic?" I said. "What's wrong with you, talking like that?"

The words dragged as they left my throat—just what my father had said, about my mother's "ghosts," and he'd been right—

Saying it was the *worst* thing for calming someone down. But as a challenge it was perfect: Sibyl twisted away toward me, flames rising.

"Oh, you still don't know what you're seeing—"

She caught herself. and turned back to Maya.

"Or you've lied to him too? Now I want the truth." She brought her flame toward Maya's face again. Maya wrenched against Dom's grip, still helpless to pull away.

Then—

"Don't we need her?"

Dom's voice broke the moment. Sibyl halted, glared up at her cousin as he held their prisoner.

Rush them? Or nudge at Sibyl's emotions? Both choices sounded ready to blow up in my face.

Then Sibyl lowered her hand. "Maya. You know where that stuff from your dad went?"

"All over the street," Maya snapped, then her flash of temper faded. "Or what I had left did. Most of it got lost in the foster system."

"You mean me?" Sibyl smiled. "All I got was enough to teach me and my cousins about fire. So, how many more secrets were in all the stuff *he* sold off?"

She stepped over, made another kick at Floyd Toomes, this time into his side where he lay unconscious.

"Greedy bastard. He's been robbing from the kids he takes in, for years. I figured he took the best stuff to the collector up the street, and tonight he tells me I was right."

The collector up the street. That had to be the home we'd been coming to see—because she'd already tried to burn her way in once.

Sibyl turned back to Maya. "So you're going to get us in."

"You want *me* to get *you...*"

A tremor of shock passed over Maya's face, before she wrenched it still. Sibyl was forcing Maya to steal her own heritage.

The Duval woman's smile stretched, wolf-wide. "Looks like this's the last night before the owner comes home, the last time getting in is easy. It's just all the alarms he's got around his stash—and burning it all up's no good. But we've seen what you do onstage with handcuffs... and you were always good at getting in places, weren't you?"

She nodded, bringing her face right next to Maya's.

"Just don't try twisting out this time." A burst of red flared from Sibyl's hand, right between their faces. Maya jerked back, trapped against Dom Duval's chest. Sibyl smirked and drew away.

"So we're all hostages?" I said. "All of us, to keep Maya in line? Sure, but after she gets you inside, what's your reason to let us go?"

"Reason?" Sibyl laughed. "How about... Maya doesn't have the guts to use fire on the three of us. So you do what we say, and don't give us a *reason* to show how fast we can end this. Or how slow." She leveled a finger at me.

They made me hoist Floyd Toomes over my shoulder. The old man was lighter than he looked, but I knew that weight would be grinding me down soon. Willard scooped up Gordon, and they herded us down the street.

The back streets we used were all but deserted. With the wind howling and the gathering clouds and cold, I saw only a few distant figures—and even the shape of us hauling the unconscious hostages got no reaction from them. Either they missed it all in the dark, or the Duvals had already tested that people here looked the other way.

It was only when the house came in sight that we paused, at a shadowed corner across the street from it. The place was three stories of wood and ornate old outlines, and I thought I could see shutters clatter in the wind. Not quite a classic haunted house... but close enough to it, when the people who brought us here were monstrous enough.

We lurked across the street for a whole, long minute, looking for anyone who'd see us approach. I kept my mouth shut about how few emotions I sensed in the neighborhood, and how empty the house was.

Then we slipped around to its back door.

Sibyl waved Maya to the door, and handed her a pocket knife. Maya crouched down and worked it in the lock—still keeping up the front that she had no magic of her own. Sibyl unfolded her wool cap down into a ski mask, but she never took her eyes off Maya.

I edged back a step, no small thing with Floyd Toomes's weight pressing on me. But it put me in place to whisper to Dom, as he pulled on a mask for himself: "You know she's talking murder. And too many people have seen you near Maya, and me." If I pulled at his emotions too... no, too risky...

"Nice try," Dom grunted.

He said it out loud, and Sibyl added "No whispering. We go in together."

The door clicked open. Sibyl took the knife back and marched Maya in, while her cousins kept me surrounded as we followed.

The beam of a flashlight reached in and glinted off shapes of dark wood. In the dim light it picked out an elaborate chair, a fancy-framed painting, a wall with irregular stains left untreated and seeping through the wallpaper. The door shut behind us, and *layers* of mustiness crawled around my nose together.

Artwork. Antiques. I followed the light around the living room, trying to picture what Helena and her company would think of these objects' history, their quality, but all I could think was *eccentric*. Sibyl had called the owner "a collector."

"Now we start on the alarms," and Sybil handed her light to Maya.

Maya glared back at her.

Sibyl held up a palm, and a spurt of flame sprang up and hung above it. "There's some more light," she added. "You don't want some alarm going off and bringing anyone here, do you? No, you *don't*."

Maya played the flashlight slowly around, passing over brass compasses and wooden masks to walk along the nearest corners and under the furniture, where sensors might be tucked away.

More deception, I realized. Anything she saw, her magic could try to yank wires or jam components in without going near it, but she wouldn't reveal that. And anything she did could mean noise—to cover that I shifted Toomes on my shoulders, groaned as if the weight were getting to me. Not hard, the way my arms and feet ached.

"No going in that way," Maya said. "But there's a gap if we go around here. And crouch low," she added.

Or she'd made that gap. We edged along the side corridor, knees bent and floorboards creaking. I tried one flicker of the Pulse to know how Maya was holding up, and when Willard stumbled I caught a spark of dark satisfaction from her. Odds were, there were no alarms to crouch under, just her small moment of revenge.

Maya led us slowly up the corridor to the next room. The light worked its way across a dining room table, and over all the corners, before she led us in.

"Haven't lost your touch," Sibyl said. "You're spotting every one of them, aren't you? If that's all it is."

Willard set the unconscious Gordon on the floor, and I finally eased my own hostage down beside him. Neither of them stirred, but at least they were still breathing.

Sibyl walked around the room, one hand hauling Maya along and the other holding her firelight over the objects they passed. Shapes of metal and clay on tables, an old mining helmet, a diary... like scraps of history that weren't quite worthy of a museum.

"You think there's anything hidden down here?" Sibyl said. "Can't be. This looks *old*—your dad wasn't into that, was he? This here is just piling up everything."

Maya glanced away at the wall.

Sibyl dragged her back toward her. "You ever look up your old man, and what happened to him? Or does it eat you up too much to ever know?"

Maya twisted her head away.

"I *said*, did... you... look?" Sibyl gave her a shake. The flame in her hand swelled.

My feet were moving me toward them when Maya snapped *"Yes!* Sure I asked around. They said he was obsessed, some project or research or something—he didn't really talk to anyone. They didn't even say if it wore him out so he couldn't fight the cancer, or he chased it *because* he was losing."

Sibyl halted. For one moment, her masked face looked back at Maya, looked at the girl she'd known. I touched the Pulse, felt a frisson of honest regret in her—

She shook her head, and the Duval anger closed over it like a fist.

"Obsessed, with weird legends and stories. And you never thought he was chasing something?"

"Chasing what? It was just... history, art, something. I was six!"

"The man went broke chasing this, and he still died—and he never *used* the magic to burn through those bills. And then he left it to you... well, at least now it's gone to someone that's not scared of it." She swung her burning hand in a circle.

She was goading Maya, trying to shake something out of her, I was sure of it. And Maya only stood there and took it.

We searched the floor, working through room after room of the collector's whimsies. Maya searched out possible alarms, and the three Duvals watched her and me, never clustering close enough for me to grab one before the others torched us.

The men did crowd in close when we started up the stairs, but Sibyl and Maya stayed well out of reach ahead.

It was at the top that Maya stepped off the landing, half out of view—and Sibyl charged up to grab her. "Don't try it!"

Ahead of me on the steps, Willard spun to watch me. I leaned back toward Dom behind me, to breathe "Is she always this wild?"

Neither of them answered.

"She can't keep this up, you know," I added. "Must be just how she is around Maya."

"Must be," Dom whispered.

Only two soft words, but just him considering it was a start.

And it let me do more. With the Pulse I brushed at that moment of worry, one touch to fuel that doubt like a single breath of cool air. No more than that now—it was too easy to push too far and leave someone with a mismatched feeling they'd just reject. Only true, crushing fear was different... and I *wished* I could save us with that alone.

As we neared the room ahead, Maya pulled back in the doorway. Sibyl snapped "What now?"

"Alarm, and I can't reach it. We have to stay out of that spot."

"*After* you stepped in it? Is that you trying to set it off and lie about it? Or, you just scaring us out of that room?"

I smothered a sigh. Damned if you do, damned if you don't.

The floor creaked. Off at a side door, a shadow ducked back out of sight—

Like the Eye had. And a cold emotion lurked there, where the whole house had been empty before—

"Come on out!" Sibyl lunged after it.

"Hold on—" Willard called after her.

Maya stole a glance up the hallway, but Willard spun back to level his hand at her, and she froze. My knees locked; an intake of breath came from Dom behind me. We were still watched, still had no chance.

Sibyl's footsteps echoed from one room to the next. I kept my muscles still, but the Pulse only felt Maya's self-control and the three Duvals' ferocity. That missing other presence *must* have been the Eye.

I could warn them, or...

Shining in from the next rooms, the firelight Sibyl carried actually brightened, hungry to set it all alight. No smell of smoke, only the sound of her feet running further and further away.

Softly I said "She's a danger to you too, you know."

Dom muttered "What are you now, a cop?"

"I...didn't say that."

There—his anger shifted, let in a hint of worry at my hint, for all that it was a lie. That might even be relief I caught in him.

I added "But I know if you're arrested, everyone hurt in the fires will be on you. And the way she's going—"

Sibyl's voice tore through the rooms. "It's here! Watch them, don't let them go!"

Fierce greed and actual soaring hope rang in her voice, and in her head. I caught another presence somewhere behind us, the Eye again.

Then the Duvals started us moving. Willard kept so close to Maya, so ready, I could only let them push us along. Past one room of meaningless trinkets, another—

Sibyl stood over a table dotted with shapes, knickknacks, materials of what looked like a random spread of silver and leather and other objects.

One motion turned toward me: a quick glance from Maya. Inside her spiked a desperate urgency: it had to be now.

"This is it, just like my bracelet," Sibyl whispered. It was the first lasting emotion I'd felt from her besides that volatile rage: hope and need.

And I reached the Pulse for that hunger and fed it, fanned it. While the violation made my stomach turn.

Before my eyes, Sibyl bent and spread her arms ready to hug the prizes to her. A happy moan came from her lips. Willard growled "Careful—" and stepped toward her, away from Maya.

I tightened my grip and Sibyl's fingers clawed at the table.

The pieces erupted into the air, flying and scattering under Maya's power. The Duvals stared, I saw—felt—the raw hurt in Sibyl as Dom Duval took a first lumbering step toward me, as Maya grabbed something from the air and spun away.

I lunged. My hand slapped Dom's arm and poured the Bones' terror into him.

He screamed, he thrashed where he stood—and Maya and I dodged behind him before Willard could blast at us. We bolted from the room.

CHAPTER FIVE: UNTIL

I raced after Maya, fighting to keep the backwash of her flashlight in view, knowing one slow twist in the unfamiliar corridors could leave me stumbling in the dark. I ran, grazed off of walls, heard the Duvals bellowing behind us. Already too close.

A door meant cover, I knew that as I saw her leaping through a heavy wood door, and I lunged after her. I slammed it shut—

As it closed, a wave of fire billowed through the gap. Maya gasped and dove away, then she rolled to her feet and raced on, toward a flight of stairs. Those stairs led *up,* not down, but we could only charge upward into the dimness above. Dim because Maya had dropped the flashlight.

Another door loomed in the shadows at the top. We tumbled through and I swung it shut, held it.

Darkness pressed around me. I clung to the stout wood door—a shock of heat struck through it and had me diving away.

A fire alarm screamed.

A thundering crash drove that sound aside as the door shook, under what must be the Duvals' impact. But it held, I could see it standing in the dimness... by the light of the doorknob, glowing hot and partly melted in place. The Duvals' blast had jammed it shut.

I braced against the door's wood to hold it together and waited for the next crash. But instead the doorknob's light swelled brighter, fiercer red. I felt a trickle of sweat on my face.

Footsteps moved behind me: Maya darting around the room trying to pick a way out when she could barely see.

Sibyl shouted over the alarm: "Now, do we burn through? Or just burn you?"

I reached for their emotions, for anything I could use, but there was only rage there, ready to crush down anything else.

The dark *thickened*... no, something swirled and stung my eyes and began to swallow the light. Soon we'd be coughing and choking as the smoke deepened.

Then the grayness whirled and fled away through the door's cracks, as Maya's magic flung it back. She stepped beside me.

In the darkness, her hands caught at mine.

Warm, tingling, clutching something between our grips, she stood close. Her face was a blur in the dark—did she want me to pull her closer, for the last chance we'd have?

Not the last.

I tightened one hand on hers and pulled the other away, to swing a fist toward the Duvals and a wave of fear with it. Someone behind the door gasped, a sound I felt more than heard with the alarm howling, but no more than that. Not with the door between us.

Something tingled, in the hand I'd pulled away.

I'd *missed* it, lost in the moment: the hard corners of some bit of metal, one of the pieces Maya had grabbed. I stared at it in the dimness, then at Maya. She let me go and looked at some small object in her other own hand.

Another crash shook the door.

I walled the thought out, tried to lock my will onto the sensation this bit of jewelry had given when I drew on the Pulse. My mind pulled, twisted—nothing.

Maya caught my wrist. She pulled at my hand, drawing it toward the coal-bright doorknob, the best light we had.

I had to shade my face from the heat, but I saw the tangle of points I held was a brooch, a star-shaped golden thing with a black stone in the center.

Behind the door Sibyl shouted "You're out of lies, you know. It's all ours now."

Maya looked at the brooch in my hand. Then she dropped whatever trinket she'd hung onto and grabbed out her phone, held its screen over the brooch. As a mirror.

Markings on the back of the prongs—were those tiny shapes letters? And a shape like a star design, and also...

Maya tilted the phone again. A faint reflection of those tangled lines fit beside their source, two halves of a whole shape.

"Is that a web?" she breathed. "I think Dad would mean..."

She closed her hand around mine again, around the brooch. Her other hand still held the phone, but she pressed the back of those fingers against the door where it met the frame.

Power flowed.

Something surged from the brooch's stone, through Maya's grasp. To the door.

"Time's up," Sibyl shouted.

Another massive blow sounded against the door—and the wood didn't as much as vibrate.

Maya spun away, as the heat swelled, the doorknob's glow brightened. They could still burn through, they'd have to, if they couldn't push it open now.

Then she and I pulled back into the dimness together. One room led to the next, stumbling our way along. We didn't need to see, we just needed something that looked like another stair down, or even a place to ambush the Duvals.

But one room after another was only a blur of open, shadowy space. No way down.

Down. I caught at Maya's arm and turned her toward the faint paleness of a window. The alarm was still screaming, so the only way to whisper was to lean right against her ear... strangely, vividly close again... I said "Can you float us down?"

"Too heavy. But—"

She waved a hand at the window. It flew open, and the wind roared in.

Then she pulled the brooch from my hand. She pressed her other palm against the wall, then tugged. Her hand remained stuck against the wall.

"Now, did I just trap myself?" she muttered—and her hand slid free again. She turned to the window.

"You think we can..."

I broke off as a crash sounded behind us, a tumbling crash like great chunks of wood scattered against the floor.

"You," Maya said. "You have to carry us down, your weight and mine."

She had to lean in close to say that, and as she did she turned her face away, but it couldn't hide the pure desperation in her voice.

Only three stories up, right? I stretched my arms as if I could shake the exhaustion away, and took the brooch into my hand.

First I leaned out the window, out into the bitter spring night wind, to twist my arm around to touch the wall outside.

A web, she called it. Or a *sticking*. My hand and the wooden wall, I pictured them connected and joined... it had to work.

Power crawled between us.

My skin clung to the wood—no, I felt it go deeper, like whole layers of my flesh were all drawn toward it.

I shivered, told myself I'd just seen Maya pull herself loose. I climbed out onto the windowsill.

Something moved, on a slanting rooftop opposite us—a figure crouching on the roof. Only for a moment, then it was gone.

Focus! I leaned my leg over and willed my knee to stick to the wall. Then my other hand slid the brooch in my pocket, and reached out for Maya.

She gripped my arm, climbed out onto my shoulders—

Her grasp slipped, her arms slid over my jacket, a gasp shook against my side as I tried to reach backward—

Her arms locked around my back, and held.

Heart pounding, I brought my free hand back to the wall, and locked it in at a level down by the first arm's elbow. The magic held that grasp in place... but now I'd have to *release* my upper grip and still hold the weight of both of us to ease us downward.

Making one hand let go left my body hollowed out with dread. Sliding down with the strain on my other hand and knee filled it with pain. Then I set a new handhold and dragged us down again, and again.

The alarm—still shrieking up beyond the window—softened, as the window clicked shut the same way Maya had opened it. But if the Duvals had already seen it, we were sitting ducks out here.

Don't think about that. Instead I clamped another grip down, hauled us down again, tried to push back thoughts of who could have been watching us from that roof. Or how cold the wall was, every time I flattened a hand against it. Each muscle-wrenching shift moved us only a few hand-spans down.

One knee came loose. It scraped off from the wood, left us dangling by the other leg and a hand—I clutched my will at the unfamiliar magic, splashed power out to make it *stick*.

Maya grunted against my back, "I'm trying to hold us up... just some of the weight, but..."

Clamp. Release. Down, as my arms and legs screamed.

The frame of a window came in view beside us. We'd made it down to the second story... and a quiet thought uncurled in my head, inside all the sweat and the roaring wind: *not much further, it'll be safe to drop soon, any time now...* Every second we skipped was a head start on the Duvals, but...

I dragged us on downward.

A hand slid loose again. I shoved it onto the wall, shoved magic into it—so little magic left in the brooch—

Maya said "That's far enough." And she let go.

Her grasp just came loose and dropped away, my heart plummeted for an endless frozen instant shaken by the *thump* below...

Then I looked down and she stood below me, close, waving.

I struggled and slid down another handhold, until the last of the power trickled away and I kicked out and dropped to the ground.

We'd drained the brooch dry, I knew as I straightened up, but the words Maya found on it could be how to restore it—

But, there was still that watcher on the rooftop.

And the Duvals. The hostages.

I whirled and dashed around the wall, staring through the shadows trying to find the door. My foot hit something and left me stumbling for a step, and it hit me that I was running *toward* danger when we'd finally made it out. No other choice.

Maya caught up behind me as I reached the back door, still unlocked.

Stepping inside was stepping into the fire alarm's shriek again, knowing it would swallow our footsteps, and theirs too. I picked my way through the dimness toward the dining room.

Gordon Weber and Floyd Toomes lay right in the corner where we left them. I reached for one, then stopped to search the Pulse.

My magic felt the Duvals reaching this floor and closing fast, heading right for us.

And another, colder presence back a few rooms away—

The Duvals were too close. I waved Maya to hide and flattened back behind the doorway, as they charged in.

Sibyl rushed in, with one of the huge cousins close behind her. I dove at their backs—*don't you turn, don't split up*—

One of my hands slapped down on each, and I let the Pulse's terror loose.

The lurch of their bodies made me shove forward to keep my grip on them, as they spasmed and howled and I poured magic over their rage to smother it with the flood of soul-numbing cold.

A shout burst out behind me. I had to spin, fighting to hold my grip as I saw the third Duval watching me.

And another shape, masked, peeking out in the room behind him—

The Duval brought his hand up. I flung up my own hand, praying fear at a distance could slow him down.

The big man stumbled. His hand jerked aside, his body lurched over as if some unseen force had shoved at him. And his pants pocket twisted outward in a flash of white, a glint of metal shot through the air toward me.

Toward Maya, as she grabbed it out of the air.

Right behind me a voice choked "You're *dead*—"

The big Duval I'd let go, Willard, was trying to stand. I slammed his head to the floor as I shoved forward, leaving him and forcing the thrashing Sibyl back and away to bring my full attention down on her.

The Pulse crashed through her. She whimpered, sank to her knees.

Holding my grip, I twisted, looked back. Willard staggered upright and jabbed a finger at me.

Light flared—and *broke* and burst apart into empty sparks. Maya stood between us, holding out the charm she'd pulled off of Dom.

"Who *are* you two?" That was Dom, back behind Willard and still staring at us. "You block it, after he grabbed it..."

He thought *I'd* disarmed him? Because I'd been reaching toward when she struck?

Sibyl snarled under my grip. She was still the real danger, and she'd always be after Maya.

I stared at where her rage-twisted face would be in the dark, and pressed down with pure, cold terror trying to flush the resistance away. This had to work.

"You think you can go after Maya?" I growled. "She's *my* student—under *my* protection—"

Another flash of light came behind us, Maya shielding us from Willard again.

But I pushed on with the lie: *"Mine!* And I've been watching you Duvals all night—just hoping for one sign that you weren't *this* far in over your heads. You think if you toss fire everywhere nobody's going to guess what you have?"

Sibyl's will shook under the assault. Her face was ghost-white, I could feel that from her mind as clearly as if I could see it in the dimness.

"You think you can just scare someone and they all fall in line? *This is fear!"*

I crushed the power down on her, anything to blast away her malice and see that they never came after us again...

Finally I looked up.

Willard wobbled toward me, toward Maya, with his heavy fists raised and Dom behind him.

"She's alright." My teeth still clenched tight, wouldn't let go. "So far," I added, and that made the two freeze.

A moan, low and weak, came from Sibyl. Inside her, I felt her drenched spirit flicker, began to steady. Embers of anger smoldered.

A siren wailed out in the distant streets.

A different ripple of fear stirred around the room. A siren, with the fire alarm still sounding here... of course they'd come.

Sibyl groaned "Just... go..."

"I'm *not* leaving you," Willard said. He shuffled forward, immense and unflinching.

I watched him advance. The Duvals were still too big, all of them... and just watching Willard's loyalty made me look down at the soul I'd been battering...

Trembling, holding my stomach down, I stepped back and let them pull Sibyl to her feet.

When they had her, Willard shot a vicious glare at me. Maya countered by holding up the device she'd stolen, her own warning.

The Duvals staggered away.

I waited, and fought down my revulsion enough to keep the Pulse tracking them a little longer. But they did go, they crept out of the house and kept going.

And the other figure I'd seen was gone too—that had to be the Eye again. He must have heard me too, that the person he'd ordered me to rob was under my protection, even getting her magic from me... I'd thrown that at Sibyl to warn her off, but now it felt like my answer to the Eye's demands as well.

"We... won," Maya breathed. "We won."

She was standing just a few steps from me. Her voice sounded like her face was shining.

I said "We did. And you, what was that, you *guessed* where Dom would carry his magic?"

She nodded.

"You could have beat them all."

"What, with this thing? I barely got it working—I think I used all its power stopping those two blasts."

And she laughed, she tossed the useless charm into the air and caught it.

She *bluffed* them. Something that must have been a laugh shook inside me.

Then I stumbled over to Gordon Weber, and Floyd Toomes. They both lay sprawled on the floor, but my hands could feel them breathing. Their pulses, the real "pulses" in their necks, felt steady enough—my first aid studies for the Plan told me that much. I still had no idea what Sibyl's drugs could be doing to them. But they were alive.

Maya said "So, where do we go now?"

"We..."

I kept looking down at the victims beside me, not up at Maya, and tried to let thoughts fall back into place.

"We think these two are okay. Johnny did say I'd need to talk to the police..." The word pulled a groan out of me—aches and trembling closed in despite all my stalling words, leaving me shaking. "Or, or maybe not about all of this."

"I know about the police." She sounded a step closer now. "Or, we could just get away for a while."

Maybe... just *away,* with her, to rest and spend time with someone who'd lived this too. Someone who said *we* like that and drew closer...

Instead of all the worries on me...

"You go." The words slipped out on their own. "I'll watch that the firefighters find these two here—I'll come tell them if they don't." How was that going to work?

"All right," Maya said, softly. "But, Gordon sold me out today, and Floyd Toomes sold part of me too. While you... thank you."

She walked away so quietly I couldn't hear the steps. If she looked back at all, I didn't know... with so much tangling in my head it was so much easier to keep looking down at the two men, and not up.

One more time, their heartbeats felt strong enough. The air down here had none of the smoke from the floors above. I settled in to drag one and then the other out the house's door into the open air.

My first time going up against other magic—and we'd beaten the odds. But my hands shook, my legs swayed, and the back of my mouth still felt like slime after what I'd done to Sibyl. And under all that, sending away Maya's support already left the night feeling empty. Too empty.

At last I shuffled out away from the house and down the sidewalk. Nobody seemed to be out watching—no firelight showed from the outside, and the hard wind beat down most of the alarm's sound. I let the wind push me up half a block, before the fire engine pulled up to the house.

With slow, careful movements, I forced my fumbling hands to pull out the Bones and close them away in the thick box... and with them covered, I finally felt some of the cold leave me. They slid back in my pocket, beside the star-shaped brooch.

But all that could be for later. Now I stood at a distance watching the firefighters rush out, just holding myself upright and trying not to think how I'd made myself a target for the Duvals, and the Eye...

Firefighting. We could have stayed and tried putting out the fire ourselves with the Duvals' charm, but Maya had drained that... So strange to think I was really finding more magic now, in the middle of all this.

The firefighters loaded one unconscious figure up, then the other. Even at a distance, they looked to be treating the two men with care, with a clear hope that they'd recover.

So it was over.

—No it wasn't, Johnny said the cops were looking for me. And the *weight* of what I'd been through, and the great loosening feeling of those burdens peeling away, all crashed back and left me fumbling and cursing as I dug out my phone.

No messages, no sign of anything. Weird, but right now I'd take it.

I turned and began the slow walk back to my bike, for the slow, careful ride home.

* * *

I half expected to find police waiting at my apartment too, but there were none. Instead I staggered out of the wind, into peace and warmth.

The cops would still have their questions, but *not now*. Now I dropped my jacket, pulled the Bones and the many-pointed brooch from my pockets, and my phone too. One last blurry-eyed glance at the phone—

A new text was waiting. Not from the police, not Maya, but Helena. The words *concerned* and *when you can* shone out at me.

I sprawled down along the bed. The blankets were waiting to wrap me up, same as the layers of wool inside my head...

But I'd always wanted Helena to care. Just, not make her worry... except, what had that text's time been? how close to now?

I leaned back and tapped out a call. For a quick message, something about being fine and tired and promising to talk soon.

Except she picked right up.

"Hello. Does this mean you're alright?"

Her voice was the strong certainty of someone who faced down the world, standing over where I could have been lying in a pit, of blankets and exhaustion.

Steady as I could form the words, I said "Sure I am. Or did you hear different?" Oh, great, that didn't sound suspicious at all.

"No. But you had a case that made you use my offices as a safe house, and then you both ran out anyway. That's not your regular irregularity."

"Guess not." Not using my edge and my training to see through people who had no clue about magic. This time, a part of me could still feel myself trying to leap back from the Duvals' waves of heat... the savageness of pounding on Sibyl's mind... My fingers clenched in the blankets.

Was that how the Scarecrow felt when he struck?

"I guess not," I said again. My voice came out hoarse.

"Adrian. *Are* you alright, really? Tell the truth."

I wanted to wave that off. This was the most confident, capable person I'd ever met, the one I'd always wanted to impress—more than impress. But today had been too big to stuff into one answer.

I tried "Maya was being stalked, yes. And her friends were pulled into that, and we tried to save them." And it had turned into *we,* so suddenly. "But they're safe now. We all are."

"That does sound a regular moment after all, for you." A hint of a throaty laugh sounded, then passed by. "Still, you don't sound like you've been winning."

"It... came close a few times. And, I did a few things that put us in danger." *I still am, worse than ever.* "I had to hurt someone. Really hurt them." I glared over at the boxed-up Bones on the table beside me.

"I see..." Helena stretched the word out, keeping me silent until she went on "And I suppose you won't say any more, will you? Still, I've had to make a few hard decisions too."

"Of course. Sorry."

"You brought it up. But think a moment, it hasn't been easy for me to run a family company that's still named Travers *Brothers.* Even when it was the only way to keep it afloat."

"I'm sure it was." I'd gathered something like that, from the hints people said about the company years ago.

"And *I'm* sure that my brother will never forgive me," she said. "But I've learned to forgive myself, because I have to. And I'm also sure that what you did was the only choice you had, because I know you that much."

"You think so?"

She had no idea about Ray and me finding the Scarecrow... about my mother... about all my struggling with the Plan. Or even how many weeks I'd tried to write her a song, just to have *something* perfected for her—I slammed a fist onto the mattress.

"If I'm so good, why's Maya out there alone now? The Duvals could shake things off any time and go after her again. And her home burned down, and the last I heard the police want to pin it on her." If they didn't pin it on me too.

"So it's like that? You're that certain she needs your help."

Her voice had an odd twitch—and I remembered the quick thought I'd had before, that she could have sent Maya to me hoping I'd fall for a client instead of her. That moment of ego felt like a lifetime ago.

"If the police suspect her," she was saying, "you ought to set the record straight with them. And that doesn't have to be some choice between protecting her and protecting yourself either; it only means working out what you're going to say before you do."

"Is that what this is? Afraid of choosing between me and her?"

"We can work out your statement in the morning. When you're awake."

"Thanks. I can always count on you," I added, "but it should be the other way around."

"Should it? I'm not sure what you mean."

Did I just say that? "I mean... nothing."

It really was late. Helena didn't reply, and the silence stretched one second, another...

A floorboard creaked in the front room.

A footstep? I tumbled off the bed, leaped toward it—

The front room was empty. And the Bones were still back in my bedroom.

"Adrian?"

The phone was still in my hand. "Nothing. Tomorrow, then."

"Alright then."

She hung up, and I scowled at the screen. So I was jumping at noises—and knowing those noises *could* be the Eye, any time. Or the Duvals could track me here too, or...

I clicked the lights off and tunneled in among the blankets. Warm, still, at long last.

If the wind would just stop brushing, pressing, against the building. If those voices would stop prickling up from the apartment below, around, everywhere. My nerves were stretched like a guitar string one turn away from snapping.

I breathed, tried to let my muscles unclench. Rest, sleep, I *needed* those now more than anything.

Except, I really had made myself a target for both Sibyl and the Eye now, to pull them off of Maya. *Helena said I'd make it a choice between being a martyr and abandoning someone.*

Like she's ever had to make that choice.

But Helena had something else right, I still had to cope with the police and what to tell them... later. All that, the police, what I'd become with Sibyl, all of it could wait for tomorrow.

Unless something came out of the dark tonight. At any time.

No good. I clicked the lights on, but the cold glow and the familiar shapes did nothing to chase the fears away. Any time, it could happen any time.

Instead, I opened my guitar case. Cradling the hard, smooth wood on my lap and fitting my fingertips on the strings gave me something to hold onto.

All the low voices of the people still awake, they were too low and surrounded by stillness to disturb with a song. So I worked a soft, soft pattern over the strings and tried to lose myself in the cycle of chords.

Helena's song would have begun

Every time they need, you show them that and more
A face that takes all in, whatever's there
But one thing's beyond me, one thing I never see
What's in your heart if I could only dare

No good, that was still trying way too hard. Those words were still just circling around how it felt watching Helena, and not what I really wanted to say. Maybe if I had a better handle on that I'd get the song right—and even sing it to her someday.

And where the hell was Maya now?

No use. Everything I did was pushing me further awake than ever.

I wiped the guitar down and set it back in the case, then gathered up the Bones and the brooch beside it and took them to the bathroom.

Just taking the Bones from their box made their cold a part of me again. They still had some power even after all I'd used to crush Sibyl—that memory made my fingers jerk back from them. But I *needed* all of that breath-chilling, hope-twisting magic I could keep.

I ran the water in the sink, and held the four dice in the stream. *"Shalassa lua."*

The cold grew, gathered, at its usual slow trickle here. Testing had shown me that the Bones drew the most power from natural water, and the handy flow in the pipes could take forever to charge them right.

And yet the Scarecrow made his den in the filthy *storm drains.* That contrast always unnerved me: was he avoiding clean water and what his full strength could be, or simply that terrified of going outside under the Eye?

A footstep sounded outside my front door. I clutched the freezing Bones tighter, readied myself—

A child's voice laughed, and a woman answered her, as their footsteps strolled on past my apartment door. I tried to chuckle and found I couldn't breathe. Of *course* I was charging a magic rooted in fear while I was trying to forget how real dangers could strike at any moment.

I kept the Bones in the water as my fingers began going numb. As a distraction, I picked up the brooch we'd found.

Just like the Bones, and the Duval charm Maya had grabbed, I knew it stored magic and it could use itself up. And Sibyl said she'd given her cousins their magic—was that like the way I'd made the Bones, just from knowing the Scarecrow's secrets?

I had the brooch. Or, it had felt like it was just the black stone in the center that held the power. And there had been words—I held the underside of the brooch beside the sink's mirror, the way Maya had with her phone.

There they were, little scratches that could be letters, two each on the back of most of the seven gilded star-points. And, I had water... if this drew power from the same source that the Pulse did.

I dried the Bones and slid them back in their box. Then I held the brooch in the water and sounded out the syllables.

"Sa-as-ka-ra-sh-u."

Nothing. Not one erg of power moved in the stone.

I looked at the pairs of letters again—maybe the one blank star-point wasn't the spot where the words began. I tried reading the letters around from different places, *"Askara shusa... ka rashu saas..."* and then reading the cycle counterclockwise instead. Still nothing.

So I still had the words wrong, or else it wasn't fueled by water at all. The other shapes on it seemed to be that half of a spiderweb that Maya had recognized, and a star.

I clicked the lights off and peeped out my bedroom window's blinds. There *were* no stars, only a scrap of moonlight behind the curtain of clouds.

The glass felt cold against my nose, sharp even after the Bones had frozen my hands. I really was letting all this keep me up... I had my hands on a whole other kind of magic, one I'd already used once... and my only guess on how to bring it back didn't even show in the sky.

The winds only blew on, cut by the sounds of cars on the night streets. I was farther away from sleeping than ever.

I tried my tablet, looking for any late news about how Gordon or Toomes were doing, or the fires the Duvals had set off. All I found was a basic report on the Sheffield Apartments, that said that whole sections of Maya's building were wiped out. Maybe my freezing Sibyl was worth it, if it made the Duvals hesitate the next time.

Outside, the wind dwindled away.

I turned the lights off again and stepped back to the window. The sky was still dark, but as my eyes adjusted I could see patches in the cloud cover, and a few glimmers of light through it.

The brooch pressed against the glass. *"Saas karashu—"*

Power stirred. I could feel it in the stone, not pouring in but gathering, like a tiny grain of magic forming a larger grain around it, a snowflake or crystal. Slowly, slowly...

The clouds shifted, and the magic's growth came to an end.

I let the blind drop back. With the room dim, I moved to an open space of wall and pressed a hand against it, and a knee. The stone's magic flowed where I touched.

And I hoisted myself up the wall, one step, two, before letting myself fall. I had it.

I *knew* the secret now, to create a whole second power of magic... a giggle of relief welled up through me, and I pressed the tablet to the wall and stuck it there.

For another test, I stretched my hand far out from my side and laid it against the paint there, and willed the wall to release the tablet. It didn't even wiggle. I considered sliding my hand closer along the wall, but instead I bore down to force my thoughts harder at it. The tablet wavered and slid down, right into my grasp.

It worked. There was probably a song in this—

A knock came from the front door. A single sharp sound in the night.

It could be anything. It could be nothing...

Softly I crept through the dim room, suddenly grateful I'd dropped my shoes when I'd tried to sleep.

The peephole showed nothing but an empty corridor. I gripped the door, readied myself, and yanked it open behind me.

Nothing. I leaned out, and saw only more empty space.

Something crashed into my back. I toppled forward, caught my balance and spun, just as the door slammed shut ahead of me.

Locked, he *locked me out*—I rattled at the doorknob, choked down a shout. It was starting, I knew he'd come...

And I'd left the Bones inside, I must be more worn out than I thought. All I had was the brooch in my hand.

The apartment corridor still looked empty, but I had to move before someone heard. I yanked the keys from my pocket.

"I told you..."

The words came from behind my door, and they sank to a whisper that made me lean against it to catch the rest:

"Now, bring me Maya Grant's magic."

CHAPTER SIX: THE OBSERVER

His whisper was pure cold, not the ice-like cold of the Bones but a heavy, deeper chill, like rock that had never been alive.

My hand flinched back from the doorknob. He'd found me, outmaneuvered me so easily... and even the Scarecrow was scared of the Eye.

"You knew what you had to do. You knew how much you had to lose."

I swallowed, tried to get my thoughts moving. There had to be a way to stall him, to pry something out of him I could use. Except I didn't even *have* the Bones to try getting in his head.

"What do you want with her?" I hissed against the door. "Maya's fighting the Duvals—and I saw you there when they torched the apartments, you were leading people out of the fire." If that had been him under that fake beard. If the Eye was even human at all.

No answer came.

But if he did answer... that would have him whispering, and leaning against my door. Did that mean the brooch's power could reach through the door and snare him against it?

So first, I had to keep him talking. Softly I said "You saw what the Duvals do. They could burn—"

"You were told to learn her magic," that stern voice said. *"You talk like you have a choice."*

"I'm trying to keep her alive! You pushed her down and called the Duvals on her." An angry edge was creeping into my words, too loud, and the Eye already sounded too far back from the door. I throttled my voice down to lure him closer. "How does attacking her go with wanting her secrets?"

Silence.

I held my breath, waiting to catch a word, a breath beyond the door. The floor tiles' chill soaked through my socks.

Footsteps shuffled along the corridor. Clumsy, echoing steps moving toward me—I stole a glance over, willing him not to notice me, not to react or come anywhere near us.

One of my neighbors, an older man in a rumpled suit, walking with shaky steps like he'd been drinking...

Those footsteps stopped at a door ahead of me. My breath whooshed out—no need for him to walk past me, he could step inside and be gone. So why couldn't I hear his door opening...

Don't look, don't make him notice and stop...

But I stole another glance. The drunk stood by his entrance, looking at me leaning with open *sympathy*—for whatever sad argument he thought had me whispering against my door. Then he opened his own and stepped inside. Safe.

The corridor went silent again. The space beyond my door sounded, *felt,* still.

My head pounded. Could that be all, was the Eye already gone?

Never assume. I steeled myself, forced out another low mutter to draw him in: "You really think I'd let you hurt her? Or hurt anyone?"

"You've seen her run wild."

That voice was still there, and still sounded too far away.

"Her? It's the Duvals that are burning everything in sight! Maya's just trying to stay alive, and save the people in her life. That and not lose the secrets her father tried to leave her."

"Find her magic. Before it's too late."

Too late? What did that mean—something about fighting the Duvals, or her father, or something else? That was more than the Eye had ever said, what else could he let slip—

I pushed that thought down. Nothing he said mattered as much as a chance to *catch* him. I laid the brooch against the door.

"How?" Then, softer: "How am I supposed to get her secrets?"

A moment after my whisper faded, I struck. I grabbed the magic in the brooch and slammed it through the door's wood, gritting my teeth to force it to the other side and join, bind, with anything leaning against it just those few inches away.

All I felt was the push of power struggling blindly through the wood. If it reached the other side, did it meet anything to catch? There were no sounds.

"Too late for what?" I tried, louder and then dropping my voice again. "What are you talking about?"

There was no answer. Nothing but the smoothness of the door I leaned against, and the power streaming through it.

Silence filled the corridor, dotted with the small murmurs of the people up late and the cars out on the street. I counted slowly to ten before I fitted my key in the lock.

One shove swung the door wide. Instead of a trapped prisoner, I saw only the familiar shapes of my apartment and the corridor's light shining in.

I lunged in, caught myself before I ran to the Bones; he could still be watching somewhere. Clicking my lights on, I glanced behind the padded chair, in the closet, under the bed—like some kid searching for a boogieman.

Better get used to it. The Eye just proved nowhere *is safe from him.*

Finally I went to the box, and drew out one of the four Bones. Even pocketing one was like a splash of cold water, the last thing I needed with me as I pulled the blankets around me. If I could sleep at all now.

What the hell did the Eye mean by *too late?* Just part of his threats against me, or was he thinking Maya would get herself killed and his only worry was her magic's secret dying with her? That sounded more like this bastard, but what if there *was* more?

The thoughts kept whirling, and the cube in my pocket spread a dull, cold ache... but I had to keep it ready...

A low tapping sound snapped me awake, lurching up in shock and already shivering. But this was close, right across the room at the window's glass. And the Eye had just been here.

Part of me knew, before I nudged the blind back to see Maya's face in the night.

She hung right there against the second-floor wall—I scrambled to open the window, then watched her step smoothly inside before I clicked on the light. Her feet didn't make a sound.

A grin peeked across her face, wider than I'd ever seen on her. "You think I've got this climbing magic down?"

Showoff... but she deserved to. "Looks like it," I grinned back. "And I did it too—but what did you do, just *remember* all that from one look at the brooch? Oh, I should give it back, it was always yours."

"We're keeping score now?"

Maya leaned back against the wall by the closet door. For a moment I thought she'd make some comment on the half-sorted clutter around my room, but she looked right through it to me.

Her smile stretched wider still. "I had a busy night."

The words jolted my thoughts loose. "Busy! You've got no idea, I—"

"I found the Duvals."

"Found?" The word tore out of me. "What did they—hold on, you didn't go *looking* for them?"

"I had to. They grabbed some of my dad's stuff on the way out of that house. And that's after looting and burning my home too," and her smile twisted down. "I didn't get close to them, I'm not stupid. But, whatever you did to Sibyl? It won't stop her."

"What I did was try to get us out alive, not cripple her. Maybe slow her down before she cuts loose again."

"I hope you're right." She moved from the wall, a step toward me, and her hands reached between us. "This is our chance to get it back!"

"What? Get it—" I caught my breath. "Wait, wait, you listen first, it's my turn."

She stopped, drew back a step. I pulled my thoughts into a line:

"First, I still think the police want to see you about that fire. I did tell Poe the Duvals were after you, and I don't know why they haven't grabbed me already. I'll see them tomorrow and try explaining it on my terms—I may even find someone I can trust with part of what really happened. It helps that I can read how they're taking the news."

I was talking faster as I went, trying to get through it all. But the last part came out with a grin to match Maya's; now I was the one showing off.

"It helps? I'm sure it's not that easy," she said.

"Oh, it never is. But here's the main thing." My foot tried to edge me toward her, and I held back—this was dangerous news now. "The Eye was here. Somehow he got in, and he used my own apartment so well I couldn't even get a look at him. And he gave me the same order, to get your magic. Before it was too late, he said."

And those were more of the Eye's tricks... still, I saw tremblings in Maya's hands, eager and excited signs that she'd been showing since she'd arrived. After hunting the Duvals.

"Too late for what?" Her voice clouded a shade.

"That's what I tried asking him, that and everything else I thought could give me an edge. He just dodged it all. And I bet he'll keep coming, and next time he won't ask."

"Only if you're here when he shows up."

That grin was back, but this time spreading slower on her face. Her head turned, not quite looking at me now.

"Come on. Those Duvals are out there, and we both know they'll keep burning through this town. This is our chance to stop them. We shut them down, get my things back, get proof to send the cops—or send the firebugs right to them, beaten. They're already weakened, and it's our three magics to their one. I'm *sure* we can do it."

She still didn't look right at me, couldn't manage to face me as she asked it. Her hands were moving, reaching toward me.

Except... This wasn't a rescue, not someone needing our help. This would be going after the Duvals themselves, and not just me taking the risks.

"You're *sure?* That sounds too perfect," I said. "Sounds like you know you won't get hurt."

"And you sound like I already have," she shot back. "That's not how we are together—you saw how we stood up to them."

"No, I mean the way you talk about..."

How could I say how eager she sounded, how hungry? I could use the Pulse to feel her reaction out—

No. "I mean," I sounded out, "is this about stopping the Duvals, or is it that you have to go after them right this minute?"

"What are you saying?" Now she glanced at me, and something flickered in her eyes, something unreadable.

"Look... I know you want to take them down. I get that you've lost parts of your life to them, again and again..."

I wasn't reaching her.

My voice sounded fuzzy to me, with the whole long day pressing down on me. And Maya just stood there, *buzzing* with reckless energy, but now her body had gone so still.

I breathed slowly out, slumping where I stood. This was no time to hold back.

"No, I guess I don't know what it's like. I never had someone try to give me magic like you did, and someone taking it away. I mean, we had our own rough times—"

Could I tell her about my mother, seeing ghosts? No, that was just one person's losing track of the line between guilt and dreams, nothing to do with what Maya was facing.

"Well, I came to college here in Jericho to get away from that, you know? But it always gets to me, seeing someone's in pain and nobody's listening. Like my friend Ray—ever since I knew him, he'd been going back and forth with depression. We were both into urban legends, monsters and all, and nothing made him shake it off like the latest hot rumor.

"So I dared him."

The words floated in the air between us, squeezed as flat as I felt.

"Adrian?"

"I dared him. To follow one sign into the storm tunnels. And we saw what was down there. The..."

"The Scarecrow."

Ray's scream in my ears—he only made one—

"I was the one who came back." I forced the words out, pushing them to build up speed again. "I even saw how to make the Bones, like having my own might be some kind of protection, you know? Or revenge, sure, I thought of that too. But he never did come after me. And I know, if the magic's going to mean anything, it's got to be to stop people up here from getting hurt."

And I won't, can't, let Maya be next. Not her.

There had to be a way to tell her, make her listen.

"I'm... sorry. I am." Her voice barely stirred the air.

Her head turned away. But her eyes flicked toward me, back, again and again as she spoke, slowly.

"You ever think... did he hear your name? Because, I know what 'Corbin' means, and I know about someone creating a role for themselves. He called himself a *scarecrow* for you, 'Mister Crow'? I don't care how strong he is, that's still a cheap kind of trick."

A sound came from my lips, that could have been a laugh.

"He never said that. It's what I've been calling him."

"Oh."

The room was still.

But a moment later she began again.

"But, don't you see, that's why we need to do this together. The Eye's out there, so we just don't sit around waiting for him to catch us. We go after Sibyl and her boys our way, without the cops looking our shoulders. This is *different,* what you and me can do together. We beat them.

"And, I've never had someone watching my back that way. It felt... nice."

The word slipped away into the stillness. Her eyes were shut tight now.

"It did."

She really thought staying together would keep us safe.

Deep inside me, another truth rustled: *I only told her part of how Ray died.*

"Soon," I managed to say.

Maya didn't stir. She might not have heard me at all.

"Soon. We'll go after them, sure. It's just... I need to do this right. The Plan was always about more than facing one threat, it was about being ready for them all. So I need to go see what the police want with me, and you. Maybe we'll get the help we need, but either way it'll be soon—"

"Okay."

Okay? I nodded, scrambled to pull my thoughts forward. "Okay then. Thanks, then I'll, I'll call you when I know how this works. You keep yourself safe until—"

"Okay." She smiled, and took a step to the side around me. "That'll be easy. And the way you are, I bet you'll turn the cops right around and the Duvals won't have a chance. Thank you, for doing this right."

She walked from the room.

That was all wrong, I *hurt* her. I had to say something, do something. I could read her with the Pulse—*no.*

But some kind of apology, promise, something... My mouth opened and closed, so many words tangling in my head...

I heard her reach the door, and walk outside. Down the hall. Away.

Maya was gone, *again,* and all I could do was sprawl down and try to sleep.

The thoughts twisted and lashed inside me. I was doing this *for* Maya, right, to make her slow down? And to get the police off her—the longer we put that off the worse it could get.

And there had to be a way to explain the Duvals, or enough of the tricks and twists Maya and I had made. That had to be easier than making Maya listen, or waiting around for the Eye's next move. At least I had the power to read the police, and more than read them.

It was what I should be doing, should have done long ago: getting real allies, resources, leverage. Taking the pressure off us, somehow.

I had to try...

* * *

The police station rattled this morning, so loud and busy. Every person there seemed to have somewhere to go and a reason to push ahead, or a reason to sit someone down and make them wait. I had far too much time to review the files of advice Helena had sent. She had *probably* been joking when she'd offered me a lawyer.

Then the words "A fire like that—half the Sheffield gone in minutes?" grabbed my attention. "You've got to have something. Or you want me to say you're hiding possible signs of arson?"

A weathered, rail-thin man was moving along the desks, with the tireless slow stride of a reporter. His face was one I'd probably seen on some of the crime blogs.

I watched the cops wave him aside. Anyone interested in the Duvals could be useful... but, I'd come here to smooth things over with the police, not link up with another troublemaker.

Instead I leaned over at the desk where I'd be just out of earshot of him, and whispered "I've got information on the Sheffield fire, and I'm trying to talk to someone before that reporter hears. The name's Adrian Corbin."

The man at the desk gave me a careful frown, then stepped away to mutter to another cop. Half a minute later, Detective Poe was leading me to a side room with two older men trailing behind us.

I'd been expecting some bare-bones interrogation room, but this space had thinly-cushioned chairs, posters on the walls, some of the basics of comfort. Until Poe shut the door and sat down in front of me, a tablet set off to the side on the table.

And he said "Where have you *been?* You call us about arsonists and then there's an actual fire—and you disappear?"

"Disappear?" Poe was the one who ignored our warning... but I was here to smooth things over, not blame.

The other two cops still hung back behind him, both men with hard faces like old granite. Poe's own round moonface seemed to contract, gathering in around the frustration in his eyes. But the Pulse felt only a simple, steady dislike bubbling in him, not the anger he tried to show. The other two cops had the same low-level churn inside them.

"Look, it was a *burning building,* you know? The worst day I've had... well, in a while," I had to add, better than sneaking one more lie past the police. "Then none of you cops called me, nobody showed up at my home. Maybe you'd already solved it."

Poe's frown etched deeper. "So you made your one call and you're done? I know grandfathers who stick their necks out more. If they had anything to say, that is," he smirked.

"Oh, I do." It was bait, but it led where I wanted anyway. "I told you then, it was Maya Grant's landlord in danger, Gordon Weber. The two Duvals had him, and we went in there to get him some help..." I shook my head. "Then after the fire, I still don't know if he got out alright."

That was true too, just leaving out how long "after" the fire I'd tried to stay with him. Poe could blame me for Gordon's condition if he wanted, but at least he'd have to tell me how he was doing.

The two cops in back traded a glance.

Poe's face loosened with a flash of amusement. "Maya Grant. Your 'client,' right?"

"Right. She asked me for help when Willard and Dom Duval started stalking her."

"That's the Maya Grant who was in and out of foster homes, and arrested at thirteen for stealing—well, I can't say."

A car, and Sibyl did that, I remembered her saying. I met Poe's gaze. He was trying to shake me, sure, but the Pulse said he had no passion in it, just going through the motions. He hadn't even touched that tablet beside him.

"Some client you have," he added. "Her home burns up, and now you don't have a clue where she is, do you?"

"I don't." More bait, trying all the obvious ways to pry something loose from me. Still, Maya hadn't told me where she'd go, just that she'd wait for my call. And Poe still seemed ready to lock her up on general principles. "Shouldn't you be asking me about the Duvals?"

"We're looking into all sides of this case equally," Poe said, but behind his eyes I felt his interest sharpen. "Look, just tell us what you saw."

"Sure. But I don't know where the Duvals went, and I wish I could send you to them.

"It all started when Maya came to me for help, with them chasing her. I told you how they almost torched the library where we met. Then she got that text from her landlord, that they'd come after him at his office."

I caught a twinge of guilt from Poe then, for the warning he hadn't believed.

"So we went in. Then we smelled smoke, the fire alarm went off—I've seen the Duvals and their fire gadgets, it's how they scare people." And they did save me from admitting I'd pulled the alarm first. "Then we tried to get people out, and find Gordon—"

"You tried." Poe leaned closer. "Because you're some kind of bodyguard, or is it a PI?"

"Just an investigator." I looked back at him, tried to keep smugness out of my voice—I could feel his anger was a bluff. "This state doesn't have license requirements anyway. And I have some free time, with what Travers Brothers pays me."

The high-powered name brought a ripple of surprise came from the two cops in back. If they didn't know I had that connection, did they know me at all?

"And you think you can do our jobs for us?"

I asked you to do your job—but anger was the problem here. Instead I said "I just try to be there, when there's nobody else."

That was still a shot at Poe, but the sparks of his reaction were low-burning ones, flaring inward as much as out at me. If he had no real resentment about me, the Pulse might start softening that into trust—I pushed the temptation down.

Poe said "Like with Jan Reynolds and her husband."

"Boyfriend," I said, but Poe ought to know that too. "He was terrorizing her, without ever laying a finger on her."

"So you..."

"I helped her stand up for herself. She never touched the bastard, and neither did I."

"Tough talk. For a blogger who writes..."

He finally reached for the tablet. The page he brought up was one of my first—one of the classic could-be-Bigfoot photos and the headline *Ten Places They Might Hide In Jericho.*

Another cheap shot, and I only shrugged. "Rumors and jokes, from years ago, but you never know. These days I focus on people I can help. Like Maya."

"Like—" I felt that anger sharpen in him, but then it turned and faded to soggy guilt. "Alright, yes, you gave us that tip. And sure enough, the Sheffield went up in flames."

"That's right. And Willard and Dom Duval did it."

"Did they? Did you *see* them set the fire?" His interest swelled, and I felt the same from the two silent cops behind him.

"Not that. They weren't walking around tossing bombs, no," I had to say, and all three cops' curiosity deflated again. "But back at the library, they were waving flames around, threatening Barry and Gina—did you get the assault complaints from there or not?"

"We did," Poe said.

The other two cops almost felt like statues now, sitting still and so sure I had nothing else worth hearing. I could try deepening that apathy with the Pulse, maybe getting Poe alone... Bad idea, in too many ways.

"So you know what the Duvals do," I went on. "They chased Maya to the library, and almost burned it... and then they came to Maya's place and it 'somehow' caught fire too. We're lucky we made it out at all. The last I saw, they were dragging Gordon Weber away, and we still don't know if he's alright."

Poe smiled. "Actually, Mr. Weber's been found. He's recovering just fine under medical care—and so is *another* associate of Maya Grant's, from *another* fire last night."

"*What?*"

I had an instant to make the gasp loud enough, sharp enough, to sound like someone who hadn't been there. And I flicked a faint wave of the Pulse at them, a hint of smug confidence for them to help feel they'd known so much more than me all along.

Then I sighed, and pulled my gaping jaw up. "Huh. Why the hell am I even surprised, with the Duvals? But, Gordon's alright? And this other friend?"

Poe leaned in. "Where. Is. Maya. Grant?"

"I told you, I don't know."

But she said she'd wait for my call—and for an instant I had to wonder, how long would she settle for waiting? And so far the police weren't nearly ready for me to bring her to them.

More likely they'd... I said "You're probably tracing her phone anyway," and tested their reactions.

Anger spiked in the cops. Not satisfaction or frustration, real irritation.

"Funny," Poe said. "Her phone isn't tracing, or answering calls. You want to explain that? And how yours isn't either?"

I blinked, brushed the phone at my belt. Maya could be up to anything now, but I knew no cops had tried calling me. What was going on here?

Then I said "I can't explain it. I guess Maya's afraid of anyone finding her now, but for me... I don't know, I did tinker with some anti-trace apps back in my conspiracy days, but I wouldn't think those were still working. Or that they'd work at all now. Just..."

It was the best explanation I could admit to, and I readied the Pulse for any chances to help them believe me.

But the two cops in back only glanced at each other, and the resentment in them rippled and shrank down. Without a word, they turned and walked from the room.

What was that—disgust at my thin excuse? Or did I just take away the last thing that interested them in me?

I turned back to Poe, the one detective who knew me a little, who'd shown a flash of guilt at ignoring me. "You know Maya isn't setting these fires, but she's the one you keep asking about. Do you really think she can give you the lead you need? Tell me you're tracking the Duvals too."

"We're considering all possible suspects. And any leads about any of them."

"You know the Duvals won't stop—and they're setting *fires*. You need to find them."

"I heard you the first time."

"Good. Like you said, any kind of lead should be worth it." And I felt at the Pulse, for any hint of openness, curiosity, anything. A few uncertain threads hung from the knot of his emotions... I pushed down the urge to tease those out.

Poe leaned back, shaking his head. "Stop hinting and talking big, Corbin. You meddled with two dangerous men, and your paths only crossed for a minute, because of sheer luck."

So he was writing me off too? "And Maya?"

"We'll see about her. If she's the victim in this, she should have nothing to fear. I'm just hoping she comes to us, before those two find her."

"And I hope I get a chance to tell her that."

Poe glared at me a moment, but the suspicion in him only crackled once and fizzled away, like a scrap of bacon on a pan that lost the last of its heat. He stood up and looked out the door.

Then he stepped back, as Helena moved into the doorway.

On her face, a genial smile was narrowing to give Poe a careful, warning look. "Are you finished with my investigator, Detective?"

"Ms. Travers..." He looked at her, past her.

Over her shoulder I saw see faces watching, looking in at the woman in the suit who'd walked right through them all.

"We're done for now." Poe turned to me. "But get that phone straightened out."

"Sure. I'll see what's going on there." At least I didn't have to fake confusion on my face for that.

I followed Helena out, trying to think what had happened there. Was Maya somehow hiding herself, and me too? Were the cops lying—no, that made no sense either. I was just too rusty on the tech...

"Adrian?"

"Sorry."

I looked over at Helena beside me. She *gleamed,* richly-toned suit and perfect face and the presence that opened a space within the station and made it look like a cluttered rat's nest. And she'd *actually come*—

"You didn't need to come here for me." My voice had a faint crack, down where nobody could hear.

"You did save my life. And I was nearby." She made that sound like a simple truth, or was it an excuse? "I wanted to see how they were treating you."

"I... appreciate it, believe me."

One touch of the Pulse and I could be reading what she felt, right then, about me.

That was an old temptation, and just feeling it was enough to squash it. I looked away, and pulled out my phone. The screen looked normal enough.

Helena said "I should be asking you, how you got so involved with fugitives and... arson, too?"

Now she wanted answers? Was I supposed to finally explain magic and the Plan and all the rest as we walked out of a busy, scrambling police station? I kept my eyes on the phone screen. "Um, are you sure you want to know?"

"Ominous of you."

Then she laughed softly.

"But alright. It's too easy to tease you about your trade secrets and your side jobs. What makes us work is that I trust you, and you've always gotten results."

Well... that was one less knife to juggle right now. "Thanks," I grinned. "Besides, if I told you I'd have to kill—"

A text popped onto my screen:

You were told what you had to do. Now Helena pays the price.

CHAPTER SEVEN: KNOWS

I stared at the text. The Eye... the Eye knew about Helena...

People moved, muttered, called out, all around the police station, all vibrating with their own reasons. And the Eye could be watching anywhere among them.

I drew on my magic. The station was drenched in constant, half-controlled fear, with sharper blades of it that pulled in the Pulse's power even more, all swirled in with the dull roars of resentment, boredom, satisfaction—

Useless. I looked over at Helena. "Let's get out of here, *now.*"

Her brow creased, like hunching up against a cold wind. Still, she began walking, matching my pace.

We pushed and swerved our way past the faces that glanced at us, and the anger or lukewarm sympathy that splashed around us. If speed even mattered anymore, with the Eye already targeting us. The thought thickened in my stomach.

But we reached the outside, the late morning sun on the parking lot and the open space crowded with its rows of cars.

Helena stopped there. "Now, talk to me. I've never seen you like this."

"Not like this, no. No danger is like this." *She* was in danger, the Eye had been warning me all along.

"And your first reaction is to move us *away* from the police?" Then her voice dropped. "Are you saying the problem is one of them?"

"No, not that. Or I guess not—"

Helena's frown tightened, with a dubious edge creeping toward her eyes.

"I mean it, I just got a real threat. See, right here." I held up the phone for her.

The text was gone.

Vanished. I tapped, scrolled, scrabbled for the message, but I found no sign it had ever been there.

Did the Eye *make* me see a text, was that how his magic stayed ahead of us, controlling our senses... the thought of what that could do began sinking into me, soaking through every resistance...

Or he hacked the phone.

He cut me off from the cops' calls, and even from them tracing it down—that had to be it. And if he did, he had all this time to listen in through it, to learn about me and Helena.

And he isolated Maya from the police too. That meant he could be spying on her right now.

So did I try to sneak a discreet warning to her, or... no time for subtlety, when she could be recharging her magic right now, with him listening. I turned away from Helena and snapped a call to Maya. If she wasn't already running for her life, or blocked off, or...

But her voice came on at once. "What is it?"

"I think the Eye hacked my phone—" For an instant I expected it to go dead right there, but I rushed on— "Yours too, it sounds like. And you know what he wants from you."

"So I'm on my own." The words had a bitter weight to them, but she added "Or, till I can get in touch again. Okay?"

"Got it." And then we'd both hung up and I was prying my pocketknife at the phone trying to get the battery out.

When I looked up, Helena was watching me with her arms folded. "I'm waiting for an explanation. Who is this 'Eye,' and why are you letting him get to you? Nothing did before."

"This is different. He's after you now—damn it all, just me knowing you put a target on you. That's the last thing I ever wanted, *ever...*"

I stopped there before any more spilled out. Stillness hung in the air between us, floating, waiting.

Another voice broke in. "Is there a problem?" and two police, a woman and a young man, closed in on us. Looking at the dismantled phone in my hands, and how anxious Helena looked beside me.

No. She had doubt creasing her face, but she wouldn't give up on me that easily.

"That depends on her," I told the cops, and I stepped back to let them slide between us to 'protect' her.

Helena's gaze hung on me, measuring a moment. Then she smiled. "No problem, except whatever's wrong with that phone."

"If you're sure..." They turned away slowly, with the lingering glances of people who were still weighing the worst-case scenario for us.

Or what they thought was the worst. I gave Helena a grateful grin, and searched the Pulse again. Her worry vibrated beside me, the two cops' resignation drew away, and other emotions whispered all around the rows of cars. The Eye could still be anywhere.

Helena deserved an answer. But the Pulse's power had always been either too savage or too subtle, so I never had a way to prove any of this.

Except now I did.

"Look, I need to say this fast." Her eyes narrowed, and I went on "Could you touch that wall over there? Anywhere on it."

"The wall? What about it?" But she stepped over to the gray wall of the station, to brush her fingers over the masonry.

I set my own hand on it nearby and called on the brooch in my pocket. Helena's fingertips froze, locked against the wall's surface.

"That's magic holding you there," I said. "And it's just one bit of what I've seen."

She was tugging against its grip, surprise deepening to anxiety. I tapped my hand on the wall again and released it, and she came free.

"Now, can we get away from here?" I added.

"Just what are you saying?" But she started walking, up the rows toward where her car had to be.

The lot had only a few people out on it, but I walked close beside her and kept my voice low. "Magic. Very real, dangerous forces, in the hands of some dangerous people. I couldn't show you before because what I had wasn't something your eyes could see. All that just changed."

"And you think this is a *threat,* because of sticking me to a wall—wait." Helena frowned, leaned back to stare at me again. "How long have you... been part of this?"

"Since before I met you. It's been mostly a sense for emotions—that I *don't* use on people I care about," I added quickly. "The secret of my success, yes. I was always going to tell you. But think about everything I've done, and ask yourself if it doesn't make more sense with this."

She only looked back at me, unreadable, unless I cheated and reached closer.

I added "I know, it's a lot. Sometimes I started doubting there was any other magic out there, but I kept prepping to deal with it. And then Maya showed up with hers, and the Duvals with theirs chasing her. And the Eye."

I reached the Pulse out around us—and felt him.

It had to be the Eye, that presence not in the crowds but up on the station's roof, just like he'd been last night across the street from us. The emotion I felt could be a match for the heartless chill in his voice.

"Don't look around," I whispered, and clamped down on the urge to sneak a peek. "I think he's watching us from the roof."

"The *roof*? You're sure he's up there?" Even surprised, her voice stayed low.

"It's magic, remember?" A weak laugh started inside me, and I rushed on "But I can't track him right, I can't catch him, and he always finds us. And the scariest thing I ever met was someone living in terror of the Eye."

No matter what we did he found us, he got around us, he could hit us from anywhere... A shiver swept over me.

I tried to lock my thoughts around some kind of plan, but my mouth wouldn't stop running. "He wants me to steal Maya's magic. And he just said he's taking it out on you."

I probed again. The Eye was gone.

Or whatever I was sensing was, if any of that was real... but Helena had wondered why he'd be on the roof. That spot had given him a clear view of us.

And I could barely recognize him by his emotions—for all I knew he'd been watching us every minute and I only noticed at the times he was standing away from crowds. The most suspicious thing I felt now was a surge of simple hostility at the end of the cars' row, from what looked like a father and son. Feelings like those were common as street lights to the Pulse.

"This can't be right," Helena was saying. "He can't be that unstoppable. Or there has to be someone you can go to for help."

"I was going to *be* the help—that was the Plan. Plus there's Maya." But the Eye's bugs cut me off from her too, at least until she tracked me down again. "But nothing we've done has slowed him down."

I searched the Pulse again, still felt the same array of common feelings around us. I could search, watch, forever and I'd never seen a way to stop him. The biggest thing I'd done so far was to drag Helena into Maya's risks.

"Helena, I swear, I'll find a way to protect you, and Maya—a trick, an escape, something..."

We'd come to a halt. Helena had brought us to a stop, next to a low, lean gray Porsche that could only be hers.

She gave me a long look. "So you're saying, this unstoppable master of magic wants Maya, and he's using me as leverage?"

I nodded.

Helena took a slow, deep breath. "So what do we do about him?"

Warm relief and pride welled up in me, and I grinned back. She was listening, after no more than a few moments stuck to a wall, because I'd earned this kind of trust.

But, I'd been so busy explaining and keeping watch, I'd never thought of the steps after that. Still, the first one was obvious. "We get you home. You pack, and you get as far away from Jericho as you can get."

Pack, did I say? Can she dare to take that long?

"Go?" she said. "I'm already late for one meeting... and you want me to run from a bully..."

"Please! He's already hacked us, dodged us, spied on us—running is the best answer I've got. And the office has, what, how many right hands that can run it for you? We have to go."

"I see."

We settled down in the sports car, and she brought the engine to life—smoother than any car I'd ever sat in, like an extension of her own will. I thought of stopping for my bike, but even riding behind her car felt like abandoning her for the Eye.

Instead I searched with the Pulse again, and looked around the car's wide, low view of the street that we pulled out into. The Eye had to be watching somewhere, and he'd know I'd try getting Helena out of his reach. Running was the only move that might stop him.

I could have asked her to head straight for the airport, but I'd said to head home first. That had been to help her agree... except for the one, cold thought that said I could let her spend a little time as bait.

After all, why would the airport be safe anyway? And, she'd been asking if she could do more.

"You're telling me this magic..." Helena's was strangely calm, as she twisted the wheel to dart us through traffic. "You can trap things together, and sense emotions, you said? And you've been using it on our projects?"

"It seems to work." I probed the Pulse around the street again, trying to direct it away from Helena—but the Pulse could never miss that growing worry in her, that sense of her dipping her toes into knowing how deep this risk could be.

"And this 'Eye' is hunting me. And you're sure there's no other way."

A groan started inside me, and I held it in. *"Believe* me... please, if you believe anything, it's that I'm trying to keep you safe. You and Maya."

She must have caught that, that moment when I put Maya up there with her, even right now. She swung us past another pair of cars, faster yet.

I added "You need to get away from here. Or go straight to the airport." But I still wasn't insisting, not pushing her onto the safest path.

"How did you start all this? How'd you become... get... learn..."

"You don't want to know. Not that one."

She put the pedal down and speed shoved me back in my seat.

Then, too soon, we pulled up by a gate, an enclosing wall, what looked like a pocket-sized estate of neat grass and elegance up at the end of the driveway.

While the gate was moving aside, I swung the car door open.

"Get what you need, to go." And, low as I dared, I added "Take your time—"

There it is, I'm really letting her risk—

My voice choked as I finished "Not too long."

Helena's eyes went wide. "You mean..."

Her voice faded away. She understood.

I climbed out, and she drove in, with one twitchy roar of the purring, perfect engine that made me want to race after her. The gate shut.

My legs were numb and trembling as I walked down the street, as I left her dark brick wall behind and began passing the next manor's iron fence. I had to keep moving, to hope—*hope?*—the Eye saw me leave Helena alone. And then gave me a chance to move.

The Pulse let me reach back and hold onto some sense of her. There she was, still wrestling with her fear, with no other presence lurking around her.

But the block, the whole wealthy neighborhood, was bigger than I'd thought. Only a few other emotions rippled within all its space, and yet Helena's thinned away and faded just from the distance before I turned the block's corner and sped up my step. I had to get *back* there, fast and quiet.

A huge, vintage-looking car drove past me, and I caught the driver's suspicious glare. I slipped off my motorcycle jacket and folded it over my arm, anything to look less like someone they'd call the police on.

Then, suddenly, a little side road opened up, leading into the back of Helena's block, running between trees and more of those walls. I marched down it, feet ringing faster on the pavement with every step.

And I felt her again—a faint, growing sense of that same reluctant worry of hers, the same blessedly clear space around her. The stony weight in my chest felt a little looser, that he hadn't simply pounced the moment walked away.

Please, Helena, get out of there soon. But this window was my only chance to draw the Eye in on my terms, if anything could. Did his magic still know I was back here? Did he use some kind of illusion, transportation, something... I still had no idea how he stayed ahead of me, or if he *had* limits, except the times I could sense him.

That uneasy presence ahead was my lifeline. Helena had to stay safe, now that I'd left her at risk like this. I'd *let* her, what was wrong with me?

The wall changed, from a neighbor's iron fencing to Helena's seven feet of deep red brick. I scrambled toward it.

"What are you doing—"

Two men in work clothes, at a gardening truck across the street, one staring right at me. I could feel his suspicion—

And a grimmer, deadlier presence was inside Helena's walls.

"Let him alone," the other gardener snapped.

The first one looked back at him—I reached the Pulse out, grabbed at their resentments as they faced each other—they were a whole forty, fifty feet away from me, but enough was still there to spike within them.

"Don't you tell me to—"

I whirled away from what I'd done, back to the wall while I had the chance. The Eye was drawing closer to her.

I rushed the wall, clamped a hand against it with the brooch's power, then a foot to kick me up higher, and I rolled over it and down onto the yard.

"Where'd he go?" came a voice behind the wall.

Twenty feet of neat grass separated me from Helena's home. I flung myself across it, knowing the Eye had to be already inside.

A broad deck stood at the back door. I grabbed the door, wished for Maya's magic for pulling locks open—but it swung wide. As if Helena had left every door open as part of her faith in me.

Somehow I held my steps down to softness as I pushed into the home's elegance. There was only the distance left between the two presences, in these airy rooms that would make my footsteps echo. Helena was on the second floor, the Eye still here on the first.

I felt him climbing stairs, before I peeped around the doorway to see him disappearing up them—just a man, in simple clothes with a black ski mask over his head, he could have been any burglar if it weren't for where he headed. I let a cold, hollow ruthlessness inside me hold me back another second, until he'd climbed out of sight of the floor below, before I padded up the stairs behind him.

Just a man in a mask, walking up ahead of me, but with that confident, silent stride. His magic would be ready, whatever it was... *everything* came down to my getting close before he saw me.

Helena's voice broke the silence: "Next thing: put my afternoon on hold. I'll explain later."

It came from the side of the corridor, through an open doorway, but the Eye was already pushing open another, closer door. He stepped inside—I felt his predator's anticipation, still blind to me closing in.

I stood beside the door. The Eye was just beyond it.

"Trust me, Ginger, you have my notes—"

The Eye moved toward her, one silent step.

All my fear, doubt, loathing, I flung along with the brooch's magic, lashing through the floor to clamp onto his feet. The power stretched across to him, too little of it—the Eye cursed—

I lunged around the doorway with the Pulse ready and my fist swinging.

The space was empty.

A broken-off gasp swung my head around.

At the other end of the vast bedroom stood a wide desk—and Helena sat behind it, face twisted she struggled under a choke hold.

The Eye tightened his arm over her throat, ready to crush it—

"Don't!" The desperate sound tore out of me. "Please, stop it!"

The arm loosened, and Helena heaved in a breath.

Then it drew taut again.

"Don't! Whatever you want—you want Maya's magic? Here. This is what let me climb that wall, and how I just tried to trap you."

I dug out the brooch and sent it skittering across the floor, to the corner opposite them.

Helena's mouth moved. She grunted something that could have been my name.

"It's right there," I told him. "You let Helena go and I'll give you the words it needs too. When she's safe I'll tell you the words *and* the power source."

Please, let that be enough for him.

I used the Pulse then. Helena's shock and horror screamed in it like an off-key siren, but I caught some curiosity inside the masked man. And quiet fear.

A faint touch of my will tugged at that curiosity. He had to want it enough—

The Eye pulled back from Helena, but he brought his fist up. Ready to knock her helpless and free him to run for the brooch.

No. I wrenched at him, clawed at the fringes of his greed. *You want it now, now—*

The Eye vanished.

I blinked, stared, but my gaze was too slow. He was *gone.*

A flicker of emotion made me look around. He stood at the corner beside the brooch, bending to scoop it up. His body was still swinging upright when he vanished again.

My gaze flicked back, but he was already there, where Helena was stumbling, toppling, out of her chair onto the floor. He reached down toward her.

I threw a wave of fear at him, saw him stagger, and I leaped into a charge at him.

He lifted a foot up and stomped it down on the floor—of course he did, and I tried diving to the side, but the wave of the brooch's power seized the floor as I landed. Something snared my foot, sent me toppling forward.

The Eye looked down at me, still out of reach across the huge room. His hands closed around the dazed Helena.

Then that grim voice spoke. "You'll see her again, when you have the *real* magic. Be ready for the call."

And they both vanished away.

CHAPTER EIGHT: NEEDS

The damn shoe and my foot could have grown roots, all just to trap me here. I slammed fists on it, snarled curses—somehow I'd let a friend get near danger *again*.

Nothing budged. My fingers scrabbled, fumbled, couldn't even close around the laces.

That ragged breathing that echoed in the so-silent house, was that *me?*

I dragged my hands back and tested the Pulse. It was like diving into ice water now, with my own fear so thick around me... but I caught two presences on the floor below, Helena's shock and the Eye's heartlessness.

As I pulled in a breath to shout at them, they vanished. Out of reach, gone beyond anywhere I could sense in this hollow street of near-empty space...

My fingers steadied, enough to loosen the shoe around me.

My foot wrenched free. As it did, the shoe wobbled, loosened—I wiggled it, tried to remember how many times I'd used the brooch, and how little I'd recharged it. No wonder it couldn't hold the Eye.

And I'd just thrown it to him. Not even a real try to buy Helena back, just a mindless plea to make him stop. And he took her anyway.

The shoe came loose. I laced it on, and shut the icy Bones up in their box for now—as if I'd ever feel warm again. Too late, too late.

Then, walking downstairs through her house, the hardest thing was to keep those feet from breaking into a run. All I needed was for the police to follow some silent alarm and catch me here.

Except, a security panel lurked off in one corner beside a tall painting. The display said simply "Disarmed."

One more sign of Helena trusting in my trap. Or the Eye hacking it. Damn it *all*... Somehow I kept my steps slow, inconspicuous, as I walked outside and found the gate button and started down the street.

Walking slower only let the guilt thicken around me faster. But there had to be a way, a lead, to find the Eye again.

And that'd go any better than this time? His magic can teleport, *he really can be anywhere!* My fingers were shaking again, harder than ever. I couldn't even reach Maya—

"Be ready for the call," the Eye had ordered.

I sat down on the cold sidewalk and slowly, slowly, forced my fingers to open my disabled phone and set the battery back inside. Even the phone's construction made it so much trickier than back when I'd been trading conspiracy blogs in college.

Finally I tied it together again, and called Maya, only to find her own phone was down.

Of course it was. I'd *told* her the Eye was monitoring us... did he want me in touch with Maya now, to worm her secrets out of her?

There might be nothing else that saved Helena.

My call's failure message glared at me. I'd just pushed one person in my life into danger, was I really thinking of trading in someone else? Because the moment the Eye learned Maya's magic, he'd be free to kill her. And Helena too, and me.

I leaped up, started down the sidewalk. I could at least get back to my bike at the police station... but I walked past the first turn left that would have taken me downtown toward it, as if that wasn't where I had to be. And yet the only other lead I had was to head home—the home I'd put at my back and growing farther away with every step—and hope Maya came to see me there. If we could track down the Eye together, or her secrets let me try something else...

Instead the buildings around me hunched lower, closer together. Bright friendly houses, marked with hedges on a long, rising hill...

I'd found my way onto Little Street.

For the Scarecrow.

The thought shot through me, knocked the wind from my lungs and left me staggering to a halt. I *couldn't* have come here, anything would be better than stepping into that place again. But *he* knew about the Eye, he was the only one who'd ever known about him.

And I'd pushed someone into danger again. Maybe this was what I deserved.

One slow step at a time, I began moving. The street murmured around me, cars on the streets and a handful of people strolling on the sidewalk, proof I was still far enough away from that site for people to be sharing lively talk and music and all the rest. I made another try to reach Maya, nothing.

But my phone buzzed.

Detective Poe, the screen said.

I stared at the letters. I couldn't even guess what kind of trouble a police call could unlock now—but it did let me stop walking toward the Scarecrow.

"Hello."

"There you are. Took you long enough." Frustration coated Poe's voice. Or this could be another bluff like this morning, and I'd never know it with him not here under the Pulse.

I squeezed over against the hedge at the sidewalk's side, and let a jogger scramble by.

"Something I can help you with, Detective?" This was the last thing I needed, but I forced my voice to stay calm.

"Damn right. You know what's going on here."

"I know? What does that mean?" *Calm, calm.*

"It means that girl of yours is missing, and I want to talk to her."

He wants me to bring out Helena. My throat seized up. *If only.*

I clenched my eyes shut, tried to focus. If I confirmed Helena Travers was kidnapped... a case that big would turn all of Jericho upside down to find her. If I could get Poe to listen to me.

"Detective, this morning I tried bringing information to you. And you ignored me, when you weren't insulting me."

"Sure. Because it looked like you had nothing useful, just your own agenda."

"My *agenda* is keeping people alive." If I could even say that anymore.

"You sniff around our cases as a private investigator, or whatever it is you call yourself. Working for Helena Travers doesn't change that."

The name slapped at me, Poe was slapping at me with the victim's own name—

Except he *didn't* mention Helena before, just that he was looking for a "girl of yours." This could still be about Maya.

Carefully I said "So that means you'll listen to me when..."

"When we've tried everything else," Poe said. "I won't act like we want you out there, but this time you may know something."

"So now you want to trade information with me."

"There's no trade here—you tell me what you've got, if you've got one speck of concern for anyone around you."

The bastard dared to say that, *today*—

Then I clamped my mouth shut. I didn't need the Pulse to know Poe sounded desperate.

"Concern for who?" I tried. "What are you saying?"

"For keeping people alive, you just told me. Now, how do we find the Duval cousins? Or Maya Grant?"

So this *was* about them... a sigh tried to crawl up through me, but the Duvals were their own separate kind of nightmare.

"I *don't know*. It's the truth. Maya doesn't trust my phone now, or hers." I'd been guessing she might come to my home again, but— "Why's this so important now that it's got you calling me?"

"Trying to make trades again? You holding out on me?"

"No, I'm not. But it does sound big."

"Sure it's big," Poe growled. "We had another fire."

Damn, damn it all. "Of *course* they would. What the hell did they get this time? And you think Maya can lead you to them?"

"That's *not how this works*, I keep telling you. I'm the cop, this is *my* job, and you keep saying you've got nothing."

"Because I do. Unless Maya tries seeing me at my place." Poe sounded hungry enough to stake out my apartment—what had the Duvals done?

"If you *are* holding out," Poe said, "and the next time someone gets killed... well, I hope you can live with yourself."

He's good. I still don't know I can live with this one. "I told you, you have everything I know about finding the Duvals. Is that it?"

"For now." And he hung up.

Across the street, a couple was strolling along, not even looking at me...

And the Duvals were still burning through the city. I dug through the phone's search screens, the news feeds, the local forums, anything for signs about another fire. Poe had talked about someone getting killed next time—did that mean we'd been lucky so far, or that someone already had?

My fingers shook too much to go on. I had to turn and start walking again.

Find the Duvals. Find Maya. Find Helena. But...

I topped the hill and saw the long slope downward, the street lined with green-rounded trees before it passed that great drain at the bottom and began to rise again, never quickly enough. People *lived* here—Little Street looked so damn harmless in bright daylight. If you drove by fast and didn't notice the hush lying over these blocks.

My feet halted on the sidewalk. To see it again, to think of crossing that last feeble stretch of open space between me and the Scarecrow's lair... My heart should be pounding enough to drive me deaf, but the world had gone still.

Move. Move, I had to. *Think of how I lost Helena.*

Someone had to go back and catch the Duvals too—no, that was only an excuse.

My feet wouldn't take another step.

They couldn't.

Instead I twisted away, fought to get my balance. *Now* I could feel the panic in my chest.

I shut my eyes, the last thing I wanted to do on this cursed street. But there it was—after all my talk about the Plan, when someone truly needed me I still froze. The way I had for years here.

The phone buzzed.

Slow as a dream, I managed to draw it out. The call came from Maya.

"I'm in trouble. Get yourself downtown, fast."

* * *

The Zimmerman Tower was built around an old business. Or it seemed to be, with that mix of smooth, molded wood furnishings under the bright plastic and carpet in the lobby.

People at the elevator needed key cards to work it... but the center of the building was a wide-open space rising up through a dozen ceilings, with stairs leading up between each floor, and I followed those steps.

The Duvals' fuming anger began to peek through the crowd of other emotions, between me and the upper floors. I marched, dodged, sidestepped, past the range of busy businesspeople along the way, trying not to wonder too much how Maya might have wound up trapped here. Charging into our enemies would get me killed before I helped anyone, before I got a chance at Helena and the Eye.

Unless this is *the Eye's plan, somehow.*

Unless this was supposed to be my time to get Maya's secrets out of her. Like I'd even get the chance to refuse.

I followed the Duvals' emotions up to the seventh floor, toward what looked like a suite of rooms branching off from the rest. One deeply frightened presence stood beside them, and one quick, controlled thought back behind those could be Maya.

The outer room smelled like ash. A man and a woman stood over piles of half-singed papers, struggling to sort through the damage.

As I watched, a pile spilled off the table. The two cursed and scrambled to gather them up, turning their eyes away from me at the doorway. One of Maya's distractions—I slipped behind their backs on into the next room, some kind of long meeting room, and peeped into the one beyond that.

"Where'd you hide them?" Willard Duval made it a low, harsh hiss. He, Dom, and Sybil pressed in around a small man with a birthmark splotching across his face.

And Maya's presence had to be just beyond that room, behind the door that was just cracked open.

"We... we didn't..." The little man's voice was too weak to finish.

"Try that again, Hammond." Sybil leaned closer.

"We *didn't* keep them!" 'Hammond' spluttered. "It was just old reports—Mr. Grant's pet projects in folklore."

"Where?" Willard rumbled.

"See?" And Hammond turned, reached toward shelves on the wall, and began digging through pages, almost burying his face in them as if he could hide from the Duvals. Willard stood behind him, watching.

Sybil turned away. I ducked back behind the door frame, but I heard her mutter "You're not getting these, girl."

So that was it. Of course 'Mr. Grant' was Maya's father, and Sybil was looking for more of his magic. With Maya already here to stop her.

"See?" Hammond's words made me peek back, to see him waving a handful of papers at them. "These are his project reports, and there's nothing here, same as on the computer. He was fired, we dumped it—I keep telling you there's nothing."

Sybil reached a gloved hand toward him, and flame leaped around her fingers. Damn it, my shock treatment might have made her even more vicious.

"That's the company talking," she snapped. "You're one of the experts he kept around him, so his bosses never saw what you dug up. You know there's more than these files."

"There's *not*—"

"You know. It took us all morning, but we know it was you. And someone tried lying to us then, and..."

The flame spurted a moment, still inches from Hammond's face. The Duvals *were* on a rampage—Poe said they'd already struck once today. They were too fierce to calm down, too many to attack.

"But there's nothing!" Hammond gasped. "It was just mythology from the countries he'd worked in. When he left I got nothing, nothing but my job here."

"More lies?" The flame moved closer.

Hammond jerked back, twisting away along the wall to keep clear of her—and his feet tangled, his arms flew up, the pages in his hand sprayed into the air.

Sybil pulled away and yanked the flame back before it caught on paper.

I drew on the Pulse—the Duvals' anger pressed around Hammond's fear, and that heat was actually throttling back, losing steam after the distraction. And I caught a flicker of pride from the watching Maya, that meant that stumble was one of her tricks.

Two other presences were at my back, closing in on me. The man and woman from out front: "What are you—"

Before the two could raise their voices, I flashed my widest, most embarrassed grin and trotted toward them.

I reached out and brushed my fingers over them both to send them a surge of fear. "Get out, get away from here!" I whispered.

They scrambled away.

But the Duvals could still have heard... I looked around the boardroom, flung myself down behind the grand table in the center. The next moment I heard heavy feet moving.

"He *might* know," Hammond was squeaking, his voice moving in the middle of their footsteps. "Van Owen might, but you can't just..."

The four of them moved past me.

I tracked them, felt Hammond's fear surrounded by their malice moving into the main office space, and Maya running up behind me. There had to be a way to stop them.

We peeped out as they started past the cubicles, Hammond walking with the three thugs so close to his back.

Suddenly he tripped, toppled, glanced off a desk and sprawled on the floor. And a flash of relief from him—this time he'd feigned that slip himself, to attract attention.

"Quick!" Maya snapped, and she scrambled the other way, crouching below desks and out of the Duvals' sight.

I dashed after her, hearing the cries of concern behind us as Hammond got the witnesses that might let him break away from his captors. I should be watching, prodding, trying to keep people clear of the Duvals, but Maya only kept moving. To the stairs, and on up.

"I knew you'd come," she told me as we dodged around two startled women on the stairs. "Now, we have to make them listen." Two flights later she led us out onto the floor.

She steered us along the railing and the open space, past several branches before she picked one. Seconds later a broad desk like a battle station stood in front of us, with a sharp-dressed assistant that could have been one of Helena's best. I knew the warning look that woman met us with.

The door behind her said *Wilson Van Owen*. The man the Duvals were coming for.

So Maya had rushed us here first. I looked straight at the assistant and said "Appointment with Mr. Van Owen. It's about Hammond from downstairs," I added. And I reminded myself how *close* the Duvals could still be, and I grabbed that sense of recognition the names roused in her and fanned it.

"He's... he was almost leaving, but..." She shook her head, and a knot of hard, stubborn protectiveness tightened in her.

Instead of fighting that drive, I fed it. "This'll be quick, or if not he'll need some time to work through it without interruptions. If Mr. Hammond does come by before we're ready, can you tell him Mr. Van Owen's gone?"

"But—"

Then we swept past the door.

Wilson Van Owen was a withered-looking old man who leaned back in his desk's chair with his eyes closed. His finger swayed in the air, keeping time with the string music that played from his computer. Books, small sculptures, and other oddities lined shelves all along his walls.

"Mr. Van Owen?" Maya said. "Mr. Hammond sent us—it's about an employee from a few years ago, Stephen Grant."

"Odd." Van Owen blinked at us, once, twice. "I was thinking of taking an early dinner..." He tapped the keyboard and the music dwindled to a hush.

I said "You should do that." I reached for that flicker of hunger and tried to stoke it, anything to help us get him out of here.

Instead, his eyes sharpened and he twisted in the chair to study us. "Now I'm curious. What brings people here out of the blue?"

Maya said "Megan Sanger, journalist—" and suddenly she *did* have the crisp, intrusive tone of a reporter, and a pad of paper in her hand. "We're working on a story about Mr. Grant's folklore research."

I added "Or we could talk on the way to that dinner." I pulled harder at that appetite, forcing down my guilt.

Van Owen's eyes only stayed on Maya. "Now why would you want to know about that?"

She smiled. "Why wouldn't we? Folklore's as eclectic a subject as it gets, but he was unique even there. I heard that as an executive here, he had a way of doing business with your associates that let them bond over their different cultures." She cast a slow glance around the variety of mementos on the shelves.

Van Owen stood up, brushed a hand along one shelf. "Are people still talking about that?"

"Some are." Deep down in Maya's throat, I thought I heard something catch.

"Then they should remember that Stephen Grant was unstable." He shot a harsh gaze across at Maya. "Never enough for him—we sent him somewhere to talk software rights and he had to know every last dragon story, every scrap of pottery or ritual drum they'd heard of. With company time, company reputation, you know. Of course we had to fire him."

Keep it together, Maya...

The Pulse let me feel her outrage, still clenched in, controlled.

And the Duvals' fury was *on our floor*, but drawing away, away down the hall... I held my fists down.

Van Owen's confidence coiled tighter, a foreboding alertness.

"Listen—" I hissed to Maya.

But she kept her gaze on Van Owen. "You mean, after his interests opened doors for all of you, that are still making you rich."

"For a time. But obsession isn't business. All his little fixations had to be discarded, to make room for real possibilities. And real art worth keeping," and he tapped his shelf.

"So you have nothing to say in favor of Mr. Grant?"

"He did good work, once. But time passed, and he lost. Lost perspective, lost his confidence, lost his health... I hear he died so deep in debt his daughter was left helpless. But her name wasn't Megan, was it?"

Maya could have been a statue, too frozen to breathe.

"You've got his face," Van Owen added. "But that's more than you'll get from us—no money, no lawsuit, no vindication. Just the truth of how we treated him better than he deserved."

That cruelty in him gnashed its fangs. The only other thing he felt was something different, a purer, sticky curiosity.

And the Duvals were still near, and Maya was so hungry for something... I pushed at Van Owen's curiosity, one way to tease out what else there might be.

"So, there was nothing worth keeping?" Maya said softly.

"A few good years... but..."

I pushed.

His eyes slotted tight. "But he's not worth any respect from us. He might be if he'd stuck to his guns, but he had to throw out his own work while his reputation was still good. He even abandoned the private research team he tried to hide from us, and those were worth hiring—you must know that if you talked with any of them. No, he might have been determined to bring his life down in flames... unless there was *some other reason?*"

The last words were a roar, a trap he'd never needed my urging to spring. Maya had no answer.

Out on the edge of the floor, the Duvals' ferocity was closing in on us again.

"They're coming!" I snapped.

Maya stared at me, wrenched out of the clash of wills with confusion scattered across her.

Then her features, her focus, drew themselves together.

I added "You get him out of here!"

But Maya looked at the door, at Van Owen's suspicious gaze on us, still unsure.

No good, no good, we only had moments and she needed more awareness to keep them clear of the Duvals, she had to trust I was still on her side...

My hand dove into my pocket and drew out one of the four Bones.

I let it fly—the sensation of my fingers opening was a shock, an echo of throwing the brooch to the Eye, and then I'd let all the doubts go and this time it felt *right,* as right as Maya grabbing the die out of the air. And the great smile that dawned on her face.

I spun away and marched into the corridor.

The three Duvals were still somewhere up at the far end of the floor, and one frightened presence with them, all closing fast. Van Owen's assistant was gone from her desk—was she the one who'd led them away before?

Picking some of them off first was my only chance. I dashed beside the railing and picked out the corridor ahead where they'd turn into view. Between there and me I saw one path branching aside, but a big wide display case lay gleaming just up off the intersection, and I ducked over and crouched down behind its far corner.

The Duvals, and their terrified prisoner, moved closer. Ready to pass my corridor and turn their backs to me.

I should have kept Maya with me, I can't do this alone, but I can't risk her too—

Another mind *appeared* back behind the Duvals. The Eye was here too, of course he was.

The Duvals came to my branch and stomped past it.

But their prisoner broke away. His fear twisted into desperation that flung him up my corridor, I watched Hammond race right past where I hid, with Dom Duval leaving the others to thunder after him.

Grabbing Dom was like grabbing the tailgate of a truck as it pulled away. But I flooded fear into him, heard him croak for breath and stumble, and I slammed him to the wall. Hammond kept running, away.

"You can't win," I said into Dom's ear. "You know someone's out there using you—the Eye. And Sybil, she's going to destroy you—"

His fist sent me spinning for the floor—

A carpet, so soft to lie on as the world spun... A voice, a low growl of "I *know!*" and the sounds stomping away...

I dove into the Pulse and away from the rising ache in my head. There, that could be Maya and Van Owen veering away from the main corridor, if I could tell which tilting shapes were real gleaming walls in my sight and which were the few presences in the Pulse, or what was the Eye vanishing around to baffle that too.

A sound boomed out underneath those. A shout, firm, calling out about *security* as multiple rigid wills moved onto the floor. The Duvals were running out of time, or desperate.

Then I was running into the still-spinning corridor—beside the railing, toward the Duvals' backs. Maya and Van Owen had to be somewhere in the side branches ahead.

My eyes cleared. Maya dashed into view, up beyond the Duvals, stumbling right into their path. Startled, off-balance, cut off by the open space stretching beside them all. The Duvals closed in.

The blurring closed around my sight again... she leaped backward, high... struck the railing and twisted over and fell...

No, no, no—

Screaming in my head. Heartbeat drowning thoughts. The Pulse coming to life, stretching past my ocean of fear to seize the quick, sharp sense of her not plummeting but hanging on just below our floor.

Catching the wall with our climbing magic. Safe.

The Duvals rushed past her, glancing over the edge and cursing and Dom waving them on and none of them looking back at me at all. And I couldn't move, move, fast enough.

The Duvals' footsteps were fading, that had to be distance making them softer... I lurched toward the railing. I almost lost her by being slow, by getting hurt, by trying to care about anyone besides...

She hauled herself up over the railing, safe onto the carpet again. Shuffling toward me. Her face was pale, streaked with lines of sweat, with those eyes staring right into me.

The movement tore *out* of me to hurl me into the kiss.

Hold her, hold her, I don't dare let go again—and her arms were *already* locked around me, our faces searching over hair and cheeks trying to meet—

Hold on.

Hold on to that warmth.

Hold on, nothing can go wrong yet if we don't let go...

Simple breathing forced us apart. But the way she stared with a whole world in her eyes...

"I'm still waiting for answers." Van Owen stepped out of a side corridor.

Then his head turned—toward the sound of people advancing across the floor. The Pulse showed me the knotted resolve that must be security guards, with an anxious presence at their back that must have brought them. The Duvals were a whole floor away already.

Maya said "This way!"

And she half-dragged Van Owen away from their path, back up the side corridor. He stumbled along, and I moved behind them trying to watch for any more surprises from the Duvals, or the Eye.

"We don't have much time," Maya told him.

She grabbed a door and yanked it open, and shooed us into a small room of supply shelves. Her presence, her urgency, filled those narrow quarters more than the boxes of paper and printer ink.

She said "Those three came looking for my dad's biggest secret. You know, there had to be parts of his research you couldn't let go."

He frowned back at her, curiosity glimmering. "Except that there weren't."

"You *know* none of you are safe, as long as it's still here."

As she spoke, Van Owen's deep-lined face began to strain, those lines sinking deeper into him as the fear worked in. The fear that Maya poured in from the Bone I gave her.

I caught at her arm, probed at the crushing force she held Van Owen in.

And opening the Pulse showed me another presence appearing nearby. The Eye was just a corridor away, and searching.

Maya pushed on: "That's your security outside—some of your people were nearly killed. And you know why."

Doubt and dread clenched around the old man's will. But the coils of emotion couldn't close, couldn't find a purchase on his mind.

"I... I told you, there was nothing worth keeping." His last words could have been spitting on her, as he wrenched away and lurched out the door.

Maya spun toward me. "Quick, help me open him up!"

"I... I think you can't." I said. "You can't tap into a doubt that isn't there. And, can't you see how weak he—"

She twisted away and dashed out after him.

I raced out behind her.

A figure flickered back behind a turn, there and *gone* to leave just a ruthless mind lurking behind the corner.

Maya's eyes were on Van Owen, and she stepped ahead of him to pin him against the wall, flooding him with fear. "You're holding *something,* that you knew people would want someday. And as long as it's here, you can't be safe, you can't."

His head shook, wilder and wilder as he slid down the wall. "No—it's all gone—"

I turned away from the Eye's corner and helped Van Owen to his feet. "It's alright, we get it." I looked at Maya. "We can't do this now! No—you *can't* do *this* to him."

And I was reaching out with the Pulse, searching to drag out a bit of sympathy in Maya for her ravaged victim.

I found only one fold of softness—and when I touched it I flinched away in shock at what I was doing.

Then a wave of rage, horror, smashed into me and left me swaying on my feet, wishing it could spit her *outrage* from my head—

Her fist slammed into my face. Straight into my nose, to wash blinding pain up in with the Pulse's assault... and the gouged-open look of betrayal in her eyes.

Then she ran. She ran, and I could only hear her feet fading in the distance.

CHAPTER NINE: LEAVE

Security swarmed in around us, three men in pale blue ready to treat me as one of the intruders. But Van Owen was more interested in asking them about who the Duvals had terrorized, and where Maya had gone. I could stand at the side and keep my sick tangle of guilts held in, until he gave me a moment of thanks for pulling Maya off him.

And I gritted my teeth and used the Pulse once more, just one light touch to amplify that gratitude as he spoke. The one broader smile it got me was enough to loosen the guards' clustering around me—so a minute later I slipped away.

Finally I could throw myself into dashing after Maya. The Pulse would never pick her out of a crowd, so I could only fling myself down the stairs hoping to catch her leaving.

Too much like the library where we first met... but this time she wouldn't be waiting to meet up with me. I had to find her, apologize to her, curse myself for bending minds like that.

My feet pounded down the steps, heels digging in to save my balance. How could *she* do this?

I'd kissed her, I'd never had five seconds to beg her to save Helena with me, somehow...

I burst out onto the lobby floor and stared around the figures in their suits, made for the front entrance.

The Eye had been listening, he'd heard the split between us... he *knew* Maya would never trust me with her secrets now, unless I caught up to her...

A security guard stepped over to block my way out. "Can I see some ID, sir? We're not supposed to let anyone out right now." A spindly man in pale blue who thought a big corporate smile counted as a badge.

"You've got no *right*," and I sidestepped him.

He moved into my path. "I've got my orders."

One punch, one surge of fear, would put out that damn smile—

Hell, Maya must be long gone by now. I forced my fists down and heaved out a breath, as if I could just expel the worst of the knots inside me.

"Look..." I sighed. "I'm trying to catch up with a girl—small, dark hair, could have come by in a hurry a couple minutes ago."

"Sorry. I'm afraid nobody like that's been here. I think," he admitted.

"Thanks. I hope you're right." I turned back and moved in around the businesspeople, catching some of their uneasy mutterings about "disruptions."

What had gotten into Maya, beating down an old man that way? And with the Eye watching—was that his work, another of his powers working on her mind?

No, not him... I stared around, looking for the other exits. Nobody had twisted Maya's head up—until *I* tried to—she simply was that eager to get her answers and defend the parent she'd lost. I should know what that was like.

Except I wouldn't even see my mother, not for years since she'd been locked up...

I shoved that thought away and moved faster, staring around. Maya was simply desperate, and the Duvals had given her bare moments to make her choices. My own worst sins didn't even have that excuse.

Damn it, I'd *kissed* her, I'd needed to kiss her. When I needed to be keeping Helena alive.

The front lobby loomed ahead again. I tried calling Maya, found her phone was dead again—of course, she'd only turned it on because she was calling me. I sank down to sit on the rim of the little corporate fountain.

Helena. *She* was still the one it all came down to, saving her.

Maya's magic for her, that was the Eye's price. That was all I knew about him, that and how he *teleported* away from anything I tried to do. But he wanted Maya's secrets... and yet he'd pushed her in front of the Duvals, and he warned me about her...

I clenched my fists. No need to complicate this: he *was* demanding Maya's magic, so anything else he did could be just ways to manipulate me into getting it.

He might even be giving the Duvals orders, too. He sure wasn't *stopping* them, no matter what they burned. But, there had been that time in the apartment fire when he'd led people to the escape—

And then he choked Helena. My fists slammed down on my thighs. I had to find the Eye's weakness, somehow, not start looking for common ground with a brutal kidnapper. I had to *find* him, *beat* him.

I was on my feet again and looking along the walls for security cameras. Those might have caught something about the Eye, if I could get Van Owen to show them to me—but the Eye had already hidden his face once. And, the thought of giving Van Owen one more scrap of information about us made me shudder.

A weathered-looking man walked in the front entrance, and the guards let him right by.

I walked up to the guard. "Looks like you're letting us through again?"

"We are." Then his wooden smile softened, and he added "Sounds like you need to talk to your girl. You know where she'd be heading?"

"I wish—"

That man who'd walked in. I'd seen him at the police station, on the crime blogs... He was walking toward a trio of guards—Leland-something was his name, a crime reporter.

"Two of them?" he was asking them. "Huge men that look like trouble?"

"Could be—"

He knew the Duvals. He had the connections to hear about this incident, or even guessed the connection to Maya... I angled around the guards toward him, my feet suddenly lighter than they'd been. At least it was something.

"*There* you are." One of the guards, a no-nonsense-looking woman, stepped in my way. "Word just came down, Mr. Van Owen wants to talk to you."

I managed a smile. "Sure..."

I could use that. Leland might not talk to me now, but if I introduced him to Van Owen, with his own story about on the Duvals... no, that was giving that vicious old man another piece of the truth. There had to be something else—

I pulled in a breath and looked over at the reporter.

Leland was walking away, around a corner and out of sight. Just one moment, I'd hesitated *one moment* and...

"Come on," and the guard stepped in my path. She waved me back the way I'd come, toward the elevators.

I started walking. First in front of her, then easing back a step to move beside her—then I whirled and ran. I heard her stop cold and swear, and I just had to get around the next corner, if I could talk to Leland—

Around the corner the lobby were four doorways, whole knots of people, a bathroom door, and no reporter in sight—

I grabbed the bathroom door and let it swing open as I dove around the next nearest doorway.

"Sir? Don't make me send someone in there." That was the woman guard's voice, from back outside the bathroom.

I rushed on to put some distance between us, staring around. I'd lost Helena, Maya, I couldn't even find a reporter...

A reporter. I stopped and grabbed out my phone.

Fingers shaking, I pulled up the blog list I studied—there he was, *Philip Leland On Crime*. With a picture and a contact email.

"I saw the Duvals attack Zimmerman. I'm by the lobby."

I shot the message off and pushed myself to a steady, safe walk away. Something, something had to work.

My phone buzzed in my hand. I let out one long breath, and answered the call.

"Your time is up."

The Eye. My hand shook to get that heartless voice away from my ear—I stared at the *Caller Unknown* marker, then drew the phone close again, gingerly as if I was holding a live snake.

Voices were filtering around me, innocent people chatting with friends and coworkers. I dropped my voice low: "Don't you hurt her, please! Helena's not your enemy."

The phone pinged softly. An image slid into view: Helena, a close-up shot that showed every line of her face, every mark of the fear she had to be fighting against.

Helena Travers should be wrestling her own troubles, not my demons. My fingers locked around the plastic's edges.

The Eye went on "I gave you your orders. Do you have Maya Grant's secret?"

I had to stall him...

Or trace him, somehow, or...

No. Any trick, any delay, could make him take it out on Helena. There was only one answer.

"Yes! I got Maya's magic, damn you."

The lie slid out all too easily. I stepped over to the corridor's side, watching the passers-by and fighting to keep my face calm for them as we whispered over life and death.

"Do you?" he said. "I'm waiting."

One slow breath, to gather all the strength I had...

"No you don't," I said. "You don't just demand this and I hand it over."

The phone pinged again—the bastard had another image ready to send me, but I kept it pressed to my ear.

I said "She's got the magic to push, lift, move, things any way she wants. It's done everything from helping her stage act to unlocking doors. If you want that, if you want one word more about that, you'll have to bring Helena back to me."

"I said, tell me. Now." He didn't even raise his voice.

"No! You either show me you're keeping your word—"

I forced the words out, like spitting out razor blades—

"Or just kill her."

My heart thundered louder than all the voices around us, but I had to say it. The Eye could kill her either way if I didn't take every chance to rescue her... but this was still me putting Helena in danger and failing her and now saying the words that finished her...

"Agreed."

My breath whooshed out. A chance, I'd really get a chance...

Then he said "Come to Little Street."

* * *

This one place... he had to want it here. *I'm really going here.*

The sunlight angled down on the streets, the houses, the yards, but even under that light nothing quite moved here, even when I was still blocks away. And the Eye had set our meeting right at the Scarecrow's doorstep.

Each step I took was off-balance, lurching and trudging up the hill. If the Eye really knew about the Scarecrow... I locked my gaze on the sidewalk ahead, told myself once again that his map showed a spot on along that, not the tunnel grate itself. Tracking my phone could have showed him I'd come here this afternoon, that was all.

Forward, forward, I kept climbing. Closer to where I'd frozen up before—back when I had a choice. Now all I had left was beating the Eye, if anyone could. Voices around the yards, or puffs of wind over the hedges, even the occasional car roaring past, none of those sounds covered the so-clumsy clatter in my steps.

The phone buzzed.

I yanked the thing up with a snarl of *I'm almost here!* rising in me, but this call showed a name: Philip Leland.

"Mr. Corbin?"

"Right here." I worked my throat, trying to squeeze the tension from it.

"Are you? At Zimmerman—where, exactly?"

"Oh hell, sorry. I got called away." I glanced around the bright, almost-normal streets, and choked down a bitter laugh.

"I think I've heard of you, Mr. Corbin. Your early blogs were... interesting," with the same dubious pause so many people used, "but now you've got a different beat?"

"Finding answers for all kinds of clients, yes." The next words came easily, this time: "So I'm thinking both of us might have information we want."

"Could be. You did call our oversized friends 'the Duvals.' You know them?"

"Willard and Dom Duval, and their cousin Sybil too—"

I clamped my mouth shut before I gave away more. The street around me sounded quieter than ever, feeling the hush of what it was leading toward. And I was walking into an attempt to bluff the Eye... this was no time to let anything slip by me.

"I said we both had something, to trade," I added. "Like you: how'd you know they hit the Zimmerman offices? That was no lucky guess."

"Oh, luck never hurts," he chuckled.

"You've got to have more than that. And me, I know who the Duvals came to lean on, and what they were after—" And that was about *Maya's* life, the thing she was racing to take back. I clamped my desperation down tighter, tried again. "That's just the start. Your turn: what is it the Duvals want?"

He cleared his throat. "I'd say they want what any bully wants: a bit of extortion, fear, revenge. They're better than most at hiding their tracks from the police, and they're smarter than they look."

There he was, still holding back. "And a group of 'extortionists' came to the Zimmerman building, and you showed up half an hour later? Or are you going to call that luck again? You've got more on them than that, I know."

"And you say you were there when it happened?" Leland chuckled again. "You've got a few tricks of your own. But you think a reporter's just going to give answers away?"

I broke over the crest of the hill.

It was *there,* the long slope down, the depression before the street rose into an even higher hill. And the storm grate that it would all flow down into, the concrete outline and the opening within it...

If my steps lost any speed now, they'd dwindle away to nothing again. I had to squeeze Leland while I still could—for the one thing that might make a difference now, any clue about the Eye.

And the Eye could be tapping this phone, could notice us any moment. Cold dread clogged my mouth, but I forced it to move:

"Alright, you're a reporter. I bet you've got that one source out there, that you're sure is lying? Or someone who won't talk to you at all? Well, I'm the special investigator for Travers Brothers. If I owe you a favor, you could get to see how to *really* get someone talking. *If* you tell me, right now—"

I was talking too fast, already partway down the hill, with the bottom growing closer every step.

"Tell me, what's really driving the Duvals? You think it's greed, or Sybil's grudges? Or could someone else be pulling their strings?"

"Strings? On them?" Leland's voice rose like he'd never considered the idea. "Hmm, let me think... there is one thing."

"*Yes?*"

The word came out too shrill, made me glance around the street. There was nobody, not one face, within earshot of me now.

"That they're still out there. With all the risks the Duvals take, it could mean someone's looking over their shoulder."

Oh. All Leland saw were bullies the cops couldn't make a case against—not knowing how untraceable their fire was, or how far it could terrify the people they targeted. That didn't put them in the Eye's pocket, it didn't give me *anything* on the Eye.

"Maybe," I said. *The Eye wasn't leading the Duvals... but...*

A fence began running beside me. It marked off the last house before the one by the grate, the one the Eye summoned me outside.

"Now why would you ask that?" Leland said. "You know their names, and you said you were there. I'll take that favor, sure, but I want to hear more."

But the Eye *let* the Duvals run wild. That told me something, if I had the strength to use it.

"Soon. Soon, I'll get back to you," I said.

"You wouldn't be trying to con me here, would you?" he asked, with what sounded like a suspicious smile.

"I guess you'll just have to believe me." Or if I never came back, I wouldn't have to hear him accuse me. I hung up.

The map the Eye had sent me could expand just enough to place its red X on the sidewalk, outside the white and brown and green house right at the bottom. I stood on that spot, saw a car roar past the grate—*don't look down there, just take in the houses. He didn't send me to* there.

Cold worse than anything the Bones did seeped through me, just knowing what was nearby. My face must look like I stared right at a ghost... but there was nobody here to see me but the rare passing car, and those never slowed down.

Where was he? All I saw were still, silent houses—the Pulse might tell me more, if I *dared* to use it here...

A sound behind me broke the stillness, a soft scraping.

I whirled to see the front window in the house edging upward. It crept up only half an inch, and curtains still hid whatever was inside.

That was him. Unless it was whatever beaten-down householder had to live in this place. To be sure, I gave my hidden observer an embarrassed wave and took a step away toward the street.

"Corbin."

Just one window... glass set in a frail brown lattice against the white frame, a heavy white curtain behind it, a curtain that edged back to allow what must be a masked head to look through the crack. The Eye's voice issued from it.

I marched toward it, over clean, trimmed grass, that someone had managed to care for right at the edge of the Scarecrow's domain.

"The house is empty now, right?" I heard myself snarling the words in my rage. "Did you know the people were out, or did you just kill them?"

"That's not what we came here for," he said.

Because we came to trade magic I didn't have—and the moment he asked for that—

"It's *exactly* what we came for," I flung back. "Who else you might kill."

It was what I'd realized with Leland, that I could still judge the Eye based on what he did, and what he allowed. It might be the start to keeping him off guard.

I drew on the Pulse. Just enough to feel the person close behind that glass, and try to miss all the rest of the power radiating over the street. The Eye was the same impassive presence I'd felt before, no anger or greed or anything I could turn.

Unless I changed that. "So which are you? A mass murderer nobody could trust in a deal, or someone only after Maya?"

He warned "You and I, we came to exchange—"

"Did we?" I glared at the mass of curtain across the window, and reached a wisp of soft, shifting doubt toward him. "I'm trying to save lives, not throw them away. You want Maya's power, but as soon as you get it you'd be free to kill her, and us too. Or am I wrong? You say you set the terms for our deal, but I'm the only one who can give you what you want—and I want to know who's dying for it." I gave him one more brush with the Pulse, softly, better to have it ignored than let him notice I was *raising* this worry in him... Firm as I could, I said, "Convince me."

Did his emotions waver at all? But he said "You saw the threat Maya can be. I need to know her magic, to contain her."

" 'Contain' that threat? I guess." I said it to humor him, even when it sounded like a lie, *felt* wrong for him.

"It has to be done," he added.

"With Maya, and not the Duvals?" Another soft push at his mind, to keep him on the defensive.

"The Duvals are thugs. They'll get themselves caught—or, is it your job to stop them?" and a twist of amusement ran through him. "You tried it with their leader."

"Yeah." He saw me try to break Sybil's will, he'd seen it fail.

My hand trembled, my focus trembled, to give him just that smallest imperceptible nudge.

He was saying "They're nothing. Even retracing her history won't make them a threat. But Maya Grant... I should have stopped her long before—"

He cut off.

I pulled the magic back, hoping he'd missed it. *But, "stopping" Maya meant killing her, he* knows *he's just admitted we're only trading Helena's life for what he needs to kill someone else.*

"Why?" I demanded. "Why is Maya—"

"You were never going to do it, were you?" He laughed, a sad dark rasp. "You'd never give up her secrets, or her."

"I..."

His emotions drew together into grim certainty. My throat tried to work, tried to squeeze some kind of lie out to deflect him from what he knew. But there was nothing, and I could only try forcing us over the impasse:

"You know I won't. You must know that, but you still came to meet me here."

Here. I finally opened the Pulse wider, searching for Helena.

At my back I felt it—the pressure of what lurked somewhere behind me, and all around, the few, quavering human presences along the street, like the few rustling sounds of the breeze that only made the stillness louder. Only that air moved here, and us.

My arms clenched in tight around me. Could that flicker of dread across the street be Helena, or that druggy daze up the hill? Where were they, why'd it have to be *here*—

"You," the Eye growled. "You made me hope you'd understand. Instead you're trying to use me."

"Listen!" I rushed the words out, clawing for every second I could get. "Listen! Helena's not your enemy. You're talking about threats—how is she a threat to anything? If you punish her for this, all you are is another murderer." *Focus, find her...*

"You think this is about Helena Travers? This was your test, Corbin. And you still don't see the dangers a Grant can be."

A Grant. Maya's family.

But I had to keep pushing back, as I searched. "And that lets you go after Maya, and drag anyone around her down too, because she *could* be a threat?"

The Eye laughed again, softer now. "You want a real enemy, is that it?"

"No enemy is worth that. You think I'll let you kill Maya, or the Duvals either?"

"Not them? Then what about the Scarecrow?"

I couldn't move. Every muscle I had locked up, left me helpless as the freezing wave poured through me. One small thought said *of course he knows,* but I gasped "You... can't..."

" 'Can't,' you think? You're going to lead me to him."

Move, think... One part of me flailed at the Pulse, still searching for any speck of hope here under the Scarecrow's grip.

A rustle of fear, close. It might be—

"Helena." My word dragged a thought out behind it, and more words to throw at the Eye. "It's Helena I came here for. I told you to show her to me. So where is she? You can't send me against a monster for her sake if she's already *dead!*"

My voice came out raw. It rang out across the empty street, too loud, with everything I had behind it.

"Is that what you think? Look in the garage."

My head turned, my upper body turned on its own, and I swayed and stumbled before my frozen legs jolted into motion. I lurched across the grass, a few steps toward the open garage beside the house.

Nothing. Just empty space, an empty car—God, those little bikes meant *kids* lived here—

A shape burst into being within the car. The masked form of the Eye sat on the shotgun seat with *Helena* held in his lap. She stared around, struggling to get her bearings, her mouth straining against the gag over it.

The Eye looked across to meet my gaze. Then they both were gone.

Helena was here. Or she had been here—I strained at the Pulse, at the Scarecrow's influence and the dread sinking into me, strained to find where she'd gone. Right now I could believe the Eye had the power to whisk her in from clear across town, and yank her away again.

"She's not hurt." The Eye spoke from the window. "I won't harm her, but then, I won't need to."

I staggered toward the window, fighting to catch one clear sense of Helena.

He went on "She'll go free, but only if we come back safe."

One sense—that was her, in the house—

"After you take the Scarecrow—"

I screamed, as I threw myself into a headlong leap, arms coming up an instant before I crashed through the window.

One instant of bone against wood, then the impact was falling away behind me and I was through, sprawling down and tangling in the massive curtains but still catching that one, vital glimpse of the Eye, enough to fall towards him with my hand lashing out and the Pulse ready.

He toppled backward. The masked man flailed in shock, then vanished away just ahead of my fingertips.

Fighting free of the curtain, I struggled up and turned for the next room—I'd sensed Helena back that way. Pain began crawling over my bruised arms and side, and I had to hope my jacket caught all the broken glass.

Heavy-curtained windows kept the house dark, to just a glimpse of pale furniture as I raced through it. Any second now could make me too late.

But Helena was there, tied up back in the corner of a dim TV room, her eyes locked on me. Ten steps from me.

Any second, the Eye could appear and grab her away. Five steps.

No—too obvious—

A reaction tore across Helena's face as I spun around, saw the Eye lunging at my back.

His hands, almost on me, my own arms out of place to grab him and my bruises screamed pain as I moved—

Instead I let fear burst out from me. One wrench at the Bones' power spilled it out, letting it explode through me and into the air.

Those hands flinched back.

And my fingers clamped down on his wrist and channeled the rest of the terror straight into him. A flood of colder-than-ice poured through me, locked my grip down harder. There were no words, not like I'd tried to break down Sibyl's resolve. This was pure mindless panic, the Scarecrow's own weapon.

The masked man staggered, thrashed and tugged backward as if his flesh shrank away from the grip. He wailed.

Then my fingers came together, around nothing.

I struggled to my feet and stared around. The room looked clear, no hidden enemy reappearing in the shadows or lurking behind the various tall chairs.

But in Helena's corner, she lay huddled in a tight ball. Frantic, shallow gasps from her rippled through the motionless room.

She'd caught the blast wave of fear too, on top of everything she's endured today...

"It's alright." My voice broke, it couldn't contain the safe sounds I needed for her now. "I'm here. You can look now, he's gone."

Her breathing didn't even slow.

And the Eye only needed an instant to reappear. I dug for my pocketknife. "Here, I'm going to cut you free..."

The several zip-ties on her ankles were closest, since she clenched in around herself. I cut through them one by one, still murmuring what promises I could. Her wrists came loose next.

Her feet slammed into my stomach.

Lying in a heap, I dragged myself upward, as all the pains and cuts from the window took the time to sink their hooks deeper into me. When she ran off, the wild look on her *face*...

I reached out for the Pulse. Nothing answered, I felt no coldness in my pocket at all. Because I'd poured all the Bones' power out in that blast.

But I heard her—clumsy, frantic steps that had to be Helena racing through the house. I bolted after her, and caught up just in time to see her wrench the front door open and rush outside.

In the middle of the front yard, she slowed. Her head darted around, staring at the open space, the gag still over her mouth.

"It's okay, Helena." I tucked my knife away and moved slowly toward her. "He's gone. He's gone—"

Then the masked figure was there, right beside her. His hands shook as he grabbed out at her.

Helena twisted away and dashed clear. A horrible choked-off sound came from her, a scream smothered by her gag. She scrambled down the yard, and the Eye turned to track her.

I charged up between them. Glancing over at him, I stretched my fingers at him as a warning—and remembered I had no magic left. But the Eye jerked backward, held his place instead of appearing in our midst.

But Helena was already too far away, clear across the yard—

Metal scraped over concrete.

I whirled to see Helena wrenching at the storm grate, the grate that the Scarecrow always kept unfastened... *Good God, how broken does she have to be that she runs* toward *the thing that's radiating fear...*

The bars slid aside. Her face gleamed once in the sunlight, pale and frantic, before she dove into the tunnel. Panicked and helpless, helpless even if she could guess who was down there. But I knew.

I stepped inside.

CHAPTER TEN: NO CHOICE

Scurrying down the tunnel meant *stooping,* crouching just enough to keep me staggering forward. It meant hearing my feet clatter on corrugated metal and echo in the tunnel's endless roundness. It meant knowing I'd never be fast enough.

A motion, a scuttling shape, darted away through the dimness where the light of the outside faded. Just Helena being shorter let her slip through this better than me.

At least the Eye hadn't cut me off yet. I crouched lower and barreled forward.

The faster I charged into the dark, the better my chances of outrunning the clutching physical truth... but my body remembered already. This was the cramped banging of my shoulders off the sides, the flood of smells from every scrap of mushed-up trash that my feet kicked through—still mostly dry, if I didn't think how many grubs and roaches would be squirming through it all. There'd be no rats down here, not in the Scarecrow's world, but bugs would be right at home.

Here where I lost people.

I clattered to a stop—with the Bones drained, all I could do was listen for her. Helena's panicked steps echoed through the dark, farther and farther away.

The light behind me went black.

Behind me! I leaped forward, away from what had blocked the remnants of light. Crashing down along the metal, I twisted, tried to brace for the Eye's next attack.

He vanished from my sight, as suddenly as he'd appeared.

No more shapes lunged out of the dimness. But, the bastard didn't have to risk fighting down here, where it was too tight and dark to teleport around. He was afraid of this place, and the Scarecrow. He should be.

The clatter of Helena's footsteps was farther now, but the sound began faltering. I spun to race on, blinking in the dark.

Too dark, too much darkness. My breathing wouldn't slow, it must have been roaring ever since I stepped in here, and every step brought me closer...

I dug out my phone, and fumbled until the flashlight app came on. The endless metal-ribbed tunnel stretched out around me, too few steps before it thickened into the shadows the glow threw out.

Running on came faster now, if I didn't look at what my feet crunched through. The light made me a target, but it was worth it just to push the darkness back. *If this counts as a light—why do I go* anywhere *without a real flashlight?*

Because I never thought I'd be back here.

Helena had still sounded too far away.

Then the tunnel ahead branched. A second tunnel led into it—and I could just hear the city outside. Bracing myself, I tapped the light off, and in the crush of darkness I could just make out hints of distant sunlight on the intersection.

Up that tunnel lay a curled-up silhouette that could be... I blinked, stared, moved toward it one slow step at a time. "Helena?"

The shape didn't move. And I blinked again and the outline cleared: not a person huddled on the ground, just a damn pile of cardboard and waste.

Breathe. Listen.

Footsteps clanged off the tunnel I'd left, far, far deeper in. I tapped my light on and raced after her.

My feet set the metal echoing again, booming out my presence and drowning hers—but even when I stopped I couldn't make her out. Had she gone that deep already?

And what do I do when I find her? Or when I hear that he *has?* I pushed on faster, faster.

Another branch formed ahead. I tapped my light off again, but this time total darkness slammed in around me. This new tunnel could be as deep in as the one I'd followed, and Helena could—

A sound moved ahead. Clumsy, soft banging sounds of a person struggling to *crawl* her way on.

Then the voice of the Eye:

"Corbin... you'll never bring her out alone..."

A single chilling thought: *He used my name. Where the Scarecrow could hear it.*

It whispered in the darkness, smooth and cold as the metal around us. He *knew* I was here, bringing a light...

Helena's footsteps scrambled away, fading.

But the Eye's voice had come from the side tunnel. He wasn't blocking me, he was waiting to jump me when I moved across.

Heartbeats pounded in my ears, bringing my breath up faster, faster. All the Eye needed was one touch to yank me out of here, to pull me back into his schemes while the last faint chance at saving Helena guttered out.

Her footsteps were already gone.

No use fighting, no use talking or letting more time slip away...

I forced my breath to slow, and took a quiet step forward.

All I had left was the darkness, the hope that the Eye was still playing it safe down here. One slow, careful step at a time, I crept across the intersection. Something rustled under my foot—

"You won't find her." Right at my shoulder.

I froze. I *froze,* like a poor dumb animal again—

But the Eye's voice was still only taunting, the rattle under my foot was nothing, he couldn't see me or hear how my heartbeats pinned me in place.

Another step, feeling my way through to silence on the cluttered floor. Another.

A dozen feet, if anything so endless could be that short.

Then I dashed into the blackness, banging off the side and fighting to keep my balance and staking everything that he wouldn't dare chase me in the dark. The tunnel thundered around me, louder every time I glanced off it. My footing turned slippery, until it *splashed* and sloshed around my ankles and sent me stumbling again and again.

It might have been a whole minute later when I caught the sound. When I slipped and struggled up on my feet, and still I heard the same frantic rhythm out there. Helena trying to run.

The sound echoed around me. Was that from up ahead, or... I tapped the light on, and *two* more branches sprawled out at my sides. Water glimmered around me, and just the sight turned my soaked feet to ice. More shadows stretched away behind me, that could hide still other tunnels I'd blundered past. How lost had I gotten?

But I heard one sound. Helena's ragged steps, slowing.

"Helena? Please, it's me—"

The steps broke faster, faster, fading into the silence.

Running from me. Even into this place.

Because I'd done this to her. The same as Ray—no, this time *I'd* used the terror on someone, I'd shattered her myself and chased her down here to die.

And I let it happen. Again.

I slumped back, slid down the cold metal side to slosh down in the water. *Everything* I'd done, the whole Plan to make up for this—sure enough all it led to was another friend trapped down in the *same goddamn place*... Because of me...

My heels dug into the floor. My legs hauled me up.

He hasn't found Helena yet—I can lie down and die later.

I picked a tunnel and moved toward it. "Helena?"

A sound moved, a frantic breath and a patter of fleeing feet, closer than I thought. Not from that tunnel, but maybe the next. I turned and splashed toward that.

Splashed.

Slowly I looked down, at the shifting, gunk-ridden layers floating around my feet. Water.

I was soaking in the power source for the Bones.

I stared, blinked, and something twitched deep down inside me. It stirred and swelled, until the laugh burst out and rang off the walls—

I had to clamp my hand over my mouth to smother it down. All this time, I could have gathered the power to resist, to track, maybe even to draw Helena back from what I'd done to her... *Smart, Corbin.*

Hands still shaking, I fumbled the three cubes from my pocket.

And one of them slipped.

It slipped between my fingers, I tried to catch at it, and my grip burst open and spilled them all away over the floating bits of trash. I stared, watched them tumble over wrappers and cups and dirt and fall into the mirk—

Hands reached out of the tunnel to scoop them up.

I jolted back, but the shape wasn't *him*. The dirty, wild-eyed figure of Helena crouched over the water, each hand clutching what must be one of the Bones. The third one lay lodged in a tangle of plastic floating at her feet. But she wouldn't look at me, she huddled at the side of the tunnel, still trembling.

"Helena."

The tunnel seemed to catch my word and draw it out in an echo. Her head darted around, staring at all sides before looking at me. Then she looked away, back up her tunnel.

Soft as I could, I said "Helena, it's me. Please—I'm here to help you."

She twisted on her feet, ready to run,

"I'm sorry!" It was all I could throw at her, to make her pause. "I'm sorry I hurt you, I'm sorry the Eye came after you, I'm sorry about everything..."

My throat seized up. I didn't *deserve* to reach her—*but if I let that matter it'll never stop.*

"Please. All I want, more than anything, is a chance to help you. You came back to see me, didn't you? And look what you've got there... can you show me? Please?"

An inch at a time, she looked back. She turned, and stretched out her open hands.

I reached to take those in mine, but she shied back. I moved again, more slowly, and lifted the two cubes from her palms. She scuttled back a step, eyes still on me. Her face looked a little warmer now.

"Thank you." And she'd drawn back from where the third Bone had caught, so I picked that up as well.

Then I dipped them deep in the water.

His water, when the whole tunnel system was choked with his power... Helena crouched nearby, a hint of her proper strength trembling on her face and already slipping away again. I had no choice here, I never had.

"Shalassa lua."

Magic trickled in, the same sharp, irresistible cold I'd felt every time I'd used the Bones. I felt no taint or difference from it in the tunnels—only the proof that it had been this same undiluted power that I'd been carrying with me ever since.

I held on, feeling the power flow through and work its chill deeper into me. More, I'd need more...

Helena edged back a step, sloshing in the water. The more I waited the more I put off facing my own ignorance at this.

Gently as I could, I said "One more time, I'm sorry you got dragged into this. Will you let me help you?"

She moved, an inch toward me.

I brushed her with the Pulse, like mental fingers against a great icy block of fear. She jerked back, one reflexive step.

No—not simply a mass of fear, she felt more like a stone figure that was cracking from veins of ice within it. There was no spell to lift or change to reverse; she'd been *hurt,* shocked by the blast of terror and all the rest. I could only send her touches of hope, comfort, as a promise that there'd be something different after the nightmare.

Helena shook, buried her head in her hands. But her eyes still peeped out at me, she let me reach slowly out and place my hand on her slime-covered shoulder as I worked. This woman was fighting her own battle here, the way she'd come to me. It had only been the Eye she'd been fleeing.

The Eye could burst in on us any moment, or he *could*—my thought shook and trembled through the magic. I struggled to warm the touch again, to not think of the endless echoing dark around us.

She pulled away from my hand. Then a weak, dazed voice came from her: "Adrian? It's... over?"

She broke off, eyes going wide as if startled by her own voice. She whirled away, and her hands batted, combed, through her hair trying to drag the muss and dirt from it.

I watched her look around and try to take in the tunnels again with a steadier gaze. We were still deep in the Scarecrow's home, and any moment could be only an instant from the Eye too. She kept fighting with her hair, tugging to tighten her clothes, but she stayed with me.

I said "I never, never, meant you to get anywhere near this."

"Stop," she whispered.

"It's the truth. The last thing in the world I wanted was to let someone get hurt again—"

"Just *stop!*"

The word rang off the tunnel pipe, echoed away into the dark. She pressed low and glanced around, cringing from the noise.

Then she gave me an embarrassed look that almost met my eyes. "And, get me out of here."

"Sure," I smiled. Now that I could.

I closed my eyes and let the Pulse search around us. The tunnels' malice still hung over us as surely as the dark... I strained to reach past that, for the more elusive threat. Out beyond the tunnel Helena had fled up, and above our heads, the emotions of the city beyond were dim. If the Eye were out there, would there be anything to sense?

The Scarecrow was certain. But if we scurried out where the Eye could see us, we were trapped anyway.

"I think," and the words came slowly, "the Eye would be outside somewhere. Watching to catch us coming out. We could go a bit further in here and get more distance from him, but that means... risks. Or we could risk sneaking out past him now—"

"We go in."

Together we moved back down to the pipe I'd been following. Every ripple of the water around our legs made Helena flinch, but she kept moving.

That was all there was: one step after another, hoping the tunnels would give us a branch far enough away from the Eye before the worst closed in. We moved too slowly, sweeping my light around the tunnel and watching the bits of trash bob and dance in the water.

That water soaked through clothes and numbed legs, left us ready to slip at any patch of ooze that might be coating the pipe, or any bit of junk that shifted under our step. And everywhere we turned the light away from, more shadows were waiting to press in.

The Pulse only gave me glimpses of the world outside, but I kept searching for a hint of the Eye vanishing around. More and more I was certain that, if the Scarecrow came for us, I'd never sense him at all.

At least Helena could push on right behind me. She didn't know the full pressure of his tunnels, but she felt the place itself. Like the *smell,* the brew of the metal walls and rotting trash that filled everything thicker than the darkness, that we had to keep drawing into our lungs because there was nothing else to breathe.

We just needed a tunnel upward, maybe the next one would be far enough...

Again and again, a splash of the water had Helena starting in shock. I reached for her hand, but she pulled back and looked away. Her eyes stayed focused now, even if they never kept still. Her clothes, that had been meant for some long-ago business meeting this morning, were soaked and stained as if the dirt down here had its own hatred for fine fabrics.

She must feel the tunnels' influence, some of it. Somehow my Pulse had shaken her so badly she'd run *toward* the fear that guarded the gate. And yet the only danger she understood here was the Eye.

The less noise we made in the water, the less it startled Helena and the less attention it would draw. But the cold sunk deeper into my legs, and that tickled shivers along my ribs and within my lungs too. Step by step, step by step, anything to clear the distance.

The thought had to be on her mind too—she asked "How far have we gone?"

"Blocks, I think. It feels farther, when there's nothing else to see." It only *seemed* like the magic twisted the space itself. I hoped.

"That can't be right. Why would they even build this much..." She waved her hand around the endless pipe.

"Why? I don't know. But first they built it, and then he must've settled in here."

"He? You mean—" She broke off.

I almost swung the light back to look at her, where I could hear her trudging along. Just her voice told me the fear was digging deeper into her now. She still didn't know...

We just had to get on out, get on out...

The water was higher now—how had I *missed* that it was almost at my knees? Keeping our legs moving was the best way to keep feeling alive in them. Helena held her arms high at her sides, trying to keep them clear of the larger piles of trash floating by. Even the sounds changed, the splashing from our footsteps growing deeper and more muted. The water and the tunnel were devouring their echoes.

Again and again, I told myself I'd felt these before. And tried not to think about the rest.

At last another branch of pipe stretched in to join this one.

Helena stared at the tunnel, her eyes unreadable. But I forced myself to stop and search with the Pulse—her fear was growing deeper every second.

And the tunnels pressed, closed, squeezed their will around us... and out beyond it, that could have been something flitting around...

"It *could* be the Eye up there," I said. "You said we should go on past a few tunnels—"

"No. No, we can't..." Her voice choked, and I turned the light toward her.

The light. My phone, the same phone we'd been clinging to in the darkness—horror raced through me.

"Helena. The Eye was tracking my phone, remember? All of this work to slip out a tunnel he's not watching? If *any* signal from this slips out, we'd be walking right into him." I tapped at the thing in my hands; I had no signal now, but it might only take one connected moment to give us away. "I just put it in Airplane Mode—but his hacking could have thought of that. I could try pulling the battery again, but—"

"No! No, are you *out of your mind?* We can't go on, we can't go in the *dark...*"

Her head darted around, faster now, searching the shadows. She was cracking. We were dead if the Eye could track us, but if she broke...

"Alright, I promise I won't." Carefully, softly, I said "How about we go a bit further down. And hope the tunnels keep blocking the signal—all this metal has to be good for something, right?"

Her gaze centered on me again. She gave a quick nod.

I glared at the bit of plastic in my hand. The only thing that held off the dark, and it might be attracting the Eye. If its light hadn't been drawing the Scarecrow all along.

We pushed on down the main tunnel. Helena's flinching at our splashes grew more anxious—no, I realized we made more noise, more often, hurrying along faster than we had. I stole a look at the phone's battery level: almost half, but how fast was the light running it down?

Our new speed brought the next branch into view soon. This time the tunnel *ahead* forked, into two similar shafts branching off. With the dimness and the water's stillness, I was only guessing that the left one led upward. No sounds from the outside reached down from either, and no light.

I reached the Pulse through the tunnels' haze, and something flickered up above that left side. That could be the Eye—we were too close anyway. I turned toward the right.

And something eased away from me, a small, sweet relief like a cold draft cutting off. When I turned away from that branch.

Slowly, testing my words, I said "The Eye might be up there, on the left. But the fear's pushing in from that way too."

"Then come on." She turned right, moving faster now.

"No, listen. I said it's pushing from there, he's *herding* us—"

"Stop telling me what to do!"

She broke off, looked down with a flush of embarrassment. But that ragged sound in her voice, fraying and ready to break...

With all the gentleness my voice could shape, I said "You want to go on, that way?"

"Yes! You said it's safer, you *know* it is."

"Then let's take it just one more tunnel down. And when we get to the next one, we'll both be ready to head out—promise?"

She nodded. Too quickly.

Then we moved down that right-hand way. With Helena walking ahead of me.

She moved too fast, with too many anxious glances behind her and none for what we headed into. If she lost control again, I'd lose any chance to get her out alive. *I can't let it, can't let it.*

The water lapped around us like a giggling.

One chance left. I watched every haunted, hunted move Helena made as we pushed closer. The light shook, as trembling dug deeper into my hands. One chance left that she'd listen to me.

The water was up to her waist now—how could she not see that? But the shadows, the echoes, the will of this place pressed closer with every step. I strained the Pulse against it, for some defense or probe or just to feel that there still were lives up above us, and at every try the darkness smothered it. The tunnel stretched on.

I worked my throat to ready my most calming voice.

I stared at the shadows, for the first hint of movement or the first glimpse of the tunnel opening.

And at last the pipe split again. One more opening that crossed our path, one more chance.

Before we reached it, before Helena could settle in to what it whispered, I said "Let me test them?"

"I... alright." The struggle was already forming on her face, control and trust against dread.

I stared at the two paths. Reaching the Pulse out beyond them was useless now, but I knew that soft pressure coming from the side path, the right.

"This way."

"You're wrong—don't you *hear* it? We stay away..." She was whispering now, turning toward the left and away from whatever was in her head.

"You promised, remember? The next one?" I reached my hand out for her. "If we head out now I promise you'll be alright—"

"*You* promise?" She yanked her hand away, and the squeezed-tight fear in her face sharpened into stabbing fury. "You can't!"

"Listen to me... We have to face this. It's not too late, but we can't go much deeper. People die down here, I've seen what I—"

"Stop it!" She shook her head, eyes clenched shut. "Stop! I don't know who you're thinking of, I'm not that weak!"

Who I was thinking of? She'd caught that—*but it's not about her being stronger—*

She ran. "You're wrong, you're wrong!" she screamed—at me, at the shadows, at something—and threw herself down the deeper tunnel.

I reached the Pulse toward her. Just like I'd driven Maya away—instead I gasped "Listen—"

"Leave me alone!"

The water caught at me, dragged at my steps after her. *No, no, no—why'd I hesitate, why didn't I* make *her listen?* I grabbed at her, found her outside my reach by three steps and too much weight of water.

I flung the Pulse out for her as I struggled on. All the warm calm and courage I could dredge up washed into her—but she was already running, and the touch broke off her, useless.

My foot slipped. In one moment I sagged forward, crashed face-first into the depths to sink and flail and somehow get a foot under me and drag myself *up*, spluttering, up into air that still pressed nearly as thick around me.

Helena was just a distant ghost at the edge of my light now. I plowed after her, fighting to at least keep her in view. Her figure shrank, grayed away...

The tunnel spread wide.

I stumbled, barely caught myself as the sight flooded through me. The one I'd only glimpsed once.

The shaft had broadened and swollen into a tunnel that vaulted well above my head, with other pipes leading to it. A mound of boards and scrap lumber lay piled up on one side, letting Helena stand clear of the water.

And lining the tunnel sides... weak light and weaker memories twisted the images, turning trash into tools into bones and back wherever my gaze went. Worst of all were the lightbulbs, unlit but hanging along the sides and proving that someone *lived* here.

Somehow, somehow, Helena and I were still alone. I clawed at the Pulse, felt nothing watching.

I dragged myself up onto the wooden hill.

Helena gave me one glance before her head began shaking, before she crouched down trying to shrink away from the power around us. "You, it's your fault, all your fault."

"Listen to me, Helena." *I know, I know it is*—but I forced out the words "We have to go. We have to, *right now*. This is where—"

He was behind me.

There was no sound.

Only the last gasp of warmth that fled from me, as his terror pierced through, left me impaled with the need to be *away* that left muscles thrashing and helpless. I toppled to the ground.

My eyes had to fight to look back. Through the haze of tears, I got a glimpse of tallness... a mix of tattered cloth, jeans, leather... one sense of a bald head before my eyes slammed shut, before he stirred.

"Attention. You bring their attention here."

Please don't speak, don't notice us... but I could hear him, every word, even with my heart thundering enough to tear me open. And I heard Helena's helpless wheezing for air.

Not again not again not again...

The voice said "A rich woman. One that will be missed. But..."

That *but* was a regret brushed aside, an executioner's voice. It would be now, and there was something I could say, some thought that tried to latch onto his words.

Just another moment to think—

I drew on the Bones to throw out a barrier of the Pulse, anything to slow his magic down another instant. It had worked for Maya with the Duvals' fire—but Maya—

Power smashed through the world.

It was total, crushing fear. It was breath choked out and heart aching to give way under all the horror inside. It was losing Maya, it was my mother, it was what I'd done to Sibyl, it was dying in the dark with someone else I'd dragged down with me, it was the Scarecrow knowing about Ray, it was everything twisting thoughts and feelings to tear themselves apart to leave only screaming meat.

The scream ripped out, echoed up, carrying me up howling and rushing at the shape.

And twisted around, wrenched around to slam into metal—*so smooth and cold.*

The touch on my face shocked me back, let me separate the wall from the clenching mass of agony that was me. But *his hands* held me in place harder than any metal.

"You ran toward fear."

He knows, he knows—I couldn't stop, I just had to say it. "Let her go." He had to, it would even dodge that 'attention' he spoke of, but he *had* to—

He said "You aren't like you were."

His words, *those* words, shriveled me, and I heard a moan and knew Helena would be awake to hear him say:

"Once, you ran before the magic touched you. I took you for dead."

I should have been. I saw what you did to Ray—it took so much power you had to recharge your magic when he finally died. Because I ran.

"Now you run toward fear. Why is that?"

He twisted me around.

Eyes stared into me—

This time his will didn't smash through. It came probing in, feeling and tasting—touching frozen shapes inside me, layer upon layer of frail icy forms as if my whole soul were made up of fears, all ready to shatter if he brushed against one...

"Go save her.

"Save them both.

"Take the rich thing, and keep her *attention* away."

And his grip on my hearing, my mind, my body, all let go. I slumped nerveless to the ground.

Helena and I were alone.

CHAPTER ELEVEN: ONLY

Save them both. The words clung to me.

Each time Helena's wild eyes looked out, I had to drag myself more together still, to keep pushing the cracks and the shaking in me down below where she could notice.

With her arm over my shoulder, I began the walk out. Helena's legs tottered and carried most of her weight, and when I settled into a rhythm she scrabbled to keep up. And all around us, the endless grinding pressure of the tunnels seemed to draw back and gnash its teeth at us where it had once been driving us down in.

All of it impossible.

The tunnels still had the same weight of water to force through, the same darkness and treacherous ground to steady my feet against. The further we moved, the more the sense of dread grew at the back of my neck again, but now it swelled behind us to push us out.

Somehow we'd come *through* it.

We'd come through the Scarecrow's own tunnels with me *not* losing someone—none of it felt real. Like I wasn't still walking hunched under the tunnel, with Helena's weight on my shoulder. I could have been floating, flying.

"Is it over?" she whispered, more than once.

"I'll get you out."

First Helena. Then save Maya, from the Eye.

Reaching the tunnel outside brought out all the caution I could scrape together... but I sensed nothing out there flitting around like our masked enemy. I kept my bugged phone disabled, and the daylight let me work the grate open with my knife and step out until the full sun.

Eye-blinkingly bright, *warm*—I stood in the light and let the voices, the cars, the blowing breezes remind me that there was a whole city the Eye could be hiding in. Later.

Helena was still shaking, but she could walk beside me now. After a block, she pulled ahead of me and began moving with a purpose. She led us into a convenience store, still trembling and soaking wet.

And she actually forced the trembling still, as she looked at the clerk and said "Can you give us a hand? We were in an accident, and I need to make a call." Then she said a few quick, controlled words into his phone.

Finally, she sank down in a corner and let that control collapse into shivering again. She took the sweatshirt I bought to wrap her in, and only looked at the coffee I set down beside her, just sat and shook and stared blindly at the cup and her own quivering hands.

I settled down opposite her and tried to close my eyes and let my own stiff, shaking muscles work themselves free again.

But if I closed my eyes, she might not be real—this miraculous proof that we'd made it out, I'd made it out. This staring, shuddering person would never be the same woman I'd known before, but she was alive.

Someday, would the worst of it leave her?

Did it ever leave me?

She glared down at that cup, and flashes of anger moved on her face. That might be the first step for her, simple frustration at how she'd been dragged around.

We weren't alone, I began to notice. Faces clustered around the store's aisles, goggling at us both and whispering. Chasing them off would have been a pleasure, but I might never want to stand up again.

Why'd he let us go?

There'd been all that talk about *attention* and who'd come looking for someone like Helena. So he was trusting she wouldn't send cops by the dozens down after him?

Or was it what he did to me at the end?

A different kind of shiver rose in me, not over my skin or down my nerves but one that started deep in my chest and twisted its way out. The Scarecrow hadn't been reading emotions or wielding that fear, he'd seen something else. Two people I had to save.

And that moment was over. *I'm out, I'm free...* but even the thought felt unnatural.

It was one of Helena's assistants that stepped through the door. A young black woman—Ginger, was it? I knew she was Helena's newest, and she had to be the quickest to win her confidence. She stared at her boss and me, with an expression I couldn't read.

And Helena drew herself to her feet. "Adrian just saved me from... well, we can decide what that is later. Now, just take me somewhere we won't be noticed." She bent slowly down to pick up the coffee, and now she didn't spill a drop.

Ginger blinked. "I can do that."

The two of them started for the door.

I called out "I wish I had—"

"Stop. Just..." Helena closed her eyes, held them shut as I saw her take a long breath, then look up. "Just, let me get used to knowing that I'm not as tough as I think. I'll be on this," and she passed me a card with a phone number.

I nodded, watched the two walk away. She wanted some distance from this, for now... I hoped that kind of humility, perspective, was what she needed.

And I had someone else to save. That meant either finding Maya and protecting her, or catching the Eye.

I bought a quick replacement phone, and a roll of wipes to scrub the worst of the tunnel slime off me. Then I stepped out to take in the street, the endless open space and the buildings and crowds and everything that broke it up into hiding places, with their emotions clamoring louder yet... finding the Eye was as hopeless as ever.

That left Maya. I reconnected the battery on my old, compromised phone, and made one more try to call her and apologize—but her phone was still dead, disabled. I shut mine down again and twisted around the corner to get some distance, watching for any mind that might suddenly appear and start searching for the spot I'd called from. Nobody did.

* * *

Entering the police station needed even more caution. If the Eye did check for me here, just the number of people inside could make him hesitate to flit around. But I still barely knew what he'd look like apart from his mask.

At least my bike was still in the lot's corner. Where I'd left it to drive off with Helena, trying to keep her away from the Eye.

There were no safe answers now.

The station had several entrances, and I picked the one that was least watched. But that still brought me into rooms full of cops and the people around them, all moving and fidgeting and looking around with nervous eyes.

It was closing in on five o'clock—I saw papers shuffled restlessly where someone thought of finishing work, and heard voices turn guarded as they braced for the evening hours ahead. Most of all, using the Pulse brought all of them roaring into my head, and I wrestled to catch whether anyone's flicker of reaction came just as they noticed me.

I'd met a few cops and clerks besides Detective Poe, and now I looked for any familiar faces. Or, simply the right kind of emotion might be an opening... anything in the nearest people I passed that wasn't anger or frustration or sheer iron determination.

What I settled on was a young man sitting in a corner of the Research section, tapping hard at his computer but inwardly radiating sheer mushy boredom.

"Any news about the fire yesterday? I'm investigating one side of that." Sounding confident was the key; I had to bet he was the right kind of bored to go along with me, not motivated enough to make trouble.

"Umm." He rubbed his too-short hair uneasily.

"Anything confirmed about the ties to the Zimmerman break-in?"

"I guess... There should be a detective on that."

A touch of cold worry bubbled in him. I could calm that, ease those fears before they put him on alert. But that manipulation was the kind of thing Maya brought out in me.

"I'll check, sure," I said. "But, it looks like the Duval cousins."

"I guess—hey, how'd you hear that? I don't see your badge."

At least he kept his voice low, and the desk next to him was empty. "I only said I'm investigating it. And I'm not trying to make trouble—but there's a woman in danger here, and the Duvals have been stalking her for days."

He pulled back in his chair, inching away from me as he eyed me like a threat. His gaze moved toward the desks around us and all the more senior workers and cops that might be within earshot. And I felt his apprehension welling up.

I reached the Pulse toward him—not to twist that emotion but just to weigh it. The fear grew as I watched, and it grew fastest when he looked away from me...

There was more to see, if I stared deeper...

I caught a sense of a shape, a frozen shape within his fear. Of eyes looking back at him, different, varied gazes from all around the station.

That was *what* scared him, I knew it at once; less afraid of my meddling than of him being caught. I added "No trouble, I said. I'll just sit off here a while, and you think about it."

"Maybe." Then he said "That woman they're chasing, was that for real?"

"Real as it gets."

"I figured. Most of my job is sitting here *not* helping."

I stepped away, moved up the room. But sure enough, after long moments he turned back to the keyboard and began typing, with a care he hadn't used before.

My hand brushed the pocket that held the Bones. I'd just... used the Pulse to see the shape of what he feared. His actual, private fears—the idea sank deeper and deeper into me, a more unsettling secret than any nudge I could give to someone's emotions.

And, I'd taken that deeper look because the Scarecrow had turned it on me. Imitating him.

Still, wasn't it imitating when I used the words he did to make the Bones, to protect myself, to try heading off some of the suffering around here?

A familiar form moved up the corridor: Detective Poe, with his round face half-covered by a folder full of papers he stared into. Even without the Pulse, I knew he was fuming.

And if he'd got word about me being down here... I remembered that clerk's fear at the idea of being caught with me. Whatever else happened, he didn't deserve me leading Poe toward his room.

I stepped into the corridor and strolled away, up ahead of the detective. He made no reaction, like his papers had him too absorbed to notice. His footsteps closed in behind me, about to pass me.

"*Mister* Corbin. I'm guessing you aren't down here looking for me."

He'd suckered me, him and his distracted look. The best I could do now was keep his attention all on me. I met his warning gaze and said "You haven't believed me so far. You don't care about Maya, but you still want to get the Duvals."

His glare sharpened a degree. "And you still say you aren't holding out on us."

He left it there, and that gave me a chance to use the Pulse: he was all knotted frustration now, nothing more open or more dangerous. I looked harder for the shape of any fears in him, but that focus I'd found before was a weak blur.

Still, everything I'd ever sensed in Jenson Poe was the steadiness and stubborn compassion of a good cop. And I needed *some* way to catch up to Maya.

The pause had stretched a moment long, as people brushed by us in the corridor. "All right, I do have something. And not only about the Duvals."

"With me." Poe waved me along and marched on down the corridor.

We passed a few figures in and out of uniform, and then Poe took a turn to the side. This corridor looked the same but seemed quieter—people hurrying on through or stepping behind at doors, not lingering or meeting each other here. He was leading me away from the centers of attention here, either keeping his talk with me out of the spotlight, or I'd read him all wrong.

A half-open niche along the corridor was filling up with boxes and a few crude plastic chairs. We settled down on two of those.

As we did, Poe stuffed the pages back in his folder, and I caught one glimpse of a photo that had to be of billowing smoke. So he *had* been tracking the Duvals.

"Alright. What have you got?"

I had real information about their rampage—so I might as well get something else covered first, bad news before good news. I gathered a breath, tried to steady a tired tremor.

"For one, there was a break-in on Little Street today. You'll want to keep your eyes on that case."

Poe shook his head. "Out in the subdivisions? Why would the Duvals be out there, more fire?"

"Not them. Look, I bet you won't get a lot of witnesses in a place where nobody dares to look out their window, but sooner or later you'll hear—"

Two uniforms walked past us, and I paused. Poe's eyes narrowed at that.

I forced it out anyway: "You'll work out that it was me."

The detective's face hardened. "You're telling me you're a thief."

"No, I'm not—"

"If you confess to a crime, I have an obligation to act on it."

"Right this minute? Besides, you know I don't have anything like that in my record. Anyway, this is a case you'll be hearing more about soon, and it's got certain bigger things involved."

Three people, talking and laughing, strolled by in the corridor. I checked my thoughts a moment; Helena would agree that some pieces of this would come out, and she could give Poe some simpler story about a kidnapping and rescue that she wanted kept quiet.

I added "You'll understand more then, But you'll see, I did it for the best reasons."

"*Reasons.* You confess to a crime, and you expect me to sit on it because you're dropping more hints that you've got some inside track on it. We've been through this—you've either got real information, or you're in the way. Or you're the bad guy."

"It's real, and I'm giving it to you." I shifted on the hard chair, tried to push the tiredness from my head. I'd seen that folder in his hand— "You're working the Duval case. Did you just stumble into me now, or did you hear I was in the building? Did you come because I was 'in the way,' or were you hoping that just maybe I did have something you could use?"

Poe swallowed. Then he gave a narrow smile, tight enough to be a warning too. "How about, you've gotten in the way enough times that somebody owes me a break for dealing with you."

"I guess they do." I leaned toward him. "Here's the other thing that changed since you called me."

"What, you found the Duvals' secret hideout?" His hand moved to wave that joke aside, but I caught a scrap of hope in his voice.

"I wish. No, but... did you get word how they invaded Zimmerman Tower?"

" 'Invaded'?" Poe's voice was guarded, not giving away if he'd heard at all.

"They grabbed one of the employees, a man named Hammond, and forced him to lead them around. They gave him the scare of his life, and they could have left the whole place on fire if it had gone south. I tracked the Duvals there, and I saw it."

Only, *Maya* was the one who'd found them, and placing myself there was almost volunteering the identity of the woman I'd been seen with... But, talking about the Duvals was only a path to finding Maya anyway.

"You saw them," Poe mused.

"They all but dragged Hammond around, the way the Duvals do that lets them walk their victim past his friends, you know? They had their fire tricks—the same flame gadgets they used to bully the librarians at Central yesterday." That let me sidestep how the Duvals' magic worked, just by mentioning the 'trick gloves' they used themselves to explain it.

Or I could tell Poe what he was really chasing.

The tired thought floated up in me: how long could I try using him to find the Duvals and still count on him not getting close enough to see more? Poe was more trustworthy than most of the cops, from everything I'd known, everything I could read.

I leaned back in the chair. No need to rush.

Poe said "Alright, Zimmerman did report a disturbance, but no details like that. If you *saw* that was the Duvals, what were they after?"

Magic. My stomach clenched—all my hints and clues, and I really had run myself into a corner. I must be more worn out than I thought, so desperate to find any pattern that led to the Duvals and Maya that I didn't see the pieces I was sharing pointed Poe right toward the magic.

Still, I didn't have to give him all of it. "Some research that Maya's father did with the company. That's what the Duvals are chasing, and it could still be the way to find them."

"Research. You mean, like the private collector whose house burned last night? Or the lawyer?"

"What lawyer?" And, "What collector?" I remembered to add.

"Lawyer." Poe opened up the folder on his lap. "The lawyer that ran from his office this morning, saying two huge men assaulted him. Followed by the fire—not that we can pin it on the Duvals. Or find the Duvals."

He held up a photo. The same glimpse of smoke I'd seen, this showed it pouring out of a window. *That* was the latest fire he'd tested me on when he'd called me.

And this time he *was* talking with me, starting to show me what he had.

"Sounds just like them," I nodded.

"The victim wouldn't talk about his past cases. But it 'sounds like' he could be the executor of Stephen Grant's will. Someone else who knew where this 'research' might be."

"Sounds like it," I said again.

"So what are they after? And I don't want to hear about confidentiality and your 'client'—what kind of old records have a bunch of small-time extortionists burning the city down?"

"I wish I knew."

Damn, damn, of course I'd given Poe too much... but it sounded like he'd already put most of it together on his own. But I couldn't simply hand him the rest, and he'd just warned me not to hide behind Maya being my client.

I added "There must be something in there. My first thought was some good old-fashioned treasure map, you know? Or that they thought it was."

"Huh. So what came after that first thought?"

"Not much more. Just that it was enough for them."

"Oh? You sure you want to leave it at that?" He gave me a long look, weighing the moment and my response.

I kept my eyes on his. "It's all I've got."

"You think about that answer for a minute. I'll be right back."

His voice made that another warning to make me sit and sweat—but he stood up too fast, hurried away, and I felt a touch of worry in him.

Then another man strode down the corridor, from right where Poe had been facing: Leland the crime reporter.

So Poe had been avoiding him, and trying to spin his moment of ducking away as another quick threat. Fast thinking, but not a sign that he was willing to trade.

Leland rushed past me, barely giving me a glance as he hurried on. After all, we'd never really met in person... but he *was* someone else on the Duvals' trail. His phone call had come closer to making a deal with me than Poe ever had.

I stood up and moved after him.

Leland was too fast, halfway toward a turn in the corridor already—I dove after him a few steps. My stiff legs balked at changing gears.

"Hey, Leland!"

My shout came out too loud, but the reporter stopped. He turned, watched me stumbling up to him. "Do I know..." He took a closer look. "Mr. Corbin, is it?"

"That's me. We keep missing each other."

Leland turned to sweep a glance up the corridor. "Right now I'm looking for someone."

And I'd just seen Poe duck away from him. I could tell Leland his contact wasn't talking, or help him find Poe...

My tired head hurt trying to play them against each other. One angle at a time, then. "I won't hold you up. But I did have some thoughts about the Duval cousins. And Maya Grant."

I saw his expression flicker then. He turned back to me, and edged over to the wall beside a snack machine. His face was almost bland now. "Alright, what do you know?" He didn't even lower his voice.

"No, you're not playing me that way." Throwing that back at him was a welcome moment of pleasure today. "You first. I told you on the phone, I can make it worth it, the next time you have a stubborn source to talk to. You'll see—or you will if you've got anything that can help me. So what do you know about what the Duvals are chasing?" Where they might go, and Maya.

Leland sighed. Of course I'd tried this on the phone call. "They want money, or revenge. What thugs always want."

A pair of cops walked by behind us, and Leland's clear voice didn't even draw a glance from them. Typical talk for a police station.

"I think you know more than that," I said, softer. "You had someone at the Zimmerman Tower waiting to tip you off, didn't you? You knew that was one place the Duvals might show up."

Now Leland's voice dropped. "Mr. Corbin, I'm a professional. I've had years to set up contacts all over Jericho, among people who know I can pay for odd tips about a crime."

No—Leland *must* have guessed the Duvals would come after Maya's family secrets. Even if he did call them simple thugs.

The same as the Eye did.

I frowned. *Anyone* would write the Duvals off as brutes—it meant nothing that Leland said it too... and that we kept missing chances to meet in person...

But I could do more than guess. I eased the sudden suspicion back behind my face, and reached the Pulse out past his so-calm expression.

More calmness floated there, only a few flickers of emotion. Not much to distinguish him from the Eye—or from anyone else.

Softly I said "Or there's a connection between Zimmerman and Maya. Same as the collector's house the Duvals burned last night."

"A connection? What would that be?" His voice was back to the same unimpressed tone—and I caught one spark of interest inside him, all reined in with what could be just professional caution. "What do *you* think they're after?"

"Something dangerous," I murmured. "That brought them to Zimmerman—and to a certain lawyer too."

Even that didn't rouse more interest inside Leland. And he only said "You're so sure there's anything beyond that?"

I tried "It would have to be valuable, right? And think, even a share in it might be worth a lot to whoever found it first."

His mind *tightened,* clenching in like a fist—but a few tendrils of greed leaked through. He edged a step to the side, away from the snack machine and toward the open corridor. Still, he said "Could be."

"It could be anything," and I leaned closer for a whisper.

He shied back. A faint, instinctive fraction out of my reach. *Fear* flashed in him and was gone.

What was that? I stepped along beside him, and added "Just think, what might be that powerful..." Another step put me up ahead of him in the corridor.

That fear spiked, and sharp anger broke Leland's control and burst free—*he knew.* Him flinching away back beside the vending machine was just confirmation.

Unless I was still wrong. "I can read anyone, I told you," I bluffed. "When I want to. But that's between you and Eye."

Cold fear hardened in him at the word, shook itself into place like a wall of barbed steel—if walls curved outward toward me, ready to trap whoever came close. He heard what I really said, because he knew.

Fists clenched, my feet shifted ready to lunge—

He *wagged a finger* at me. Like warning a child.

I dragged myself to a stop. Right, as long as he saw me coming he could just vanish away. He even had the snack machine at his back to screen that moment from most of the corridor.

But he was still here, he had something to say. I still had a chance to read more from him.

"Kidnapper." My throat clenched around the word, holding in my rage. "Monster. Like I said, you're just a murderer."

"Murderer? Seriously, who do you think I killed?"

What spiked in him was a touch of hurt, not full outrage, not like an innocent man. And he spoke in the low voice of the Eye—no wonder Leland had avoided whispering before.

A quiet footstep sounded, up in the corridor. I watched the distance between me and Leland. When that person came closer, when they could *see* him around the machine, would thm watching make the Eye freeze an instant before vanishing away from my attack?

Leland's face had gone as hard as his voice. He whispered "The Scarecrow is the murderer. You're the one who chased Helena into his lair—"

Hold back, wait for the distraction—don't let him get to you—

"Or did she make it out?" he added.

Closer, almost—keep your face still—

The footsteps were behind me, in view.

And Leland was gone. Already gone.

I stared at the empty wall, frozen and coiled to strike, breath caught and muscles locked, heartbeat pounding as the simple, light steps of some woman strolled by behind me and moved on.

Leland reappeared—faster than a blink, not even a pop of air, fast enough to make it feel wrong to think he'd been gone at all.

"I'm not the one who hurt your friend." His voice teased at mockery now. "And the Scarecrow would have never harmed another living soul, if you'd just come with me to hunt him down. But no, not you—even trading for Helena Travers couldn't make you see the real threat."

Threat? Come hunt *with* him? Just more of his tricks to throw me off—that would match the iron ruthless I felt in him.

I answered "So you took Helena to *save* us from the Scarecrow? You're some kind of protector now? And you're still letting the Duvals burn through the town."

"Letting them? Now who wants someone killed?" That mouth tightened into a faint smirk.

"Funny. But you can *teleport*—how many hundreds of ways does that let you spy out a story, get secrets, get anything you want? With all those ways you can watch the Duvals, don't talk like your only options are killing them and ignoring them."

I caught a throbbing smugness from him when I made my guess about his magic's easy life. He said "The Duvals are easy. You don't see the real danger, do you?" Sharp, cold bits of fear emerged in his mind like claws on a beast.

"And what's that?" He'd dropped hints about Maya before.

"Talking with police, and reporters... and you're teasing them about magic too." His fear swelled as he said it. "You can read people, or twist them around. You're smarter than the Duval cousins. Walking the streets where the Scarecrow won't."

His fear sharpened in him, and it held rock-steady, as certain as if I was already a monster.

"You don't know me," I said. He was still just trying to rattle me—but how did that quaver get in my voice?

"I think I do. You're some kind of protector now?" he added, my own words. "No, you're manipulating everyone, even here with the cops."

"No." For all his lies, I could still sense the hard cruelty behind them. Of course a liar would see lies in anyone else, and try to break them with it. And no bullying bastard was going to tell me what my sins were when I knew them too well.

He scoffed "You believe that? You think you even know who the enemy is?"

"Besides you, you mean?"

"It's not those Duvals you're so afraid of. They're easy to track, if you jus—"

He vanished.

In mid-word, he was gone, and I blinked, stared, tried to turn around. Then the hand caught my back, and the world broke apart.

CHAPTER TWELVE: ACCEPTING

Empty, whirling emptiness—shadows, diving backward through shadows that had to be, *had to be* walls, and plunging out into open space— No way to scream, that was the one mercy if this grip kept me from breaking loose and being lost in this— Hurtling through air, air, air—

Wind, real wind, brushed real skin again. I clambered up on actual, flesh-and-blood legs again, and they even remembered how to balance.

Space swayed before me—whole steps away, I could see now, I stood on a flat roof above the clattering, churning sounds of the city.

Leland crouched behind me. Except there was nothing there, my mind was going... then he *re-appeared*, he'd simply vanished again out of reach.

Now he stood on the next roof, with a whole ten feet of open space shielding him from me. But that was close enough for him to smirk at me, and speak with almost a normal voice against the breeze:

"Look down at that street. See anything familiar?"

My thoughts were still spinning, but I glanced over the edge. It was all more mad *pieces*, moving and meshing between unmoving shapes... then sight snapped back into place. That was a real street, those shapes were cars flowing along at three floors below. Heavier traffic flow even past those battered houses, softening daylight... still early evening. The same time as when Leland had grabbed me; just knowing that was unchanged helped steady my head.

And one of the sounds in the open air was a siren. Some place a few blocks to my right was pouring out smoke.

"Looks like those three did it again," Leland called out. "It's how they cover their escapes—and do you seriously think they'll last long that way? But here, take a look down at your left."

He'd brought me to the Duvals? I stared harder at the street below, but at the edge of my sight I watched where Leland stood. I had a body again, and fury burning through it.

Looking down was meaningless anyway. It was just a stream of different cars' roofs bumbling on past a few unkempt houses and small apartments.

"Yes, I thought that was promising," Leland said. "See down there, what just pulled over?"

A gleaming, oversized car too well-off for the neighborhood had just halted beside an empty-looking house. The slight figure that stepped out could only be Maya.

Now, while Leland was staring at her—I dashed across the roof, all my strength hurled into driving my feet against the short tarred distance I had. The roofs' gap loomed ahead to force me into a leap.

Too far. Too slow. Too weak, I was sinking in the air...

The far roof caught my feet, at a sideways tilt that left one foot flailing in air while the other finished kicking me forward to dive at Leland, hand first.

He vanished away.

I tumbled to a stop with my weight crashing around me—of course my damn footsteps gave me away when the Eye only needed an instant to escape. I fought my way to my feet.

A hand closed down on my ankle.

We plummeted through madness—but solid walls burst out around us again just as the horror closed around me. We'd swooped down, right across the street.

A dirty green aluminum-siding wall lay beside me. Another stood at my other side, the houses sectioning off a small corridor just a stone's throw from the grumbling traffic.

Leland was right there behind me. He held a finger to his lips, and pointed to the window.

He'd dropped me right next to that same house. I glanced at the dirty glass, and saw Maya moving slowly, softly inside. And voices rumbled inside those walls, low angry tones that Maya crept toward.

The Duvals.

While I was still standing around outside. I rushed forward, for the front of the house.

And Leland stood in front of me, crouched and all set to grab me away *again*. I slammed to a stop.

He whispered "No—you have to understand—"

He pointed at the wall, at the windows. Behind me.

I edged backward. Rushing the Eye always failed, but I had the Bones ready in my pocket to search for some kind of hesitation. Anything to keep Leland or me from barging in on whatever Maya was up to.

I could feel the three Duvals further back in the house, near a window, and that window had a crack in it. When I leaned close I could hear them inside.

"Got everything?" Sibyl said.

"We still keeping the papers from that collector?" Dom said.

"Everything."

They stood over a set of boxes, suitcases, and scattered clothes of all kinds. Willard was trying on a dirty raincoat, and then a man's blond wig.

Trying to change their looks—as well as two huge slabs of looming muscle could blend in, anyway. And they'd torched another building up the street, to draw the police off, Leland had said.

One doorway led to the next room. Maya's face peeked in from there.

If she was watching them... I realized one closed suitcase was cracking open where it lay, eased open by her magic.

Willard Duval glanced at it, eyes drawn to the motion, but then he looked away.

Did Maya really think she could *rob* them, right now?

But the suitcase edged a fraction wider. Sibyl waved her cousins over for something, and in the moment they turned away a sheaf of papers shot from the case and out her door. Without one rustle.

And in the Pulse, the Duvals really were distracted, buried in petty annoyances and missing it all. Maya was all razor-edged focus.

I leaned against the wall, fear and thrill whirling in me. She was doing it, she was pulling this off right out under their noses.

Then Sibyl's head jerked toward the doorway. She roared in savage rage.

I flung myself at the front of the house—something tangled my leg, I got a glimpse of Leland tripping me before he vanished away and I rolled down and up again.

Through the window I saw Dom banging on the connecting door. She'd sealed it, the same way she'd done with the brooch once—

He slammed his fist into the wood, and the door exploded.

A wave of black ash burst—I ducked from the window, spun toward the front again, but Leland was there glaring that same mocking warning at me. Somehow I halted, gathered the Pulse to try some way to slow him down.

Then Maya's voice came from inside: "Now, are you three ready to talk?

That sound rang with confidence, and the Pulse felt a wave of courage within it. Just the feel of it drew my glance back to the window.

Dom Duval stood in the charred remains of the door—trapped. He wrenched his legs and cursed, but his feet were stuck to the ground, and the other two were cut off by his bulk plugging the doorway.

He said "You should have run," and he slowly raised a hand toward Maya.

"More fire?" She laughed, she *laughed* at them. "And what if it spreads over to you?"

Specks of fear moved in her, clear as pale fireflies to the Pulse, but her will kept them caged tight. And the Duvals' anger dimmed a moment.

Then Willard stepped up behind his cousin. "We *own* fire." He waved a hand at the doorframe, and the embers around Dom went dead and harmless.

"I own it too, remember?"

She was bluffing, her stolen fire weapon was drained, but her will was as firm as if she held a dozen of them.

Then she added "And then there are the cops just a few blocks up. You think they aren't looking for more smoke? And no matter what you do, Dom is stuck there in all of it."

Sibyl waved Willard aside and took his place behind Dom. "You always were too smart."

This time a moment of fear swelled in Maya. It never touched her voice: "I've had to be."

The two women glared at each other, around Dom's trapped form.

I crouched lower at the window, afraid to breathe. Maya was really trying to trick her way out of the Duvals' grasp...

And the Eye was still in my way, watching and listening with that same unreadable expression—to the Pulse, he felt tensed, *poised* for something. Back in the apartments, he'd shoved Maya down in front of the Duvals, and now he must have a hundred ways to ruin her escape.

But he only pointed silently to the window, for me to watch.

Sibyl's fingers drew slowly into fists. "You only want all this *now,* when we make a grab for it? You had your whole life to find it. It's magic, it's your own family!"

Maya looked right back at her. "My life, that's right. I've been asking about it for years—just not burning the clues down."

"Then you don't want a change as bad as we do. Or maybe you *wish* you'd noticed the same magic I did, the one that lets us smoke the truth out. Is that it?"

Sibyl laughed, low and dull like an old wound stirring to life.

Then she added "It's what let me know what you don't. About how your father died."

One glint of anger was all Maya felt. She answered "You want me to trade for that, right?"

"Better. It was in one of the lawyer's files, that you didn't have the balls to take. Kid, the last months of his life your dad was bleeding money on the nastiest kind of debt. And *I* know that name, he's in with the Mob now. And you're still so sure nobody killed your father?"

Maya gave her a long, level stare. "This again... you sure imagine a lot, about a man you never met." The edges of her voice softened, but the firmness never faded. "I told you, my father's last years were all about dying, from the cancer that ate him alive. You want some big enemy for him? I know he was simply doomed, and desperate for anything that could change that."

Unless, the way the Eye talked about Maya meant he had... I focused the Pulse on Leland with all my strength, but all I picked up from him as he heard her story was a watered-down kind of sympathy.

Sibyl laughed "So you have to be *sick* to want more than you got? The old man had money and all of it like we never will—it just wasn't enough for him." Her voice settled to a lower, predatory tone. "Well, you're here too. If there's any chance of more magic, you still want it, princess."

Hard, misshapen envy gleamed within her. She'd only ricocheted off being Maya's sister, not any part of this magic or this family. That only made Sibyl want it more.

"Alright, yes!" Maya snapped. "Yes, I still want answers. I want you to stop burning them up trying to grab them away from me. But what do *you* want?"

Her finger leveled right at Sibyl.

"I mean it. Are you really out for more magic—like how to trap someone in place instead of frying them?" and she waved to Dom in the doorway. "Or would you walk right up to it and still go stab me in the back just because I'm me? Could you even stop yourself?"

And Maya locked her gaze on her, so close it had to be more than a question. She'd be using the Bone she got from me to read Sybil's reaction to the idea, or trying to read it.

Sibyl's resentment rippled, the flames shifted, and they *dimmed*.

"You think I'm too crazy to make a deal, kid? Or I won't catch you if you run out on us? Wrong again." Sibyl shook her head. "We can find out right now."

"What's that, a challenge?"

"You show me. We know just which loan shark was bleeding your dad. *I* know he's still in the business. I know where he'll be tonight. You want to see if he took something from your dad? Or he took *him* away?"

Instead of answering, Maya reached out a hand. She tapped Dom where he slumped in the doorway, and he staggered free and stumbled forward.

"Deal. But we do it my way."

She was *calm*. Firm, all fears shrinking down, glimmers of anger and greed reined in... I couldn't make the pieces fit, I could never get past Maya's surface. What was she *doing*?

Out beside me, the Eye whispered "Now, you see what she is? Do you?"

I couldn't answer.

* * *

The four of them walked across town. The April sun was already setting, and the shifting tides of people on the street gave the Duvals and their "partner" cover as they maneuvered through crowds and back alleys, avoiding any notice from the police.

But the Duvals' fierce, banked anger—and having three of that kind of beacon together—let me stay as much as a block behind them and not lose their trail for long. Even if I began to, the Eye would step out of onlookers' sight, vanish away, and then return to point me toward them. And when Leland did walk near me, he kept well out of my reach.

I was only waiting for that first flicker of need from Maya; I kept telling myself that. Or I'd stop the Eye when he made his move against her, as if I could ever close that distance in time.

But I couldn't lose her.

Every time their path twisted, and I had to slow down and let those furnaces of violence pull back ahead with her, the deeper the worry dug into me. Even the Scarecrow had seen it, I needed to get her through this alive.

But all the while, the Eye looked away toward her like it was the people around her that needed saving.

Sure, they're targeting another person who might *know her history or her magic. Sure, Maya already used the Bone I gave her to squeeze Van Owen...*

The shivers wouldn't stop coming. She said this would be done "her way"—that had to be safer as long as the Duvals let her work. *Yeah, keep telling yourself that too.*

The streets grew colder and the sky grew dimmer. Blocks of dirty homes melted into half-closed shops, and finally to quiet stretches dotted with bright lampposts. All the way out on the wealthy edge of town.

So of course that was when a police car pulled over. I could just make out one cop leaning out the window to study the two women and the two huge men.

The two cops' suspicion rumbled, even clear down the block from me. The Duvals sizzled with menace, and Maya stepped in front of them—her emotions too tight and controlled to read much at all.

Leland said "You think she'll give them to the police now? Or make a break for it?"

His smirk made my fingers twitch, but he still kept himself that one extra step out of my reach.

Maya was swinging her arm in some grand gesture. The Duvals were still holding back—

Light flashed. A burst of pale light nothing like the Duvals' ruddy fire. Was that one of her other skills, the stage "magic" I'd never seen? But I couldn't hear what she *said* to them, and she could only use the Pulse to persuade so far.

Then the officers' suspicion faded. They drove on, and the Duvals' anger settled back like a holstered gun.

Maya might have saved those cops' lives. I turned to throw that in Leland's face, but he was gone again.

Only minutes later the four stopped outside one of the streets' pocket mansions. One of several buildings stretching out in different shapes in the night—but this one had brighter lights inside and a handful of cars out front. So few, for so many lights; the sheer space in the driveway said how many party guests had someone else to drive their cars away.

The mansion had a few trees and bushes around it, but not a single fence, as if the world should already know to keep its distance. And it had concrete, a wide moat of pavement separating the building and trees from the nearby homes.

I saw one of the Duvals wave a hand at the place and caught a rush of dark satisfaction from him. His first thought could have been to light the whole building up and see who came out.

Maya stood swallowed up among the three larger figures, for one excruciating second after another.

Then she started toward the mansion. The three Duvals spread out toward the edges of the property—where they'd have lines of sight across the concrete to any side where she might try creeping away.

Leland was missing. He could be ready to spring *anything*.

But I could track the Duvals. Two of them had already circled out of sight, and the last stayed near the street.

I scrambled forward to crouch down to keep one car between me and that telltale anger. When he paced to the side, I darted out to behind a bush that someone had sculpted into some miniature tower. Then I reached the limousine that sat nearest to the mansion, and caught the strains of party music from inside.

Maya was still up ahead, strolling toward the building itself. She wasn't looking back.

"Hey!" My voice barely carried in the night, and she only walked on as though she'd missed it. Or even knew I was there, and still blamed me for pulling her off of Van Owen.

Then she glanced back. She walked toward me, the lights behind her shadowing her face, until she stood beside the limo that sheltered me.

She hissed "What are you *doing* here?"

"Getting you out of here! The Eye's lurking around here, and he hates you!"

"He would be," she sighed. "If you want to help, stay out of my way."

"So Sybil can burn answers out of someone else? A man with, what did she say, mob connections?"

"You were *spying*—"

Up close, her snarl was as clear as daylight.

Then, softer, she said "And you're still here—"

"What are you doing, girl?"

That sharp, carrying hush had to be Willard Duval. I felt him moving up, closing in on my cover.

Maya marched out to meet him, as he said "Just get on with it!"

Whatever she answered was too low to hear.

Something moved at the corner of the house.

Someone walking into view—I caught one trace of the bored but still-sharp attitude of a guard, and scurried behind the corner of the limo. If he came any closer, hiding from him would mean stepping into Willard's view.

But the Duval was already walking back toward the street. Tracking him and the guard let me keep the car in front of them both.

Maya slipped behind a bush to let the guard amble by, and she strolled back toward the building.

Then she paused, just at the edge of the manor's light. She reached in a pocket, and I saw her tinker with something—and then drop it to the ground.

It bounced. It bounced across the pavement like a scurrying small animal, carried by Maya's magic right to my feet. A crumpled-up bit of paper.

When I unrolled it, the letters were big and broad enough to catch even the faint light:

SNEAKING HIM OUT – AWAY FROM THEM

Maya wasn't with the Duvals. This was a rescue, that she ran right under their noses. A rush of warmth leaped in me.

I looked up, watched her draw near the mansion. Enough light came from the windows to catch the clothes she wore—still an underwhelming mix of a drab coat, mismatched pants, and still the same shapeless hat. She was dressed to hide from the Duvals, so did she think she could talk her way into an event that had limousines lined up outside?

Instead, Maya stopped short of the door. She took a long look around, pressed her hands to the wall, and I watched her scale up to a quiet-looking part of the second floor. A window swung open to welcome her.

The woman had an answer for everything. Hell, her recreating the brooch's magic outdid my realizing how to make the Bones—she'd done it just from a glimpse of that brooch.

But it had been a glimpse she had in the light of her *phone;* of course she'd snapped a picture to keep the clues. I had to choke down a laugh at my missing the obvious.

Except... she'd climbed up to my window that same night. She'd worked out the magic's secrets, but how had she gotten the right stone to use them on, in the middle of the night?

I stared up at the window she'd disappeared into. Her tight, measured emotions were already hard to pick out from the guests below.

"Hey! Who's there!"

A man strode forward—the guard again, he'd just stepped around the building. He was a thin figure in the dark, a nervous voice, and his hand hovered too close to the spot inside his coat that held his weapon.

It starts with an excuse— "A waiter," I said. "Or I was supposed to be one here, but I got all mussed up and they left me out here with this. Not fair!" I spread out my arms and hoped he could see some of the tunnels' lingering stains in the dim light.

And I hooked the Pulse into him, digging in and clawing to draw out a moment of pure pity to shake him out of his routine. And I was twisting people up *again.*

"Not fair," I said again. "I really need this job."

"I should... bring you in..."

I heard the hesitation in his voice. Why let it be his problem? "Sure, let the wait-staff in the back throw me out. If the guards let me see them at all."

"Well... come on."

He led me around past the glimmering windows, toward the back entrance. I shrugged off my coat and the night air had me shivering, but at least it let me make a better impression. Staying near could keep me closer if the Eye struck at Maya—but I only had a minute to get my explanation in order. The manor's discreet little staff entrance came up fast.

The door opened, we swept past one room bright enough to make my eyes water, and then the kitchen came in view. A broad workspace where several men in suits scrambled around with trays, pouring drinks and stacking snacks—

A young man by the door was fumbling with a set of trays. Just a moment's wave of fear had him spilling and crashing them all over the floor.

"Sorry I'm late—couldn't get changed—I got this, you get back out there—" And I pulled, pulled, at the flash of sheer desperation in him.

Some decisions only give someone a moment. "Thanks," he muttered, and grabbed at another tray.

I scooped up a cloth and began wiping up the snacks where they'd fallen. The only way now had to be to keep moving, to scrub and grab and stack and work so fast that none of the staff broke in to stop me, and stay ready to run. The stocky, commanding woman in the center of everyone's operations eyed me without a word.

Noise from beyond the room overshadowed the kitchen's cramped rattling and whispers. Voices, laughs, and the same swirling party music I'd heard were in full swing; glimpses out the door showed the party-goers busy in their own world. Whenever I stole a moment to sense the Pulse, I felt the swarm of emotions, satisfaction and boredom and lust and all the shades of soggy drunkenness.

If something happened, if I saw, heard, sensed, a flicker of trouble with Maya, at least I'd be nearby. As I scrubbed plates and passed out glasses for the others to carry...

A sound, a murmur, came first—several voices raised in surprise. I glanced out the doorway.

A shimmer of beauty gliding by in a gown of sea-green, that she must have pilfered from upstairs... dark hair knotted into some arrangement that only magic could have woven... Maya walked beside a tiny old man, whispering to him. The anxious, slowly-escalating glances he made around him told me, she was using the Pulse to craft fear within him. *Come with me if you want to live.*

The rising dread in him blew through the crowd's swarm of emotions, enough to let me track them moving all the way out to the edge of the house.

I grabbed up my coat and rushed for the back. *Fast* was everything now, reaching the yard and jogging through the night air around to where they would come out. The Pulse showed the Duvals were still off at a distance, and I had enough nearby brush and shrubs to avoid their sight for now.

Out at the front, the long black limousine was rolling backward toward the mansion's door.

Cars, locks, now walls... The thought of Maya slipping in anywhere suddenly tore at me, and all the danger around us only made the question fiercer. How *had* she made a climbing stone so fast?

She darted out of the car just as I reached it. She made for the mansion door, just twenty feet away.

I had only one moment alone with her—the thought pried the question loose: "Late last night, when you climbed up to see me, where'd you get the gem for it?"

Her stride faltered, for one instant. Then she glanced back and said "Only place I had time for."

So she stole it.

She pulled the mansion door open. The frightened old man who shuffled out looked even more wrinkled and worn out up close, nothing like he'd been part of ruining Maya's family.

As he stepped outside, a voice from behind him called "Hold on—"

Maya swung the door shut, and tapped a finger on its frame. Someone behind it grunted and thumped trying to wrench it open.

Then she turned to the old man. "Quick—you might be in their crosshairs right now."

We half-urged, half-carried him to the limo. I helped him in and sat beside him, while Maya dashed for the driver's seat again. The engine whispered and churned softly to slide us away.

A huge, masked figure stepped into the headlights, his empty hand taking aim.

Maya slammed the car to a stop. A smaller shape loomed beside the passenger door, masked and pointing at the door. Maya let out a single, soft groan, and the doors clicked open.

The old man wheezed "What is this—"

Sibyl climbed in to settle next to him, putting him between her and me. "This, Mister Beltram? That," and she waved to Maya in the front, "is Stephen Grant's daughter."

In that moment, I caught no emotion from Maya, only a vague rippling. Shock still gripped her face... she'd had to let the Duvals in... but now they had her enemy...

The Duval from out front climbed in beside her, nudged her shoulder. And she faced ahead and brought the car lurching forward into a slow glide down the driveway. Out the rear window, the third Duval was closing in behind us.

The old man lashed out—"Beltram" swung his fist around to catch Sibyl's masked face, and he lunged from his seat.

Sibyl caught him and slammed him back in place.

"Don't touch him—" I tried, but she only leaned closer to him.

"Stephen Grant," she repeated. "His girl wants to know what you took from him."

Her hand struck up a flame. The orange glared shockingly bright in the enclosed space of the car, and it had no smell at all—except the rush of sweat it roused.

Beltram gasped "What'd I take... from him, from... just money, just what he borrowed..." His face had deep lines of fear carved in it now. To the Pulse his fear shone brighter than Sibyl's fire, too panicked to lie.

Maya said "You can't just demand—"

"Start remembering," Sibyl said.

I was up from my seat, leaning down to tug Beltram aside and scowl at Sibyl and her fire. "That's *enough!* He's telling the truth, I can tell!"

She only brought her burning hand around, toward me. "You stay out of it. Our girl up front is the one who tells us who's lying. Or I keep asking my way until I can see it too."

"Not now!" Maya said. "Glad you trust me. But, I'm using up my *supply,*" she added.

That single Bone's magic. She meant, she had too little of the Pulse left to read Beltram... Sibyl would keep scorching him unless Maya got another Bone, or the secret to restoring it...

If I trusted Maya with that. If anything could back Sibyl down.

"No," I said. "You're not getting more. Both of you, look at him! All of this has gone far enough—"

Something clanged against the car. One sharp metal slap... and a muffled gunshot outside.

I looked around the windows, saw Beltram clench his hands around his head and Sibyl searching the night too. Out the rear window, the other Duval was turning away, looking back at a figure in a shooter's stance, as he blasted another bullet at us. One of the guards.

We'd almost made it out.

The big man pointed his hand at the shooter. A far brighter flash of light tore through the dimness.

Sure, that Duval just has to dazzle him and he's harmless...

Then I blinked back the spots from my eyes. One afterimage lingered—but it stirred, that one flaming outline was still flinging out its arm in the instant before the shape all burned away and broke apart, gone.

Nothing remained.

Beltram began wailing, moaning.

I crouched staring across at Sibyl, at her cousin outside, at the faces they'd covered before they moved in.

The car lurched—I tumbled and fell across the seat as we stopped. The Duval riding shotgun had shoved Maya from the wheel, and the door opened to let the murderer pile in beside Sibyl.

"Now go!" and the man up front drew back to let Maya pull the car forward again, smoother and faster every moment.

Sibyl glowered at her cousin. "I *told* you about overkill."

"Sorry..." His voice, and the sudden hunch of his shoulders at her rebuke, made this Willard Duval. "I thought, I thought if there was no body..."

Killers. We were crammed into a car with three masked, fire-throwing monsters.

Beltram's moans rose into screams, shrill screams that beat against the car's space like being locked in with a wild animal. Sibyl grabbed his arm.

"No!" I caught at Beltram's shoulders and shot Sibyl one warning look before I dove into the old man's terror.

One hard wrench ripped the top of it away—more fear was surging up, but the sudden half-calming made him halt, eyes staring in surprise.

Sibyl peered at me, with what might be approval behind the ski mask.

The car slowed, just then. That and a glance at the windows, the cluster of lights, showed we'd reached a bright intersection, out in public—

My hands slammed down on Sibyl's and Willard's arms. Rage blasted through me and into them as pure frozen terror—and for one instant before it struck I savored the flash within Sibyl's eye-slits as she knew what was coming, before the screaming took them both.

Beltram was limp when I grabbed him, when I wrenched at the door and glanced up front to see if Maya had made her own escape.

She and Dom weren't alone.

Leland in his black mask sat on Maya's other side. *"Now,"* and his words froze us all for an instant, "now, do you see what they are? What they all are?"

He was speaking to me. The Eye spoke with the stony, brutal voice of someone proven right.

When the moment ended, the Eye had vanished—with Maya in his grasp.

CHAPTER THIRTEEN: TRUTH

"Where'd he—"

"The hell—"

Shouts and curses exploded through the car in the wake of the two vanishing.

But my lungs couldn't get air. The Eye had finally done it, he'd taken Maya...

My chest broke free to gulp in a breath. If he got the Duvals too I'd have nothing—

"Look out!" The words ripped out of me. "He could be back any second, *any* second!"

Old Beltram managed a groan: "But... what..."

Sibyl roared "Drive!"

"Can't!" Dom turned back from the driver's seat to stare at us—even the mask couldn't hide his helplessness. "There's no keys. *She* made it work."

Maya's magic. The secret the Eye still wanted.

I held onto that thought as I said "We're sitting ducks in here. We have to lose him, while we still can."

Sibyl turned, fixed me with her gaze. "You think you're in charge—"

"*I know* what we're up against!" I shouted. "You want to sit in a stolen limousine and wait? Come on!"

I threw the door open and raced to the sidewalk. The three Duvals followed me, leaving poor shocked Beltram behind—if that saved him from the Duvals, if the Eye ignored him, I'd done some good here.

That bright-lit intersection glowed ahead of us, but Sibyl twisted away from that, and the three were off like an avalanche racing back up the dimmer sidewalk, back into the quieter residential neighborhood we'd been leaving. I charged after them, after the killers. They yanked their masks off as they ran.

But all of us ran watching the shadows and the cover for anywhere the enemy could reappear. I held onto the Pulse to catch any sense of a mind appearing out of nowhere, or anything lurking up on another roof.

Or maybe I was wrong, and Maya had already beat him. *If she hasn't... please, Maya...*

We thundered around a corner, to where quiet houses and trees put us out of sight of the car we'd abandoned. The Duvals settled to a fast walk, the two huge men heaving for breath. The dim residential street echoed with our footsteps.

Sibyl crowded in at my side. "Alright, Corbin. Who *was* that?"

"That? You just met the Eye."

I tensed for some shudder of horror, that she'd heard of him the same way the Scarecrow had. But she only said "What the hell does that mean?"

"It means what you saw—he *teleports,* so fast he could be anywhere. He's that strong." Way stronger than me, alone. I added "He says Maya's a threat, and you three are..."

Actually, he thought they were nobodies.

Sibyl must have heard the catch in my tone. She grabbed at my arm, slammed us to a stop. "We're *what?*"

It happened the moment she stopped: a shape, a man was there behind her, and I yanked at her grip to jerk her forward and away as I yelled.

The Eye reached out for her back... and a wash of red flame burst backward, a wave of blind power from her that made Leland flinch away and me spin clear to cover my face from the heat. Fear spiked in him.

"Damn you—" Willard boomed and swung up a fist, but there was no target there.

All around us, the street was hushed again, sounds gone as quick as Sibyl's light had faded. The houses' lights and the few cars up the street shone on blindly as if they'd missed it all. Every presence the Pulse tracked was blandly, harmlessly still as well.

I broke the silence. "I guess you three are on his list too."

"He can try," Sibyl snapped. "But you? Yeah, when it's your turn up, good luck scaring *that* maniac off."

She turned away, she motioned to her cousins and gathered to break into a run—

But Maya needed—

I flung back "I've got better odds than you do!"

Sibyl slammed to a stop. It could have been the warning or the insult, but the words had sunk their hook in her. "What was that, Corbin?"

I thrust a finger at her. *"I* can track him, some. Hell, I know how he's tracking you right now."

She leaned toward me, near as tall as I was. "Oh, just like that you've got the answer?"

"Stop talking tough and *listen!"* I stepped around her, to take in her cousins too and block their way. "Sure you've got a big gun here. But you're slow, blind—you *need* my help. And I need you to save Maya."

Sibyl snorted a laugh. "Save her? Out of our way—"

"I said *listen* to me." I paused for a breath, searching the Pulse.

Right as a presence appeared across the street.

She snarled "Out of my way before—"

I reached a hand toward her. Sibyl jerked back, an instant of fright bursting back into fury over her weakness.

But the Eye was just watching, crouching in the shadows by the opposite fence.

"He's here," I hissed. "Quiet now—he's across the street—"

Dom roared "Gun!"

We bolted. I caught one glimpse of the Eye aiming before we flung ourselves up the sidewalk. The first shot shattered the night stillness, then another rang out—but none of us went down.

He's shooting at night, from a coward's distance with a singed hand... please, please let our luck hold out...

Sometime after the fourth shot, a car alarm broke out howling. A car on the street swerved and screeched to a stop up the block from the gun's flashes. Lights flicked on at porches and windows all around us—and the Eye was gone.

"It's your phones!" I panted. "He bugged mine, he can track yours."

Sibyl gave a wordless curse and tossed an object away over a fence. Moments later her cousins sent more phones after it.

Then we ran, me working the Pulse even though it made my balance wobble. Still nobody stood out of place or appeared out of nowhere...

Another turn appeared ahead, and the Duvals twisted around it to send us back toward the brighter streets we'd left. Now they were leading the Eye *toward* more people who could get cut down by his bullets, and the idea didn't slow the Duvals down one step.

But there were no more shots or ambushes, and we made it to the noise and the light at the edge of the shopping district. We slowed, gasping, looking around the streams of people in the lights. A bus stop and a bench waited ahead.

Honest, ordinary people. While I was fleeing with three criminals beside me, trying to keep them alive and in line—away from destroying anyone else. If that was what it took to save Maya.

The babble of emotions pressed around me. One steady, hard presence *could* be up on a house's roof, if that wasn't the noise drowning out my sense of locations...

A great hiss of motion brought a bus sliding up.

And we couldn't stay on our feet all night. I waved the Duvals toward it. Willard rumbled "Now what—"

"You could be right, *people* are keeping him away." The bus looked almost half full, no place for someone to just appear or vanish unnoticed. And if the Eye tried to tail us from outside, his supply of magic had to have *some* limit.

The several people in line fell back when the Duvals pushed in. Then the cousins stopped at the fare box with a pointed look at me, and I had to throw some bills in for all of us.

We moved to seats at the back, and the kids who'd been there scurried away from Willard and Dom's glare. Even if Leland risked appearing here, he couldn't get behind us.

When the bus pulled forward and got underway, Sibyl leaned in close to whisper to me "Alright, Corbin. What else do you know about this 'Eye'?"

She was challenging me to produce something useful... but I still met her sneer with a low "His real name. What he wants. And my magic can sense some of his moves too. You want to survive, you work with me to find Maya."

And that sneer twisted deeper into her face. "There it is again. Don't you get it?"

"Get what?" I tried. "That you're scared?"

"That you lost. A blitz attack like that? If the Eye wants Maya dead, she's already..."

She left the word hanging for me.

Dead. The thought was a frozen shroud that had been hanging over me ever since she vanished. I stared straight ahead, taking in the mix of ages and faces in the people along the bus, all murmuring or sitting or going through their own business not hearing who we whispered about. People who didn't know her, who didn't care.

"No she's not."

I forced the words into the air, and my faith with them.

"If the Eye wanted her dead, he'd have done it long ago. Sibyl, he *captured* her. I told you, he wants her magic. He's been fighting to make me steal it from her since..." Since yesterday, a lifetime ago. "He's already kidnapped someone once to lean on me."

"So that's it. He wants to drag the secret out of her, same as we do with old man Beltram."

Her tone changed as she said it—she understood the Eye's move, she almost respected it.

Don't make me regret this, Sibyl. "You're the ones he wants dead, all of you. You want to survive or not?"

The woman didn't even blink. "Huh. First I'm sharing with my 'sister,' now I'm saving her ass."

The seat creaked under Dom's weight, leaning in to join us. "So you got a plan?"

This time I'd learned from getting Helena to listen—I had the next step ready to say. "We track him down." And Helena, the thought of her made me remember the Eye had already made one enemy nobody would ignore.

Sybil's nose twitched like it had caught a bad smell. *"Can* you track him? No, he wants us, we nail him when he makes his move."

"You saw how that worked. And you saw how slippery he is. Sure, we can try being ready for him, but that's still just betting our lives on who's faster."

I had to draw my voice in to keep words like that away from the woman in the row ahead, and all the other passengers spread around the nearby seats. "Ready" meant ready to kill Leland, the same way as Willard had incinerated that guard—but, this was to save Maya, when Leland was probably torturing her for her magic's secrets. A sickening twist tore at my stomach. And that torture would be the only reason he'd keep her alive, until we found her.

Sibyl leaned closer. "So start with what you say you know. The Eye's *name.* You think I forgot you said that?"

Just hearing it, killers asking for an enemy's name... I froze.

Sibyl scowled, looked away, a motion that could just extend onward and pull her out of her chair to leave me on my own.

And I was in too deep already. "He's a crime reporter. Phillip Leland."

The words left a stillness behind them. The low, familiar rattle and murmur of the bus felt more distant, as if the secret had pushed those sounds away.

"Leland," Sibyl muttered. "Maybe I heard the name."

"He's probably been watching you for a while." *And he said you were no threat, until tonight.* "Trouble is, he knows I know, so this won't be just catching him at his home."

"Sounds like we do trap him. You make the perfect bait."

"And I told you he'll slip right out of it again, you know he will," I said. "We can't keep our guard up forever—we need to catch him when *his* guard is down. So we track him down, with everything we've got. Like the biggest name he's pissed off, and how she can get us some off-the-books help from—" I saw where my thought was going, too late— "the police."

Sibyl's hand clamped onto my wrist, big enough to go all around my jacket's sleeve. "You're bringing us to the cops."

"*I'm* going to the cops. And I'm not telling Poe much—I can't, Leland's probably got them bugged, just like our phones. All of you can keep your distance, I'm not trying to trap you. I thought we had a truce."

Sibyl snorted a laugh. " 'Truce.' One little word. You think I believe that?"

"You know why you can believe me: we're hunting someone who can be gone in an instant. Of course I need all the help I can get, and that means you and your fire, you know? It's the only chance Maya's got."

Dom turned to his glowering cousin, and Willard behind him gave her the same quick, trusting glance.

And I could have been reading their emotions all through their debate. Not that it would give me any more to say, if this wasn't enough.

Then Sibyl pulled her hand back from me.

"Alright then. But we make a stop first—" and her gaze sharpened— "all of us. Or you got a problem with that?"

* * *

The bus rolled on for another half hour, before we climbed off and switched to another. And I called the private number Helena gave me, and found a message:

"Some rest is doing me good. But if there's anything you need, ask."

At least she could sleep. For us, the night stretched deeper, with the crowd on the bus thinning out as more time ticked away, and we drew near the city's edge. Sharp needles of worry ran through me to keep my eyes open... and yet I kept lurching upright to find they'd sunk down anyway.

The quieter the bus and the streets became, the surer my searches were that we'd left the Eye behind. Or he was busy prying Maya's secrets out of her, with all the torture he could invent. He had to be, I kept telling myself, it was the only reason she'd still be alive.

If the Duvals' damn detour didn't take all night.

When we climbed off the bus this time, it was to walk down the road out of town. The night was dim and silent, with a blur of trees and hills around us. I recalled something had happened outside the city, long ago, but the roads all looked alike now.

The longer our steps on the asphalt sounded into the night, the more the thought came back to me that the Duvals could have their own treacherous reason for bringing me here... except, the Pulse didn't catch that level of hatred in them. Instead, the three spoke so little they must take the silence between each other for granted.

So there was no warning when they stepped off the highway. I followed them in among the brush and the rocks, parallel to the road. Those huge feet made less noise than mine did now; they'd come this way before.

Then Sibyl raised a hand to halt us.

My flash of worry ended when she said "I'll watch Corbin here. You watch your backs," and her harsh voice softened with genuine warmth.

Her cousins only nodded, and moved off into the countryside. Without another word, she sat down on one of the rough lumps of rock around us. I settled onto another.

The quarry. This road must lead by the Mansfield Quarry, I decided. Was the place still in use, so the Duvals might have friends there at night? Or they could have stashed more of their fire magic out there.

Except... I'd tried writing the quarry into one of my urban legends pieces once. But there weren't a lot of ghost stories there, even for a place that had once been shaken by a riot.

What if this place is something else? I glanced at Sibyl, unmoving and unflagging. The Duvals had needed to come out here, but they kept me from seeing what they actually did. Did that make something like the quarry the source of their magic?

A quarry, and a bloody riot thirty years ago, where nobody had fully explained what had set the workers off. Could that violence have been caused by magic there, or something the riot did powered the magic...

I bared my teeth in the dark. I was sitting in the wilds beside a woman who set people on fire, and I went right back to puzzling out rumors and connections. At least it drew my thoughts out of the same cycles of worry.

Something shook the brush. Willard and Dom moved out of the shadows, too fast—anxiety clung to them.

"Someone's down there," Dom said. "Nobody's ever down there!"

"So you came back, good." Sibyl motioned us all in together. "Quiet now, and I mean *quiet.*"

We started down along their path again. Bits of loose rock moved under my feet, while the huge Duvals picked their way along with slow certainty.

Shapes formed out of the dim brush ahead. The rocks stretched higher, as the ground began sloping down. Slowly I made out the looming sides of the Mansfield Quarry.

A chain fence stretched around it, but Sibyl went straight to a spot where she folded the mesh back to open a Duval-sized doorway. The edges of the break looked like melted wax shapes in the dimness, burned through long ago.

Far ahead, the Pulse picked up two people. One surged with fierce need, the other was a mass of dark pain fighting to hold it in. "Down there—I think that's the Eye, and Maya!"

"It was there, yeah," Willard muttered.

We crept down into the quarry.

As the rock walls rose around us, the smell of the countryside faded, except the whiff of dust. A few wooden frames still clung to the huge facets of rock, as if they were holding the stone bluffs in place instead of being built to cut it away. The only sound was what little our footsteps made.

A push from Sibyl sent me forward. I scrabbled for balance, for silence—she wanted to rush us *now?* I crept on past a patch of cracked rock that looked laced with shadow.

Leland's voice broke out, low and fierce and echoing. "Just one! I only need one!" The hunger in him echoed louder than his voice. "You see all this, you know what it does every time!"

One step, then another. We couldn't make a sound, not one rattle of stones... Those emotions came from down against one of the rock faces ahead. Where an outline moved.

"Don't you see? I have to stop this! I just need one more magic, to stop it from happening."

One shape stood over a... that wasn't shadow on the ground. It was a figure in a blanket, with one pale—bare—foot stretching from under it, shaking in pain.

My fingers clenched. What did Leland do, *strip* Maya to disarm her and then throw her a blanket so she wouldn't freeze as he worked her over? I stared at the taller figure, wishing I had the fire to turn him to ash.

Maya groaned "You can't, can't..."

Her voice was ragged—what had he done—

A rock clattered behind us, then a second footstep.

Leland hadn't moved, I sensed nobody there—

But Dom Duval whirled around, and his blast exploded the night into red, into flashing spots when the dark crashed back in, and then another flare. Silent as an instant sunrise.

"Don't waste power!" Sibyl yelled. "Where is—"

I dropped to the rock, dust puffing up at my face. The Duvals crashed around in the dark and tried to watch for the enemy.

I searched the Pulse.

"They're gone! Both of them—but he could be back any second!"

I huddled against the rock, blinking to force the afterimages from my eyes. That blur, or that rocky shelf, could be where he'd reappear with his gun. Unless he was afraid of hunting us in the dark too.

Those footstep decoys, those could have been Maya's magic. I strained the Pulse around us. The Eye could take Maya's devices off her and use them a hundred ways to outwit us, but he still needed her secrets to maintain their power.

And he'd been *here.* This didn't sound like a trap, but he'd come to the quarry anyway, he knew...

Someone flickered into the countryside, far beyond the quarry. I opened my mouth for a shout.

Light flared—above us, a colossal *booming* light, a crack like the world splitting apart, and all of it, great masses of rock, broke loose and tumbled down.

Behind us. The blast has *to be back behind us or I'm just an insect clinging to the ground waiting to be crushed...*

Hands ached, knees ached, my ears were left with a dead hollowness by the time I could make myself believe the ground was solid again. And felt the endless, choking dust blocking out the world.

He could have more bombs up there. To cover anywhere except the same spot—I stumbled toward where the landslide had settled.

Sibyl shoved me back. Her mouth opened in some bellow of silent rage.

That part of the quarry, was that where Sibyl had pushed me past before?

The silence faded from my ears. And all the while, the Pulse caught nothing, no sign of the Eye striking at us in the dust.

"He's long gone."

I could hear my voice now, strangely normal in the ear-shaken aftermath. Sibyl glanced over, she heard me too.

"He planted one bomb, back above there," I said. "Sibyl... what was he trying to bury?"

She didn't answer. But her fury blazed brighter than I'd ever felt it.

The Eye had been ready for us. He'd buried that one spot in the quarry, and now the Duvals had no way to recharge their magic.

CHAPTER FOURTEEN: OUTSHINES

Willard staggered toward the mass of fallen stone, waving at the dust that choked the darkness around us. The pile of it could have been taller than him. But he grunted, bent, and tossed one rock aside to clatter over the others, while flinty shifting and popping sounds were still breaking from other parts of the fall.

"No! Someone heard that blast. We get out of here!" Sibyl said it like a curse.

We raced off through the dark. The dust fell away behind us as we slipped out through the break in the fence, then on through the rocks and brush into the night.

No shout, no siren, no sound of reaction came through the night so far. The Pulse felt nobody out there—and no enemy burst out of the dark to ambush us. We were alone.

Willard slammed his fists together. "Bastard said he needed more magic. He took out ours—"

He stopped. Sibyl hadn't made a sound, just glared at him in the dark, and then I felt that glower turned on me.

Now I *knew too much,* when they were the ones who brought me here? So they hadn't counted on the Eye's demolition blowing another cover off of their magic. I clutched for words to make them see how none of that mattered, not when the Eye still had Maya and he could attack us at any moment.

Sibyl said "He can pick us off any time, Corbin. How do we nail him?"

I let out a breath and those desperate thoughts, and tried to speak steadily again. "He could have a hiding spot anywhere in Jericho, if it's just a step away for him. We have to put pressure on him now, while he's focused on Maya." That was the closest I could bring this to asking to *save* her in time... but I felt one flicker of Sibyl's tight frustration softening just then.

Willard added "While he's beating her secrets out of her? Yeah, all we need is him jumping around us *and* he's got all her tricks too." He kicked at the ground and a pebble rattled away.

"That's right," I pushed on. "He's already got the whole city in his reach. That means it's time to bring the police in."

Rumbles sounded around me, as the huge shapes pressed closer in the dimness.

Sibyl growled "This again—"

"*What part* of 'he can be anywhere' *did you not understand?*"

The words shot out of me, ringing away through the brush. The Duvals flinched back a step, and I scrabbled for the calmer point I'd been trying to make.

"Look, I'm not asking you to walk up to the cops yourself. But we *need* to track down where Leland is, and keep the heat on him. Maybe there's time to save Maya."

I'd let that slip out—before they could see how much of my urgency only came back to that, I turned straight to Sibyl and pressed on:

"That means we need actual cops tracking him down, who can find every place he owns or knows in half an hour. And today I caught him right in the police station, and he vanished us away. That means there are some recordings there that prove Phillip Leland went in and never came out." I spread my hands. "It's the only mistake we can catch him at, and our only chance to put real pressure on him."

"By showing the cops about magic." Sibyl gave an angry grunt. "Then we're as good as dead."

"You *are* dead if Leland's free to keep chasing you. He *shot* at us, even if he kept his distance that time. Now, I know a detective that'll listen to me—he'd want to catch the kidnapper, not stop and tell his chief about vanishing men. I'll see how much he needs to know."

"You forget something?" Sibyl laughed. "You see a lot of cops on the street now? Your guy better be on the graveyard shift."

"I'll get him," I snapped. Or else Maya could be dead by morning... I clung to the memory of him keeping her alive.

Willard said "That or we just go to this Leland's home and..." He broke off. "Hell. He knows you saw him, right? So he's gone."

"You're right, you're right," Sibyl said, and then she took a step toward me, and sparks flicked from her hand. "Just don't forget. You sell us out, we'll find you."

"I know. Just like Leland's sure to find *us,* if we don't get the drop on him soon."

* * *

In the dead of night, the loudest things on the streets were the worries filling my head about what could come next. Sounds pattered away on distant blocks or came rolling by with each isolated car... but none of that kept me from the same half-formed fears of what I might have to say to the police. And even those were easier than wondering if Maya was already gone, or if Leland would guess at our move and be waiting.

At last, we drew near the hunched, bright-lit shape of the station. I tried the Pulse, looking for a first reminder of what attitudes I'd be trying to sway. Even at the city's emptiest hour, parts of the place buzzed like trapped wasps with the night's tension.

A jab at my awareness—two other presences *appeared* beside it.

"What?" Dom said.

I waved toward the lower, dimmer building at the station's side, almost empty of people. "He's here. They *just* appeared here."

The narrow courtyard was still, I could track only a few people apart from the station itself. We moved toward the side building—then pulled back behind the station's corner as a cop walked past, heading straight toward our destination.

He was staring at his phone screen as he stomped by. And I caught a few words from him: "...*knew* the cameras were crap..."

So cameras were going out right when Leland snuck in... what if he'd already wiped the images of who'd walked in today? The officer unlocked the building's door and marched inside. Leland and his prisoner would have the whole space to dodge him—

Willard dashed forward, grabbed the door before it swung shut. He waved us forward.

"One chance," Sibyl muttered. "Leland hears us, we're dead."

Inside a police building—the Duvals really were crazy. Or desperate. I dashed with them to the door, and we stepped inside.

A sign on the wall said *Archive,* in the "sparse" fluorescent lighting that was eye-wateringly bright after moving outside. I tracked the cop storming away deep into the building. Leland and Maya were actually closer, up a branching corridor—and Maya's will was still pushing back knots of pain.

I darted down that corridor, quick and quiet. The Duvals followed with their masks already on. The cop was far away, and Leland had to be behind that door at the end.

The door was locked.

Damn it, we couldn't be this *close and still shut out.* Unless Leland was so distracted we could slip in—

And he and Maya vanished again. He whisked them straight over to another room on the floor, so casually he seemed not to know he'd left us behind.

"Leland's moved on," I muttered.

Footsteps sounded in the main corridor. The cop was on his way back—and we stood in a short, dead-end corridor just one glance over from where he'd pass by.

Willard clenched a fist and turned toward that intersection. Sibyl stopped him with a wave.

Instead she held a finger over the door's latch. A single flame sprouted, a knife of pale fire brighter than the flickering fluorescents above. She gave a low grunt of effort sharp enough to be pain.

Then the door swung open and we piled inside.

We had a glimpse of old racks and file cabinets before she shut the door, closing us into the dimness and the deep smell of paper.

"Impressive," I breathed, and searched the Pulse. "The cop's heading out... wait for it..."

Then the cop was walking outside, gone. But if Leland had crippled the cameras here, that couldn't have been a two-minute fix—the cop could be back any time.

I led us out and down the main corridor. For now it was just us here, and Leland and Maya. Their door was right ahead.

And it was locked too. I gritted my teeth and waved Sibyl forward, listening.

Leland was saying "Yes, now *this* is where they put it—see?"

"Oh, police have a folklore file? Urban legends?" Maya had to be gritting her teeth, to speak through the pain.

Right at my ear, Sibyl breathed "Think they'll notice?" She pointed at the door. I edged back to let her cut.

That step back still let his voice reach me: "No folklore here. You think what happened in that quarry back then was anything but hard fact and plain human hatred? What happens every day?"

Sibyl's flame worked into the door, not a quick slash this time but a slow, stealthy cut.

Maya said "What are you getting at?"

"Look here!"

Something clicked. I heard what could only be a file cabinet drawer rolling open with a clang.

Leland went on "Your magic does open up so much. And you think you can leave me with just these scraps of it—" His emotions spiked with a flash of greed. "Here, you see the name on that access record?"

"So my father asked about a riot. So?"

"One riot? Here!" Metal rolled back again. "And here. Requests about mass murder... suicide..."

"Requests," Maya said. "That one's about before he was born. Sounds like he did your job, reporter—"

"Don't you see? He knew! These did the same thing as the quarry riot."

Sibyl's flame snuffed out. Her gaze was locked on the door, on the message beyond it.

"He knew. *Any* site of enough violence, and the right words, can make fire talismans..."

A low, soft gasp came from Dom. His eyes were wide with shock.

I tapped Sibyl, nudged her toward the door again. The sharp, hungry look on her face ignored me.

"He knew that," Leland went on. "And he kept looking—and you still think the world needs you searching out more magic?"

"He was *searching,* that's all. He was no monster. I... was six, but I would have known."

I pushed Sibyl again. She only waited, leaving the door untouched as she soaked the knowledge in.

Leland said "But he knew, he had to know what kind of horrors it could lead to. And he still left signs lying around—even your foster sister got one, and look what she's done with it."

"So you shoot her? Or were you having your fun watching them play and waiting to steal it, right up to the moment *you* decide they've gone too far?"

"I..."

Leland's voice wavered, I could feel him writhing on the inconsistency she'd caught him at.

Then the brutal certainty tightened and closed over it, like cement settling and filling in a grave. I shoved Sibyl again, harder.

Leland said "I'm shutting them down. You think you can distract me? Anyway, those three would have burned out on their own. None of them are the kind of danger you are."

Sibyl whispered under her breath, "Burn out, huh?"

Her knife of fire lit up along her finger. This time it was a scalpel that slowly edged into the lock. There was no smell, and only a soft wave of heat escaping her ruthless control.

Maya said "But you're the only one who could use all the magics, right?"

"No! Don't you see, I never looked for the words for that fire, I don't *want it!*"

"Sure you don't." Maya actually laughed, low and harsh.

She was challenging him, daring him—playing every card she could find to make him stop and answer her. Fighting to keep him from finishing her.

"You..." Leland fumed. "You've stared right at this, how can you not see it? The fire spreading, that lunatic and his fear tunnels? I don't *want* to trust myself with your telekinetic power, but—"

Something clanged, the sound of a file cabinet slamming open. Then a second drawer, a third, then all three closing together.

"But there's just so damn much it can do to keep the magic covered up. Don't you see, someone needs to stop this?"

"Someone like you."

"Me. You *have* to see it—I'll do it, even if I have to learn a second magic to stop it."

"Stop what?"

"Stop *everything!* Before they go starting fires just to make more places than can build fire—or that thing comes out of the tunnels... it's still just starting! Hell, your father—"

A flash of need spiked through Maya's pain as he went on.

"Grant almost *sent* a package off with one of those talismans, chasing some rumors in Lavine. *My God!* You know what his teleporting could have done if he could trust the leap?"

He stopped. The corridor went silent.

"But... you *don't* know," he said.

And he laughed, cold, bitter, as his mind... sank down, drained away the tight-packed layers of determination and left him still and empty.

"Oh, you're clever. You play along, you fight me and you tease me that you could understand, you hold out your magic... I never appreciated how long I'd been keeping watch all alone, until I had someone to tell it too. And you used that."

No, no, no— I stared at the line of heat creeping up the lock.

"I did *what?*" Her word spiked, managed to sound offended, as if that could convince her captor now.

Leland didn't even pause; his words had to be for himself now. "You had me believing. But you, you can't see what it'll do, can you? You really are just like him. And I took your mind cube and the rest of your talismans and you still had me believing. But you'll never see what you're starting. Just seeing you squeeze old Van Owen—you think you can get away with that? That you'd never pay a price?"

A tide of fear rose in Maya now, but her voice was steady. "Listen to me..."

"No more listening, no more lies. I should have done it the first minute. Goodbye, Grant—"

I slammed into the door.

The instant my shoulder touched it, I felt the horrible, certain strength of the lock, knew that our stealthy cutting could never have been enough... Then metal snapped and I tumbled in.

Framed by rows of file cabinets, Leland stood over where Maya lay huddled in a yellow blanket, his gun leveled right at her. My rush swept me on with every muscle I had throwing me forward. Some sound, motion, moved behind me as the Duvals began to follow, ready to get him.

But Leland's moment of shock burst into reflex, and he swung the gun up toward me instead of vanishing, instead of shooting Maya. All in an instant, I knew I'd never reach him before he pulled the trigger.

Then the gun flew up as Maya lunged upward, arms and shoulder and everything blocking him and clawing for the weapon. A curse tore from Sibyl behind me, cut off from her target. I lunged on the last steps with my fist driving straight at Leland.

They vanished.

I spilled through empty air and slammed to a clumsy stop. The room was still—only my gasping breath, and the first steps of the Duvals crowding inside.

And one muffled cough.

Beyond the bulk of the file cabinets, the room's corner opened up for a tiny reading table. The sound came from back there, squeezed down and sheltered behind the cabinets—the Pulse showed them both.

"He's right there!" I pointed.

"Ready..." Sibyl glanced at her cousins.

The three Duvals started forward, hands raised to strike, heads darting around trying to watch how every direction could be where their enemy came from next.

But they had it wrong. Leland didn't need to ambush them here, he only needed another moment to get his bearings and be *gone*. Or shoot Maya—and the sounds behind the cabinet had just gone silent.

"Stop it!" I said. "Leland! Let her go, and I'll show you *my* magic's keys. Reading people, searching for them, it's all yours..." Hands raised high, I began walking toward the corner.

Not a sound answered. My footsteps could have been echoing in an empty room. But I felt curiosity stirring in Leland, swelling.

"I mean it—"

Rage flared in him. I ducked back from it as the gun jabbed around the corner and boomed out. A wild warning shot, but the thunder smashed at my senses and set my ears ringing.

Another sound broke through that—lower, screened off, but *outside,* from the whole world beyond the building:

"Jesus, what was—"

"Move—"

More voices were out there, closing in, and the Pulse caught a wave of shock and anger from what had to be a swarm of onrushing cops.

Then a shout came from behind the cabinet, and Leland fell, toppled, tumbled into view headfirst.

I lunged at him, but he vanished as he hit the floor, like a bubble bursting.

Maya crouched alone behind the cabinet—she'd finally had her chance to fling him away. Around us, the room looked clear.

But the police echoed through the Pulse and my aching hearing, closing fast. The Duvals traded a look between them, between their masked faces. And they dashed from the room.

I turned away, tried to wall out the sound and walk over to Maya, but I kept glancing around for the next space where Leland could reappear on us.

Maya... she wasn't wrapped in a yellow blanket, it was some knee-length rain poncho Leland must have brought her. After he took her pieces of magic and most of her *clothes*.

"You alright?" I breathed.

"I..." Her voice died away. Her face was lined with blood, and outrage.

She crouched down to bring the poncho's plastic folds closer around her, and then held out her hands together. A zip-tie ran around them.

"Got it." I grabbed out my knife and cut her free. Her skin was cold when I brushed it—it would be, after hours like this. Another cut freed her bare feet.

"That door took you long enough." I caught the tremor in her voice, so faint.

He'd left her no real clothes, no magic, no hope, but she was still fighting... I could listen, just stare at her, until...

Leland's still out there. I wrenched my gaze away from Maya, and we started toward the door, watching every direction around us as we moved.

A storm of voices had been raging outside. Now Sibyl stood in front of five, six cops with their guns on her, her empty hands raised but leveled at them as they shouted *on the ground, lie down!* One of her cousins stood behind her.

She wasn't budging.

"Don't be stupid!" I yelled at her.

Then the other Duval touched her arm gently—even masked, it had to be Dom—and he whispered something, and guided her down to kneel and surrender. I watched, tried to think what our "truce" meant now. The cops were raising their guns toward us too.

A boom rang out behind us. The sound of a door blasted open—I glanced back to see the last Duval dashing outside and away.

"Don't move! Show me those hands!" one cop bellowed at me, and I raised them.

Maya stepped beside me. Bleeding, wrapped in the poncho that could be hiding a dozen weapons, but just the wounded look on her as she raised her hands made the cop *melt.* "You alright, miss?"

"I... hope so," she said.

"There's someone else around here too," I said. "He's different, he could be hiding anywhere, *anywhere.* He wants us all dead. And these two were..." I looked at the captured Duvals and tried to find words.

"Let's get you out of here."

The cop didn't put away his gun, or his watchful look, but he and a second officer guided us away from the Duvals. Sibyl lay still as the others cuffed her, glaring at Dom and us.

I kept watching around as we walked; two cops was no protection at all if Leland came back. Just stepping outside had me blinking at the sudden wide-open dimness. The air hadn't been this cold before, had it?

Maya stepped closer. She leaned over, and whispered:

"Leland said he's going after Helena. She's seen too much."

"What—" How, how could Leland even find her—no, this was the Eye, of course he could.

But why would he tell Maya—

A shape lunged out of the darkness. A single, huge figure charged up behind the cops and with one motion swung his massive arms to sweep their heads together with a sickening crack. They slumped to the ground.

"C'mon!" Willard snarled. "They got Sibyl and Dom, we get 'em out!"

"We can't—" Wrong thing to say, and he advanced on me as I said "Think, there's four cops there, you can't—"

"Come *on!*" His voice was halfway to a roar. I edged sideways, between him and Maya.

A gunshot blasted through the night, a second, more.

My body was already moving to fling me toward the building's side, toward Maya and toward what shelter it gave from the shots above it.

We reached the wall, as yells and warnings burst around us, police trying to orient on where the shooter was. The Pulse had a clear sense of Leland, up on the roof and already drawing back away out of sight as they searched.

Our chance. I grabbed Maya's hand and led her in a dash across the courtyard—tugging her, watching for the moment her just-freed legs slipped—but she never slowed. I caught one glimpse of Willard dodging away up along the wall before we reached the cover of the parking structure.

The station itself would be just beyond that. Once we were right inside with the police all around us, Leland would have to back off. Or he'd go after Helena, the one person the cops would have to listen to.

Maya slowed to a walk. "The police? You think we'll be safe with them?" It was a question, but a dark, doubtful one, pitched not to echo in the parking structure's open space.

"Best we can do. And we call Helena—"

I felt Leland appear then, somewhere beyond the next wall, too close to the crowds inside the station—I focused, struggled to keep that one new presence from fading in among the others' mental noise.

Maya stopped with me, following my gaze at the wall.

"He's waiting up ahead," I said. "We walk on to the front of the station and he'll be right there."

I looked around the gray walls of the parking structure, tried to picture the other ways through. Or we could walk right up to him and try making it too public for him to act. His presence was... near... a buzz of emotions, too many for my worn-out nerves to make a picture of who might be in view of what.

Maya said "Or we get out of here," and she pointed to a corner of the building. Where my motorcycle stood waiting.

I looked at her—barely *dressed* in that poncho—but she was already padding toward the bike.

You're crazy. Or else you think I can ride us through anything... I tried to hold my fix on Leland behind us, and peeled off my jacket for her. Even without it I felt suddenly warm.

She scrunched the coat on over the poncho, and I unchained the helmet from the bike for her. Now all we had to do was walk the bike up near Leland and then roar away before he could react.

Thinking, tracking Leland, I almost missed the Duval fury barreling toward us.

"*There* you are!"

Willard's bellow boomed off the concrete. I waved at him to lower his voice, but he only closed in. His mask was off, his face twisting as if his emotion would burst his skin at the seams.

"You think you can *leave* Sibyl back there? You just use us and you're gone?"

"Leland's right outside!" I hissed.

Maya added "We'll meet you at—"

"*No!*" he snapped. "No more lies. We break them out right now or—"

I searched for Leland's presence again, trying to feel past Willard's rage.

I must have glanced away—Willard roared "Where you think you're going?" And he grabbed at Maya.

My hand swung out at him, fear gushing to my fingertips, and Willard jerked away out of my reach. His face had gone from red to pale.

In the corner of my eye I saw Maya climbing on the bike. I stepped toward Willard and thrust a palm out at him. He dodged wildly back, stumbled, and crashed down along the asphalt.

Then I whirled and rushed for the bike. Her arms locked around me, and we roared for the street.

It was the craziest, most desperate race I'd ever tried—both of us clinging to our balance and so much of our flesh unprotected against what one slip would do, and knowing we'd already lost far too many seconds since Willard started shouting...

But we made it to the street. We swung down the dark, streetlight-dotted course and wove between the few cars, Maya clinging tight and matching the shifts of my weight as I fought for the perfect, steady balance we'd need to stay *moving.* Too fast for Leland to touch.

When the second turn loomed up I had the space to swing wide and make a smooth, clear right turn that only cut our speed for a few key seconds. Every twist we made might throw off Leland's line of sight and shake him. I blinked and squinted my unshielded eyes as the rush of cold air tried to drag tears from them. Maya's balance and her grip fitted tighter every moment.

A red light loomed in the emptiness of the street ahead. I slowed, weighed charging through it or twisting around right again—headlights moved through the cross-street and I had to pull over. One slip dodging those would spill us over and crack our skulls.

Maya lifted her feet—her poor bare feet—from the bike's pegs to rest them on the pavement. "Too close," she murmured. "I... I guess Sibyl's more Willard's sister than mine."

"You know she is." I watched the traffic. How could this street have so many cars at this hour? Leland couldn't be that far behind.

Helena! He's got another target! I grabbed for my phone and hammered out a call to her.

The phone rang... rang...

The light glowed green. I twisted in the saddle ready to pass the phone to Maya, when the voice came in my ear: "A-Adrian? What is it?"

"The Eye's after you again."

"What?" In mid-syllable the sleepiness fell away from her voice.

"We think he found you—get out of—"

He was *there,* right on the walk beside me, Leland reaching for me and making me sway away in the saddle, trapped—

Maya's hand knocked his grab aside. I roared fury and clutched at Leland's arm, and he was gone again.

"Hold on!" I shoved the still-live phone into Maya's hands and shot us forward, with all the speed as the engine could give. I dodged one car, wove around another, twisted through the safest left turn I could find and raced down block after block in the night.

Memories nipped at me as I moved. Leland could have been reaching for me just now, or for my phone, as a way to track down Helena... But he could get both, he could appear anywhere to grab us or shoot us, any moment.

Any. Moment. Just the thought of staying *that* hair-trigger alert made my nerves twitch as I steered us on, blinking to keep my eyes clear. We had to get away... or his magic had to wear out sometime, it had to have *some* limit.

"We should..." Maya was shouting at my shoulder, trying to speak over the engine and the wind.

"What?" I dropped the speed for a second as we slid beside a huge blocky truck.

Her voice was the fiercest voice I'd ever heard from her: "We should trade secrets. More power for both of us."

The bike wobbled under me, the slightest twitch before I straightened it. Her magic, mine—

We were racing down the street at night with the Eye behind us somewhere. Even if we got away, there'd be no time to make it to the river, or to whatever charged her magic either...

"You hear me?" Maya shouted again.

I swept us past a yellow light, and then I kept the throttle open, thundering past one car and then another. With what the Pulse could do, with how Maya had turned it on old Van Owen for her own reasons... and Leland still playing his games...

I let the engine's roar drop for a moment. "Best if we don't," I heard myself say, in the sudden, shocking lull.

Her grip went tense around me. I twisted the throttle again and we roared around the truck and on.

Another block, another... the further we went, the more chance Leland would lose us. This was no time to think about Maya trying to share the best thing she had in her life, or all my doubts about how she was around Van Owen or the Duvals. Maya Grant was too many shifting pieces for even the Pulse to sort out.

But I'd hurt her, I knew I had.

A light flared in my mirror. Bright blue, with a siren and a police car closing in behind us.

Of course. Charging through the city at full speed, even in the dead of night... we wouldn't have to look for the police because we brought them down on us. And trying to lose them with just one helmet would be worse yet.

I eased the throttle back to let us settle toward the curb.

"What are you *doing?*" Maya said.

I brought us to a stop, and the police car halted a distance back, under one of the many taller buildings around us now. I turned to tell Maya we had no choice.

Her helmet was just lifting away from her head. She leaned close, breath on my face in the cold night.

"Then," she whispered, "just *gyo-din na vath.*"

"What is..." Inches closer and I could kiss her again—

"Gyo-din na vath, and you press some onyx onto a big enough mass of metal. That's how." Her smile, small, bright—

She looked away, of course she looked away when her gaze held so much within it—

"Off the bike! Both of you... please," and the cop's voice turned uncertain as he finished. He'd been standing at a distance and calling out to us for whole seconds now, I realized. His wide, craggy face looked softer, as if even he guessed he was looking at something far beyond his depth.

I blinked, and words fell into place again. I looked at the cop, and at his partner back in the car. "Phillip Leland! He's been stalking us, he tried to shoot—"

Movement struck, a shape lashed into existence, and Leland was behind the cop cracking the butt of a gun into his skull.

The cop toppled over with a twist of pain frozen on his face. I tried to kick free of the bike, and Leland was gone again.

One hoarse grunt made me spin around. Now he sat in the car beside the second cop, and he'd slammed the man's head into the dashboard. His gun thrust out the window at us.

I froze, still trapped astride the saddle with Maya behind me. The street around us swept by, dark and quiet with the few people in reach hurrying away. Both cops' minds felt scattered and lost from the brutal blows.

Leland stepped slowly from the car. His gun never wavered.

I tried leaning over to shield Maya—a useless motion with the bike saddle holding us in place. Leland's emotions were as unreadable as his mask now, all tight and closed.

He took one quiet, sideways step, around me. Toward her.

"Listen—" My word came out too fast, anything to stall for another moment. "You, you've been keeping watch against magic because it's dangerous, right? That's what I've done, that was the Plan... if you just don't hurt—"

"I told you." He shook his head. "You'd either get me Maya Grant's secret, or you'd lose—"

His hand lashed out, without even breaking the rhythm of his words.

It latched onto Maya's arm, and they disappeared. My helmet fell from her vanished hands to the pavement, abandoned.

A motion drew my gaze upward, along the side of the tallest building. Up along that wall of black glass, two figures stood on a tiny ledge, swaying and stepping apart. Five long stories up, and directly over where the pavement dipped into a steep ramp leading down under the building.

For an even longer fall.

He'd do it. My heart thundered in my ears—I could just make out their silhouettes high up there in the night, but I remembered Maya's voice as she whispered to me. The last thing she said.

Leland pointed a hand at her. Maya lurched and teetered on the edge, shoved by her own stolen magic—

"*NO!*" The scream ripped me inside out, but it had to reach them up there. "I *got* it!"

And he heard. He waved again—the damn showoff—and she tipped back and flattened against the wall. I gasped in a breath, but Leland had already vanished again.

I knew what I'd see before I looked down: Leland would be in front of me, gun ready. I let my gaze linger on Maya for a moment longer, hoping somehow the Eye would keep his word.

Then I looked down to glare at him.

"Onyx. She said she used onyx, pressed against 'a big enough mass of metal.' " I used her exact words, to give him every scrap of help I had. "And, *Gyo-din na vath.*"

Even in his mask, I could guess Leland was smirking at me. Then he reached in his pocket and held up a small pale stone—that must be the weapon he'd turned against Maya, the thing he could use but not recharge. Until now.

He disappeared. I looked back up, saw Maya leaning against the wall. And Leland back in place beside her.

His hand reached down, to touch the huge steel beam of the building itself. That had to be enough metal... then he'd say the words, and he'd feel the power...

Leland stopped, held up his hand before him, and he stared down the building at me. A word fell down through the night: "Lies!"

Then Maya was moving, scrambling across the ledge to grab at him, catch at his arm and fight to hold the gun away—hopeless, useless, but she kicked off and hurled herself backward.

Off the ledge. Dragging Leland with her.

CHAPTER FIFTEEN: ILLUSION

Five floors up... the two fell, tumbling and plummeting for what would take whole endless seconds... the smaller figure still turning and fighting to hold on...

Of course. *Please, Maya, please be right...*

They vanished out of the air. *Both* of them, Maya pulled along into the magic by her grip on Leland.

A gasp and the sound of a fist on flesh yanked my gaze around. The two of them sprawled on the pavement, just ten wild steps from me, Maya still clinging and struggling to hold him off balance.

Then I reached them. One hand clamped a hard lock onto his gun hand, my other arm snaked around his for a more complete grasp, squeezing in beside Maya as she held her own grip.

I opened the Pulse.

Leland shrieked, struggled, but I locked my hold and my power down tighter. For Maya, for Helena, for everyone he'd terrorized—

The world shattered. No hands, no body, nothing but hurtling madness and motion through nothing, everything, and *bumping* against it as the lines of us stretched too frightfully thin, but still holding, holding on with nothing to hold on to—

Real again. But all that real weight hung in empty air.

I saw flashes of ground whirling below us, hundreds of feet below as we began to fall, tumble. I locked my arm tighter on him, heard Maya struggle—

Emptiness and pain again, shooting through chaos and scraping through, grinding and fading and—

Solid again, and falling—

The ground slapped up into us. Flying to falling to hitting just as I was tensing up, and something lashed out at me and wrenched itself away. Leland was free.

I twisted, found I had the weight to roll for my feet, but my balance was all wrong. No, the floor *was* tilted, an angled roof—

Leland crouched three too-long steps away, throwing Maya off his arm. Behind him stretched the roof's edge, and dark empty ground just below it.

Dark silence, a silence that crashed into me. The last house on Little Street.

Of course, when he vanished us he'd been drenched in the fear, so his memory could have guided us here again by reflex.

Leland's gun rose.

I felt the rage in him sink away, as stilled and deadly certain as when he'd passed sentence on Maya. Out of reach, out of time.

"So *do it*," and my voice choked to say it, choked to say there was nothing left.

Maya said "Like you killed my dad?"

Leland froze. Some emotion turned in him—but no sharp guilt or concern, barely anything real.

"I *know* you did." Her voice rose, fierce and certain as a child's now, and nothing like her tighter true feelings. This had to be her one last distraction.

Leland heaved a slow, deep sigh. "No, no... Is that what you really think?"

Maya only glared back at him.

"No... You should know better than that." Leland chuckled. "Of all the things you think you know about Stephen Grant? That makes one more you have wrong."

Something moved, behind him, down in the shadows of the ground below. Something I felt like a trickle down my spine.

"Your father was *dying*," Leland said. "Of course it was the cancer that got him—he didn't even have the strength to charge more teleports. Near the end he tried to send talismans out to anything that might be another Spellkeeper, just to trade for another chance at hope... You'd think he'd know better, after that fear-breathing maniac. But that freak was the one who stopped him sending those."

And the shape drew closer, out below us, too dim and ominous for sight to focus on. I locked my gaze on Leland, on his gun, as if anything could keep me from feeling as the cold bit deeper.

"Fear," Leland said. "Your father was simply afraid to die. And that his daughter might get the same cancer someday."

Maya's breath caught.

"And when all his study failed, he simply gave up." Leland shook his head. "So broken he didn't see his off-the-books researcher grabbing the secret for teleporting. He was beyond caring. And so the worst of the magic was over."

Leland shivered then. Starting to feel it.

He raised the gun again.

"Over. Except for him," and Maya pointed.

Nobody would have looked there, anywhere else. Here nobody could have dared not to.

Leland glanced around, to where the shape in the night below was drawing near the house.

He moaned, jerked back from the roof's edge.

The gun twisted away as I dove at him. *No ducking away for you*—I grabbed him, wrenched him around and slammed him down on the roof.

Maya started toward us—and she screamed.

She shrieked, she stared away down off the roof, staggering back. That force was beating down on *her*.

Something numb crept into my fingers. I could only tighten my grip as Leland thrashed under me. A clatter sounded like a gun falling away. Maya stared, down off the roof, at...

I grabbed at the Pulse's fear and flung it at Leland, but the flood of terror poured past us and crashed the other way. Too deep to dive through, too strong to escape...

It lapped around us now. The Scarecrow stood *below* the wall, I felt it like my own leg dangling into a nest of claws that began climbing upward—

Leland shuddered—and we exploded away.

Terror burst into chaos, storms and shatterings as we flew away, away, tumbling and bruising and stretched snapping-thin as the flight turned too weak, feeble and faltering and—

And he, he, shoved at us, tried to force us away—

We held on and the space dumped us out together.

Something broke inside there, I knew that was true as we crashed to the ground again. But Leland wrenched, kicked me, and he twisted free again.

Wind brushed at me. Open air, high up, around us stretched the high flat roof of a building with others pressed close around it in the thick of downtown.

And Maya was still with me, clambering to her feet with her face pale as a scar. Somehow she'd pushed through the Scarecrow's power and grabbed onto Leland in time.

Leland raised his hand—his empty hand, his gun was gone.

He waved. *Goodbye.*

Then... he was still there. Still standing in front of us, unarmed, and stuck.

So it finally happened. Those crashings through space with all of us in tow must have worn out his magic. Leaving him trapped.

He whirled, and dashed for the building's edge.

"Don't—" I shouted, but he was already leaping.

Out into open space he flew, toward the next building over, soaring out and arcing downward and straining toward the wall beside us.

Words flashed back to me, Leland's words:

You know what his teleporting could have done if he could trust the leap?

Was *that* the key to gathering this magic, not water or metal or anything except a real leap through true open air? So simple, so within reach—the Eye was unstoppable.

He was halfway across when Maya thrust out her hand.

The leaping figure shook, twisted. Its curve changed and steepened and bent down, *down.*

Pushed down, out of a leap he should have cleared. Something flashed over Maya's face—sheer, feral rage, but her eyes glittered wet.

Leland fell short of the wall. Then he fell.

A tiny shape broke away from him as he plummeted, and it rose up toward us.

Before Leland hit, I looked over at Maya again. She had turned away, from it, from me.

Then a simple, distant *whump* sounded, far below.

The figure lay there motionless. No emotion in him now; there would never be again.

And the small shape that had been torn away reached our roof to settle into Maya's hand. A phone.

"Come on!" She turned across the roof, toward the access door that led inside and on down.

Then she swayed on her feet, drooped and slumped to the asphalt. I rushed to her side—pain and shock were still dug into her face, trying to work themselves free.

She dragged herself upright, leaning against me. The door clicked and swung itself open wide.

"You had your magic, the whole time?" I said. "How? He searched you, right?"

"Like I can't pick a pocket. Or maybe I swallowed one of my stones." She pulled away from me and stepped through the door.

We made our way down the steps, one flight after another, and the shock seemed to drain away from her the deeper we went. Our footsteps echoed in the stairwell as if we had the whole building to ourselves.

Maya had *faked* being powerless, the whole time... or she'd given me a few nudges of help, but never let Leland guess...

And she fooled me too. That one moment that she'd given me her magic's secret, it had all been another trick for Leland—it *had* to be aimed at Leland...

If the building was deserted, the street outside was hushed, with all its sounds low or far away and leaving this moment for us.

When we looked for Leland, I had a sudden worry that somehow the empty body I'd seen would still get up or vanish away. But he sprawled right there on the grass between the buildings, unmoving. I gazed at the so-still figure waiting for this moment to become real.

Maya murmured in concentration.

Leland's coat stirred. One pocket turned itself inside out, then another, and an array of small objects began to float out and parade through the air across to Maya. With steady, hypnotic care, her magic rolled the body over and searched through every piece of his clothes. I saw her gather up notepads, small stones, the Bone I'd lent her, and a set of keys with a shock of colored feathers at the fob. And one tiny device that had to be electronic.

That broke my silence. "Is that a bug?"

"His. The one he slipped into my poncho before he let me escape."

"*Let* you... so he..." Our ride for freedom played through my mind again, and every twist it had taken. "Him going after Helena was another bluff, to make us desperate? So, he heard what you said was your magic? Or else that thing didn't pick it up. Or it did, and he took you up to that ledge anyway just to test me, or you."

"That sounds like him," Maya nodded. "I put the bug back on him in the fight. I thought we might make him say..."

She tapped at the phone, the one she'd pulled off Leland before he hit the ground. Scrolling and searching a moment, she held it to her ear. Finally she scooped up the handful of objects she'd gathered, and brushed a tentative finger over the keychain's feathers.

"Got it," and a broad smile spread across her face.

"Got what?"

"The words that I'll need. To find whatever else is out there, and see how to change—"

She stopped, and her smile softened into a crooked sort of curiosity.

"Well, I'll have to decide on those." She stepped back from me and began walking. "But I bet it'll need some muscle."

"It? I don't get it, what are you..."

"It starts by keeping my 'sister' out of trouble."

The building's door swung open for her, and she lunged forward and darted through it. And it slammed shut behind her.

When I touched the door, it was locked.

Through the glass, Maya turned back toward me. But she looked away, avoiding my gaze one more time.

"Hey! What are you thinking? *Hey*—" I shoved at the door, pounded at it, as she walked away.

I spun around and ran around the building, searching for other doors. The Pulse showed Maya thrummed with layers of anxiety and satisfaction, all traces that told me nothing. But what she'd said, the way she'd locked me out...

The Pulse only let me track her, as she climbed to the top floor. As she launched herself out toward the building beside her—a leap pushed along by her own magic, or just a leap of faith.

Maya landed against the opposite wall.

And vanished.

* * *

I walked the streets, not certain where I headed now. The night was colder than ever—and Maya had my jacket too. But the Bones were finally back in their box, and I could walk without their constant chill at my pocket.

The street where Leland had ambushed us had been empty. The two cops he'd left unconscious were gone, no doubt picked up by other police and recovering, I hoped. My bike was gone too.

They'd find me, they'd want answers. Tonight I was just too worn out to give them.

And if the cops took me in, I'd be nearby when Maya broke the Duvals out. The thought turned and twisted in my head, refusing to fit. I owed the cousins too, for everything we'd tried to do together, but...

A weak laugh floated out of me. I'd fought to save Maya from the Duvals, and in the end she was rescuing them.

They were killers, they'd burned that guard to ash just to chase signs of more magic. And I'd seen Maya terrorize Wilson Van Owen for the same purpose—using the Bone that I gave her, that she still had. Like the Scarecrow had murdered Ray with the same magic.

No. Those pieces couldn't match; I'd seen, felt, Maya's regret when she forced Leland down. But she had her own plans for all the magic she'd gathered, and the Duvals, and whatever else she went looking for.

And now even the Scarecrow had let me go once, and then he'd come out after Leland, and Maya. And then Leland, and Maya's father, had known him once... I tried to turn that over in my mind.

I'd had a Plan—use the Pulse to help people, and search out any more magic, friend or foe. Instead I got Maya, saving the Duvals, and maybe saving us all from the Duvals if we left them under her guidance.

Yeah, keep telling yourself that.

The apartment building loomed through my haze, a familiar orange, and I knew I'd been simply heading home. With one out of two tasks completed: the Scarecrow—the Scarecrow!—had told me to "save them both," and I'd lost Maya.

"*No,*" I breathed. She wasn't lost, I just didn't know where she was headed. For now. And Helena was...

I shook my head. The woman who'd inspired me for years, and I'd barely given her a thought after our call was interrupted.

And Maya had held onto that phone when Leland struck, so they probably found it lying beside my bike. But I still had my original one—the Eye wouldn't be bugging it anymore.

"Adrian? Tell me you're alright!"

Her words *splashed* in my mind, rippling through the thoughts I'd been trying to settle. I sighed "I guess. The Eye is dead."

"You mean..." She stopped, then began again, more slowly. "You don't sound like someone who's won. Did you have to... get rid of him? Is Maya..."

"The Eye meant well, that's the hell of it. He tried to keep us safe from the Scarecrow, and other things that could be out there. Like I..."

Wanted to. Have to.

"But Maya? I don't know what she'll do anymore, not for one more minute, not if it got her closer to knowing her past. And it *could* be in a minute—she can appear anywhere now, she's got all his power. And I... I even gave her one of the Bones, I helped her, why couldn't I *see it?*"

The last of it gushed out and left me empty. I walked faster now, fumbling out the key for my apartment ahead.

Helena said "I'm... sorry."

"Don't be. It's not over yet." I just had to reach her.

Finally I reached home, and stepped inside.

One of my chairs stood facing the door. My jacket lay on it, neatly folded, with a tiny green box perched atop it. A jewelry box.

A small yellow note was taped to the box's side:

So we'll be even.

Within it lay the missing Bone.

AND THEN...

Thank you for following the first of the Corbin Cases. Keep reading for a look into Adrian's next step into the secrets of magic: *A Bone To Pick*.

If you enjoyed *Roll the Bones*, would you please take a moment to leave a review so other readers can enjoy it too? Just the first sentence or two that comes to your mind. It would really mean a lot to me.

And, you can learn more about upcoming books, the characters and their abilities, and other supernatural tricks of the trade at www.KenHughesAuthor.com[1]

KEEP READING for the next look at Adrian, Maya, and discoveries that will change everything.

---

1.   http://www.KenHughesAuthor.com

PREVIEW from A BONE TO PICK

My phone's buzz drew a glare from the police closest to me. Even when they had me sitting here and waiting in the station corridor where the harsher voices were distant doors away, the ripple of glances showed they were keeping an eye on me.

A jailbreak last night would do that.

But I picked up anyway. "Adrian Corbin. How can I help you?"

"It says you have experience investigating... things with an unusual side?" The voice was a young woman's, the tone an insistent need that still faded into hesitation.

"That's right."

The faces that had glanced toward me were still watching, eyes glittering resentment as I carried on as if I weren't hip-deep in their suspicions already. But I'd let enough lives slip through my fingers.

Besides... I opened my mind to the Pulse for a moment. A tumult of emotions crashed into me, steel-firm resolves and the churning of angers and frustrations and endless degrees of fear from what would be the visitors and suspects around the police station. But the closest emotions, the officers sitting near me, felt more like general cop suspicion, not the anger or contempt they might have if I were an actual suspect—

I shoved the magic away with a wrench of will. So many sensations jabbed a needle of pain in my head, still shaky from last night's whirlwind of escapes. The phone at my ear was quiet.

A shout, and another raised voice, broke out in argument far up the corridor beyond the desks—probably the holding cells. Detective Poe was still keeping me waiting.

To the woman on the phone I said "Answers, or protection... I've provided those to people, or helped them find the best place for whatever help they need."

"I guess we need..." Then the embarrassment dropped away from her voice as she rushed on: "The clinic I work at, I have a friend who's getting attention for some of his techniques. And those, I guess they come under what your website says, *unusual.*"

"That's what it says." I'd just thrown that wider description onto the site this morning. Was this call something real, or just the first of a flood of random worries that had nothing to do with people in need or actual magic? *Not that I'm the one to judge, after some of the things I've blogged.*

She said "We've been getting—"

Shouting swamped her voice, from out at the front of the station. "Hey! How long d'we have to wait here?" was the loudest, with a burst of other voices around it. Three uniformed cops had just walked out from the inner corridors, trying to join the unusually few officers who tried to contain the flow of visitors.

The noise settled to a lower roar, and I pulled the phone closer. "Sorry, can you say that again?"

"I said we've been getting... I suppose they'd count as threats."

"Threats? Are you in danger right now?" *Please don't be fire... but that would lead to where the Duvals escaped to. And Maya.*

"Not like that, no. But some of his patients have gotten so demanding that, well, honestly I'm afraid of where it's going."

Detective Jenson Poe stepped in beside me.

His round, moonfaced features should have made a hostile glower difficult, but he was a professional. And he must have heard me talking about handling threats, under all their professional noses.

I looked past him—focusing on a bare patch on the wall between the posters and frames helped me draw encouragement into my voice. "Then they probably are a problem, if you're reaching out for help. Too many people never do."

"It's just... I've seen patients get attached before. And Ian deserves the attention, with the strides he's making. But they make me worry something's going to go bad."

"Sounds like I should come see for myself."

Even from the corner of my eye I caught Poe's face quirking into a deeper frown, just to hear me mention leaving.

Then his head flicked over, looking away up the corridor toward the holding cells. Of course they'd put me near here to intimidate me.

But the woman's voice lightened with relief. "*Thank* you! We're at the Summerside Clinic."

"Got it. I'll be there—once I can," I had to admit. Unless I was reading the police all wrong about me.

"Ask for me, Lucy Nichols. And, I'm sure we can talk about your fee then as well."

"Alright. We'll see if you have a problem or something else, and how I can help you deal with it."

When she hung up, I looked up at Poe beside me.

"All done now?" His voice had only a small edge in it, when he could have taken me for mocking him.

"Sorry for the delay. A client needs help, you know?" I smiled my best apology to him.

He settled down in the chair opposite, and the moment gave me another instant to draw on the Bones in my pocket. The Pulse brought another crash of too many emotions, but no press of true anger or certainty from Poe. That only told me so much.

The detective leaned close, too close, bringing his scowl right up to me. It let him speak softly to push back all the noise around us: "Mister Corbin, do you know why you're here?"

Because I came in before you police got around to coming after me. But I let that go and got to the heart of it:

"Because the three Duval cousins dragged me into the police station archive last night. Me and Maya Grant with me."

I tried to fill my whisper with simple, honest frustration about what we'd been through. But Poe's face flickered in reaction—he'd seen something under that.

"You broke into the station," he said. "An officer was *attacked.*"

Then his eyes clenched closed. I didn't need the Pulse to know he was swallowing his own embarrassment—I'd been here with him just hours before then, and he hadn't taken me seriously.

He looked up again. "We had you all, captured together."

"Captured with them, sure. The Duvals were the ones with the masks. And they had Maya stripped down to a damn rain poncho by the time they caught me too!"

That hadn't been the Duvals' work, but they'd done worse—they were murderers and arsonists even in that time when we'd had a common enemy. Blaming them for the whole night gave me no guilt at all.

"So they forced you into the station. And what were they looking for—that made them 'drag' you two along?"

"Looking for? I'm still trying to figure the Duvals out." A couple of half-formed lies formed in my head, about them framing us or destroying records, but the less I said now the better. And I could hardly tell him how the Eye had been there trying to force Maya's magic from her.

"Innocent and ignorant, is that it? You don't get it—you were *caught with* those arsonists. And Willard Duval escaped, and he injured an officer—"

Injured? So the cop's alive?

"—and you two fled the scene!"

"Of course we did, someone was *shooting!*" I snapped back. "Of course we hopped on my bike and roared out of there, and I guess we kept going."

"You fled the scene of a crime. Clear across town, until you were pulled over by more officers, and then *they* were assaulted. Are you telling me that was Willard Duval too?"

"It wasn't us. Someone in a mask, and we barely got away from him."

But cold fear was welling inside me, that I'd tried shrugging off too many damning moments. I risked using the Pulse again—uneasy, buzzing irritation slammed into me from Poe, still nothing more certain.

Something moved off at our side. A motion, a slowly shaking head from a cop with a bandage around his skull, as he looked at me.

One of the two cops that the Eye had ambushed on the street. At least the way we'd disappeared out of there must have cut off any trails to how we'd wound up.

The detective said "You are a problem, Mr. Corbin. We write you off as a nuisance and then you're part of breaking into the station. An officer is hurt, you run, more cops are attacked... and then you come back and *break your friends out of jail?*"

He snarled the words from inches away.

I jerked back, and remembered to gasp. "The Duvals are *out*, all of them?" I shook my head. "You couldn't have *led* with that? Listen, I've been warning you about them for days, and you think I helped them escape? They're no friends of mine, and Sibyl Duval hates Maya."

Or she had, but the two had called a truce, and Maya's last words to me had been about using her new magic to break them out.

"Nice story... if it wasn't a *police building.*" Poe's voice darkened. "You think you can walk in under all those cameras and then lie to me?"

"Lie?"

But the Eye had been disabling the cameras... we found *him because of his sabotage...*

Poe's eyes bored into me. My insides squirmed, tried to pull me shrinking back.

A bluff. It had to be—Poe would never be this lax if he'd seen the Eye vanishing around those rooms, or any real glimpse of magic. I faced down the detective's gaze.

Then he looked away. Over at the bandaged cop, who was shaking his head in wide, clumsy motions, and swaying on his feet as he did.

"Something to say?" Poe asked him.

"I keep telling you, we were watching him and the girl. He's not the one that hit us." He brushed a hand over the bandage.

I said "You alright? Both of you?"

"Hey, he only got our heads." He laughed, an awkward but honest sound.

Poe spun back to me. "You can drop the concerned act. We have you on video bringing the Duvals into the archive."

Act?

But, me talking with the officer was taking time I could be using—I let the Pulse reach out to them again.

Frustration, tight impatience... I still caught none of the confidence he'd have if he'd seen anything more. Poe *was* bluffing.

"I told you, I didn't 'bring' them. And I sure as hell didn't break them out. I don't know what you think you saw, but it wasn't that."

Poe glared at me for a moment, two...

Then he exhaled, and his shoulders slumped like all the purpose had deflated from him. For a moment that sigh sounded like the opening of an apology.

"Alright," he said. "And I've got a real jailbreak to look at—we'll go through the details another time. You can go."

Did he say... I lurched to my feet, the chair scraping against the floor.

"*But,*" he added, "I want a report about that call you got. Someone's getting threats, you bring that to the actual police. Or I want your explanation why this isn't police business. And I want it today, understand?"

"I understand. Or when I can sort out whatever's going on—"

"Today," and his eyes narrowed. "And we'll go over every second of last night too. Now get out."

"Okay." I turned away, then stopped. "Listen, I think you impounded my motorcycle last night—"

This time a small grin tugged at the detective's mouth. "Then you better get those reports in, right?"

I caught a look of actual sympathy from the bandaged cop. But then, he had seen the bike Poe was locking up—and how desperately Maya and I had been riding when we got pulled over.

I started out, but I stole one more glance back at Poe, thumbing through screens on his phone while he got to his feet. He'd always seemed like a decent cop, and his tricks now had to be him struggling with an impossible situation. Sibyl, Willard, and Dom Duval had been starting "unexplained" fires all over Jericho, and now it must seem like they'd literally vanished out of their cells. Because they had.

A ripple of voices came from behind me, hushed just as suddenly. I looked back.

Far up the corridor, three older men—high-ranking police, just from the way they moved through the station—had stepped into view. They were heading away now, but between their backs I could make out the slim, business-suited figure they clustered around. Helena Travers still looked pale, but she looked to be walking with more of her natural confidence again.

So Helena was out in public again, probably already giving her own explanation for being kidnapped by the Eye—and *surviving the Scarecrow.* She and the police were drawing away, so she hadn't seen me. My feet twisted on the floor to start me toward her.

But something about those cops made me halt. They were hedged in around her, respectful but close enough that they had to be keeping her isolated. Keeping a lid on how the most photogenic CEO in town had been kidnapped, and the only one to rescue her had been me.

Then I looked at Poe again.

I'd *told* him I was part of another big case he'd hear about soon. Was he throwing me out so she wouldn't run into me and make me the hero of the hour, too protected for him to question?

Still... in the long run, I needed Poe's goodwill more than I needed to make this easy. I walked away.

* * *

Walking out of the station after last night, my legs missed my bike all over again. But sinking down onto the bus stop gave me a chance to rest, and to fit the Bones back into the thick little wooden box I kept. Just shutting the four enchanted dice away and cutting off their constant cold eased some of the cramps in my muscles.

According to my phone, Summerside was a community clinic that had been in place for some years. Not that large, no controversies or troubles... if I'd ever come across it my work for Travers Insurance, it must not have been memorable.

I climbed onto the bus. This could be nothing more than some clinic business and a bit of nervousness, an easy fix—when I could be supporting Helena, or looking for Maya trying to understand why she wanted the Duvals...

Once I thought I heard Maya's voice on the bus. And I twisted around in my seat and stared, only to see a whole different woman behind me. *Get it together, Corbin.*

After several stops and fighting off a creeping doziness, I scrambled off onto the corner of a shopping center, a site busily alive in the morning spring air. The clinic's sign hung on one long building at the edge of the central mall, alongside shops for shoes, haircuts, and seafood. A narrow flight of steps lay wedged in between those.

I caught voices ahead as I climbed, that grew louder at the end of the corridor. Beside the door was a simple black sign with small white letters slotted into it. It listed several doctors, with no sign of an "Ian," or a "Lucy Nichols."

The room beyond that door was wide, big enough to keep the dozens of people I'd heard spaced apart in long rows of chairs. Kids shouted in one corner, an older couple chattered trying to arrange crutches as they sat, and a TV up on the wall played local news for anyone who'd look up. A busy community clinic.

The man at the reception counter looked half-asleep already, shuffling through requests from patients and from the space behind him. A woman in a wheelchair was just rolling away from him, but a jittery-looking young man was already rushing up before I could grab a moment there. It gave me more time to look around and try to think what "threats" could be brewing here.

Finally: "Can I speak to Lucy?" I tried, hoping a familiar sound was the best way in.

The receptionist squinted as if his eyes couldn't focus on me. "Sir? Is there an issue with your care?"

"Not that. She called me—or I could speak to Ian—"

"If you'll take a seat, I'll see when she can get to you."

He took my name, and I eased down into one of the soft chairs. No surprise this crowd had everything slow.

I listened another moment to the changing murmurs and small spikes of this many almost-calm people together. Then I reached to my pocket and slid the box open.

The cold of the Bones hit me again, but I needed every insight I could find. What the Pulse brought me was messier than the police station: fewer people crammed together, with more of the bumpy awkwardness of pain and worry but less of the jagged fear that the Pulse was so good at catching. I struggled to feel through that jumble for any hints of threats or trouble...

It was still just a tangle of emotions, like swimming through muck. Nothing stood out as worth knowing, and I had no idea what I was looking for anyway until I talked to my "client."

"The fire broke out—"

I yanked my head around and stared up at the wall's TV. Smoke billowed out and hid much of the building it streamed from; the banner said the news was live.

The Duvals again? Maya had said she'd keep them in line—no, just that she had her own needs for them. Or this could be an ordinary burn and not their magic at all.

The screen was across the room, so the sound came and went as the crowd's voices changed. I stood and walked over, listening for any mention of *sudden* or *unknown* or any signs of arson.

Something sick moved in my stomach, and I held it down. We'd beaten the Eye himself... but really, Maya had beaten him, and I still didn't know what she was up to now.

But she joined up with the Duvals—that can't be good. The bruises and the long, late struggle from last night dragged at my flesh, and I couldn't even *find* Maya now. The news skipped on from the fire story to some political piece.

The clock on the wall said twenty minutes had passed already.

I sighed; this was going to take a while. I slid the Bones back in their box to let me warm up again, and turned back toward a closer seat.

"Just send him out, damn it!"

After she said it, the middle-aged woman shrank back in her chair, as if startled by her own voice and the prickles of soft resentment from the people around her. The receptionist glanced up, uncertainty on his face, before he choose to look back down at his screen. I picked out a seat near the TV.

"Send him out!" This was a man's voice, harsh enough that he knew how to make a threat. "You stuck me here for an hour already, I can *feel* the damn stitches tearing. I want to see him *now*."

Lean and mean, that was the look of the scarred man clutching the chair's side. My fingers itched to unbox the Bones again, but the way his eyes monitored me and the rest of the room made me hesitate to reach for a pocket.

The receptionist said "I'm afraid we've been backed up this morning." He leaned forward at his counter, a motion that blended looking at his screen with a settle-down gesture toward the patient. "If it's been that long, I'm sure you'll be called soon—"

"*If?* Hell with that!" He surged to his feet. "You're seeing me now. And make it the real guy if you know what's good for you."

"Please..." the receptionist tried, but nothing more came from his mouth.

The lean man stomped forward. I closed in on him from the side.

"You better," he said. "I have friends that won't be happy to see me stuck here."

Casually as I could, I said "You know how many people can hear you?"

He pivoted toward me, shoes squeaking on the tile. He wasn't big, but I hadn't thought he'd be that quick. "You call *that* loud?" he said, just soft enough set up the shouting to come.

The Bones were still boxed up, no way I could read or influence his emotions. That kept me honest.

"I just think," I said, "that there must be a dozen doctors and staff back there, you know? If they all hear you, they're *all* stopping to worry if they have to do something. That's a lot of slowing down, and it's all holding up you and your..." I gave him a measuring look. He was acting strong, but I could see a grimace of pain on the edge of his face.

"You think so, huh?" His fists were tightening. The room had gone silent enough to make out scattered murmurs of reaction.

"You made your point. Best thing now is to let them get back up to speed, right?"

His gaze flicked over me, taking in my middling build and riding jacket and all. My arms twitched at my sides ready to fend him off. His own stance had him favoring his left side, if it came to that.

But he grumbled something and twisted around, back to his chair.

I stepped over and leaned against the wall, feeling the sag of the first jabs of adrenalin trying to drain away again. The scrapes and bruises from last night felt all too fresh.

I'd come looking for threats, yes. Still, that bully hadn't even been the one to start the shouting.

He sat quiet enough now. I teased open the Bones' box until the iciness hit my pocket again. The Pulse caught a glower of small, coal-like anger, but nothing larger.

And around him... more of the busy churn of tired frustration, nagging pains people tried to hold down, dizzy worry...

No, there was no way reading the room would tell me what was going on.

The door inside stood right next to me. I could hear the crisp, professional voices with the patients beyond it.

I've waited enough—I came here to help them.

I stepped through, looking for a nurse or someone to talk to.

The corridor stood empty, mostly a row of closed doors along it where the voices came from. "Now squeeze your fist," I heard from behind the nearest.

I strolled on, feeling for any stronger emotions to go with those sounds. The smell was gone, I realized—the small tinge of all the people up front that the AC hadn't quite covered.

A graying man in a white coat stepped out of the door ahead, leading a younger woman. He eyed me a moment but then turned away to lead his patient outward.

I followed in his wake, slower. The next doorway was open a crack, with the sound of a busily-clicking keyboard.

"My mother's a lawyer," came a voice behind me. "She'd know every one of the reasons you shouldn't be back here."

He looked young, more a trainee than an assistant even in his whites. His left arm hung in a blue sling, but the Pulse felt a hard suspicion in him that didn't go with his fine features.

"Ian?" I tried.

"No. Here, I'll take you back out."

He gestured back—with the sling—and I opened my mouth.

A door opened back behind him, and two figures in white stepped out.

"Please, get back to your reports—" the older woman said.

"She asked for me."

"I said I'd handle it," but the man was already walking past her. He looked young, darkly handsome in the moment before he cleared the door to the waiting room.

I caught a faint sigh from the trainee in the sling, as I let him start me back toward that door.

Sure enough, it swung open again, and the other aide led an old woman with bandages on her arm inside. She walked quickly, but swayed on her feet—the young man had to catch her elbow with a gloved hand to keep her up.

I told him "I'm looking for Ian."

A glow of surprise, and pride, spread on his face. "I should be with you in a minute."

"No, no," the old woman told him. "You take a look at this, it feels better already."

The trainee stepped in front of me. "If we just step outside—"

"I'm here about Ian," I said. "And Lucy Nichols—"

"Here, I bet—"

The woman reached up to the patch of bandage on her forearm, and peeled it away.

"See? It's all gone—and they said I'd have a scar too. Gone!" She waved her arm in the air, stumbled a moment.

And a sharp *grin* lit Ian's face, then vanished just as fast.

It can't be. But the Pulse showed it: a bold warmth of sheer pride hidden inside Ian. He'd caused that recovery... just like Lucy and the voices out front had hinted. Actual, genuine healing magic.

God, I thought I knew what trouble was before...

ABOUT THE AUTHOR

"Whispered spells for breathless suspense."
Ken Hughes dreams of dark alleys and the twenty-seven ways people with
different psychic gifts might maneuver around each corner. He grew up on
comics and adventures before discovering Stephen King and Joss Whedon,
and he's written for Mars mission proposals and medical devices, making
him an honorary rocket scientist and brain surgeon. Ken is a Global Ebook
Award-nominated urban fantasy novelist, creator of the Shadowed Steps
books, the Spellkeeper Flight trilogy, and more.
Don't get him started on puns.
KenHughesAuthor.com.

Lightning Source UK Ltd.
Milton Keynes UK
UKHW011017070223
416609UK00006B/1444

9 798201 383176